EMMA'S TAPESTRY

ISOBEL BLACKTHORN

For my Aunt Sandra, and for all those left behind.

ACKNOWLEDGMENTS

This novel could not have been written without the involvement and keen interest of my mother Margaret Rodgers and her own detailed research of our family tree. She has many recollections of my great-grandmother which helped me give shape to the character of Emma. I would like to thank members of the 1841-1939 Beyond Genealogy Discussion Group on Facebook who helped me unearth the story of my great-grandfather. My warm gratitude to Reverend Ray Robinson of the Wimbledon Spiritualist Church for providing me with my grandmother's Baptism record. I am enormously grateful to Philip Wallis for his encouragement and insights which have made this book so much the better. Many thanks to Karen Crombie for her editorial comments on the first chapter and her enthusiasm for this project. And my warmest thanks as ever to Miika Hannila and Next Chapter Publishing.

AUTHOR'S NOTE

The timeline of this story is true and based on extensive genealogical research. My great-grandmother Emma Katharine Harms, born 19 January 1885 to German parents in an unknown location, was a devout Spiritualist, faith healer and highly regarded private nurse who cared for Jewish heiress Miss Minnie Adela Schuster in the last years of her life. Miss Schuster's affection for Oscar Wilde is noted by historians. Adela's portrait of Oscar Wilde is as close to the historical record as I could make it. However, the letters from Oscar Wilde to Adela Schuster referred to in this story are pure fiction.

The first chapter of this novel was shortlisted for the Ada Cambridge Prose Prize for biographical fiction in 2019 and appears as a short story in *All Because of You: Fifteen tales of sacrifice and hope*

1939

DRYLAW HOUSE

A bell rang, the jingle making its way down the stairs to
where Emma stood. She was forced to ignore it. Gathered in the hall with the servants – butler, chauffeur, cook and
maid – she was awaiting her turn to receive a national identity
card, stamped and her responsibility to keep safe for the duration of the war. The mood was grave and laced with apprehension. The woman seated at the console table wrote with much
care. Mrs Davies, the secretary, watched on. The bell rang
again, a trifle more impatiently. Emma waited.

The housemaid received her card and returned to her
duties. Emma watched the woman inscribe the chauffeur's
details onto his card. With every word, her heart beat a little
faster. Her palms felt warm. When Mr Webster walked away,
card in hand, she strove to maintain her composure. Mr Holt,
the butler, was next, followed by Mary Stoker, the cook. Only
Emma remained.

'Mrs Emma Taylor,' Mrs Davies read, her tone authorita-
tive. 'Nineteenth of the first, 1885.'

This was all the woman wrote on the card. The rest, her

marital status and occupation, would be kept in the register. Emma's mind flitted to her daughters, to their husbands, to what loomed for them all.

'Very good, Mrs Taylor.'

She pocketed the card she was given.

'Emma!'

The bell jingled and jingled.

With a quick glance at Mrs Davies, she hurried up the stairs. Miss Schuster might be eighty-nine in years, but her mind remained youthful and sharp and her will demanding.

Upon entering the room, she saw immediately the cause of the bell ringing. Miss Schuster – Adela, Minnie to her friends – lay askew, the bedcovers half off her. It appeared to Emma that she had tried to rearrange things and gotten herself into a pickle.

'I hope they shan't be bothering with me,' Adela said, breathless and flustered as Emma straightened out both her patient and the bedding. 'I shan't even be leaving the house.'

'I expect Mrs Davies will be taking care of it.'

'And you have yours safely pocketed?'

Emma gave her hip a soft pat. Adela fixed her with her gaze.

'Did Mrs Davies tell them we shan't be here long?'

'She told them Cottenham House is where we all live.'

'Cottenham.' She trailed off. Then she said, with fresh concern, 'Did she tell them we shan't be at Drylaw?'

'She did.' The woman hadn't been the least interested.

'Not at all reassuring, though, is it? War will soon be upon us, again. I won't be here to see it. But you will. You must be strong.'

'Best not dwell on such things.' She didn't want the conversation to settle here, not on the prospect of the war. 'Are you comfortable? Can I fetch you anything?'

'A new heart would be nice.' She issued a soft chuckle.

Emma sat in the chair by her bedside and reached for Adela's hand, cradling her wrist, feeling the pulse, counting. A little racy, she thought, but it should settle with rest. She'd been nursing Adela for about six months and had become accustomed to her frailties, the slow deterioration of her heart. Accustomed, too, to sitting in Adela's spacious bedroom, with its high ceiling and elegant furniture. The sort of furniture only the rich can afford, all finely turned wood and stylish upholstery, although not modern, not even of the century. Long before she grew ill, Adela created for herself another boudoir of flamboyance, similar to her bedroom at Cottenham House. All swirls of colour, the wallpaper, the rugs, the soft furnishings a riot of movement inspired by William Morris. Not a restful room and not to Emma's taste, yet there was always something to get lost in, something to absorb the mind if not quieten it.

She tucked the old woman's hand beneath the covers and smoothed a lock of stray hair from her face. She was still handsome, despite the deep wrinkles and the folds of flesh about her neck. She had kind eyes and a perspicacious turn to her lips.

As though aware she was being studied, Adela muttered something incomprehensible under her breath and her eyelids drooped.

Emma sat back. Her gaze drifted, first here, then there, settling at last on the curtains, the brocade, noticing a touch of fading at the opening, the result of a keen summer sun. Autumn now, and the days were shortening. She preferred summer. The dying were always happier in the summer months, eager to hold on. Winter brought gloom to the spirits and the long nights were wearing, the curtains almost always drawn. She was certain she had lost most of her patients in the winter.

Adela's breathing became rhythmic. Emma took in her

sleeping patient, a small mountain beneath the quilt, rising and falling. Adela was a large woman, so large her friend Oscar Wilde nicknamed her "Miss Tiny". Emma imagined her laughing with him, wearing the name with good-humoured grace. Adela said he also called her the "Lady of Wimbledon", a more flattering title. In Emma's mind, Adela had always been a lady, if not in title. Even now, at her age, she never faltered, never slipped and most certainly never complained. She was always charming, always knew what to say. Ever since they met at church many moons before, Emma had found much to admire in Miss Schuster. She regretted only getting to know the Jewish heiress so late in her life, when much of her vibrancy had left her, after her world had shrunk to just the four walls of her bedroom.

Few visited. At her grand age, many of her contemporaries had already passed on. There were no children. There had never been a husband. Emma wondered why she'd never married. Perhaps her size was off-putting or she preferred the single life. Surely she had had suitors. Here Emma sat, as she had sat with many patients over the years, so often at the end of life, always wondering what adventures they had had, the highs and lows, successes and tragedies.

It was much easier to dwell on the lives of others than on her own turbulent past.

Adela's breathing slowed. At times, all she needed was Emma's company, a presence in that room that had become her universe as she ever so slowly slipped from this world.

Emma reached into the wicker basket at her side. Her fingers met cane, and she extracted the oval hoop. Blue silk thread dangled from the shuttle. A thin band of plain blue sky capped a simple garden scene. She was keen to finish it. The wedge-weave tapestry would look pretty on her mantelpiece and the work was small and light enough for her lap. She drew the shuttle in and out of the warp, tugging gently, careful not to yank the thread, keeping the tension just so.

Time drifted by.

The door opened on the dot of nine and Susan tiptoed inside. They exchanged a few words in low whispers. A serious and plain young woman, Susan had her youth, if not experience, on her side. She was employed to be the guardian of the night shift.

'Sleep well,' she said as Emma left the room.

She didn't think she would. She might have gone downstairs and shared a cup of tea with Mrs Stoker in the kitchen, but she was troubled and sought the solitude of her room, where she could pray.

Pray for her daughters, for their husbands, for the safety of them all back in Wimbledon. Her youngest, Irene, was with child and Emma said a little prayer to keep it safe, hoping the world in which they lived and moved would not be destroyed, that mayhem wouldn't descend, that it would all be over quickly and peace would reign. She prayed, too, for her other family far away, whom she had not heard from in so long.

She sat at her dressing table and slid a hand in the pocket of her uniform, and took out the card. Her name, date of birth, some numbers and a stamp. Her identity. She hoped Adela held on to life a while longer; here, Emma felt secure. She put the card in her handbag. The clasp made a muted click as she directed her gaze at the room.

Adela had insisted she took the main guest room next door to her own and not, as was customary, a room in the servants' quarters. She was privileged, a matter Mrs Davies, who had a much smaller room in the east wing, brought to her attention whenever she could. Emma took no notice. Not since Singapore had she dwelt anywhere so fine and she was grateful.

As she readied herself for bed, she wondered what the

future held for her now another war loomed. The last war had proved difficult but not unbearable for her, as it was for many, yet her troubles, brought about by the happenstance of her birth, formed a dark backdrop and, in the finish, tremendous loss.

Would this time be different? Worse? She was here, an alien in England, a country at war with her own, and not as she was before, a British subject by marriage living in far-flung climes, in Singapore, in Japan, in America. Memories crowded her, chattering voices, distressing scenes. She shook them away.

She did not care to think of the past or indeed too far ahead, for such musings inevitably involved death and now that war was here, death loomed far larger than Adela in the room next door. She went back to thinking of her patient. She would do better to keep it that way. Nursing held her in the present, which was where she preferred to exist.

The following day, Adela was as bright as a button. She was always at her best in the morning. Unlike Susan, all bleary-eyed and eager for sleep. Once the two women had heaved Adela up on her pillows Susan left the room. Adela chattered while Emma drew the curtains and attended to the blackout fabric that Mr Holt had attached to the window frames only the other week. Adela watched.

'I have no idea why we must bother with those things.'

'Because we have to.'

'We shan't be here long.'

'Just you rest, Miss Schuster. It really is no trouble.'

They'd come to Guilford to enjoy the last of the summer and then to shut up the house for the winter and gather various items precious to Adela, most importantly her signed copy of *The Happy Prince*, which she had inadvertently left behind on her last visit and could not bear to be without with war on its way.

Done with the curtains, Emma returned to the bedside and propped Adela up even higher on her pillows, just as Mr Holt knocked and entered with Adela's breakfast.

'I'll take care of this,' Emma said, meeting him in the centre of the room and reaching for the tray.

He glanced over at the bed and raised his eyebrows a fraction as though about to mount a challenge. Then he said, 'As you wish,' and he let go as Emma took the weight.

Tea, a soft-boiled egg, toast and marmalade, and a small bowl of bottled fruit. There were two cups. The teapot was brimming.

Emma set down the tray on the trolley table and poured before the tea stewed, adding a dash of milk. She preferred coffee but had learned to enjoy tea. The English loved their tea. She discovered how much in Singapore. Even in the heat, the English drank hot tea.

She helped Adela, whose unsteady hand was not as adept as it once was at finding her mouth. Emma's own, gentle and guiding, helped steer from bowl and eggcup and plate all that Adela could manage to eat. It wasn't much. Then they sipped tea together, Emma sitting on the chair at Adela's bedside.

'Is the sun shining today, Emma?'

'I believe it will be.'

An expectant look appeared in Adela's face. Emma knew that look. She smiled to herself. The dear old thing loved nothing more than to voice her reminiscences of the times she spent in Torquay, at Babbacombe Cliff. They were heady, joyful days. Back when Emma was a small child growing up far away in Philadelphia, Adela and her mother would travel from Wimbledon to Devon to stay at Lady Mount Temple's manor house.

'Georgina was the perfect hostess and you would journey far to find a more interesting woman. You know, in those days, people took interest in the most fascinating things. Unlike today. Today, things are much too grim.'

'What was the house like?' Emma said, pretending she didn't know, guiding Adela's thoughts back to the past.

'Just magnificent. Rather like this room, Emma. Can you imagine an entire house festooned with such floral prints as these? Not to mention the most glorious of paintings! Those pre-Raphaelites could surely paint. Remind me to tell you about the pre-Raphaelites, one day. Such interesting people. And rather wicked, at times.' She giggled and Emma saw a flicker of the youthful Adela in the old woman.

'And then, of course, Constance would come and bring her dear Oscar. That was how we met, you know, Oscar and I.'

She broke off, lost in a private world for a moment. Emma waited, expecting more. Every day Adela sang the praises of her precious Oscar.

'We did have a lot of fun in Torquay, although when Oscar came, we didn't leave the house much. There was simply too much going on inside it to be bothered with outdoors.' She laughed. 'I suppose the others took walks. He was such a wit. What was it he said to the customs agents in New York?'

'I really have no idea.'

'"I have nothing to declare but my genius,"' she said, more to herself than to Emma. 'That's it,' she added with a self-satisfied smile. She paused and patted the bed. 'Sit here where I can see you.' Emma stood and moved her chair forward, facing her patient, and Adela went on. 'Now, Georgina knew how to put on a good séance. Have you ever been to a proper séance? They are nothing like the after-service sessions they put on at the church.'

Emma pretended she had never heard the story. Of a large, circular table in a darkened room. Of hands joined together and resting on the indigo velvet covering. Of the charged feeling. Of the strange utterances of the medium as she slips into a trance. Of the messages that would come through from the dead. Of the squeals and screams and tears and fainting. Emma pictured the drama with ease. For those adventuresome aristocrats, a séance was little more than a parlour game. Spiritualism for some had always been reduced to a parlour game. For others, for those missing departed loved ones, a séance was not a game, but rather a genuine means of contact and a source of solace and hope. And that was the way it should be, Emma thought. Yet she resisted now, as she always did, the urge to defend her faith to a woman more interested in the frivolous and the social.

Adela's concentration slipped and her memories faded. She rested her head back on her pillows. The dear old thing had so little energy for anything much.

'Read to me, dear,' she said breathlessly.

Emma took away their teacups and picked up the book by Adela's bedside, the only book ever there. This was the second time she had read *The Picture of Dorian Gray*. She suspected once she arrived at the end, she would be required to start over again. But she preferred it to *The Happy Prince*. Early in her stay, on Adela's insistence, Emma had tackled *The Importance of Being Earnest*, but the two women soon agreed it was beyond her capabilities to deliver the dialogue with any finesse. As a consequence, unsurprisingly, she had never been asked to tackle *Lady Windermere's Fan*. *Dorian* it was to be.

Emma managed to read two whole pages without interruption. As she turned to the next, Adela broke in with, 'Mrs Taylor. You haven't told me what name you started out with.'

Her non-sequitur took Emma by surprise.

'My maiden name?'

'I don't know it.'

'I prefer not to say.'

Adela lifted her head off the pillows and scanned Emma's face before letting her head fall back.

'I've embarrassed you,' she said lightly. A lightness belying tenacity. Then, 'Don't you like your name?'

'It isn't that.'

'Then what is it?'

'Please, Miss Schuster, I would rather not have to tell you.'

'Oh, but I insist. You needn't fear. I shall not laugh and I shall not breathe it to anyone. I shall no doubt forget it, in any event. Do tell!'

There was no choice. She was too honest to lie.

'Harms,' she said softly.

'Harms?' Adela boomed. 'What on earth is wrong with Harms? Much better than Taylor, if you want my opinion.'

'I suppose Taylor is somewhat...'

'Common. There, I've said it. Do forgive me. I prefer to think of you as Mrs Harms.' She took a breath then added conspiratorially, 'It can be our secret.'

Emma was relieved and hoped the conversation would end there. She picked up the book and inhaled, preparing to continue. She hadn't had a chance to utter her next word when Adela said, 'Where is he? Do you ever wonder where he is?'

'Who?'

'Your husband.'

'He passed away, Miss Schuster. I am sure I told you.'

'Yes, yes, I know that,' Adela murmured vaguely. 'But has he ever been in touch?'

'No.'

'Pity.'

Adela said no more. Seeing her patient had expended all her energy for now, Emma closed the book.

The conversation had left her unsettled. And she quickly

told herself these were unsettling times. Unsettling for more reasons than Adela could suppose.

Too much long buried now bubbled under the surface.

She thought she had succeeded in vanquishing the memories but, as she moved her chair back beside the bed, Adela's probing stirred in Emma sensations she at first did not recognise. Something laboured its way up in her, a slow and steady climb, and she felt the pressure like heavy footfalls in her belly, at last pressing down on her heart, a heavy pressure weighing her down, an iron searing that vital muscle until the pressure no longer burnt, but ached. Moisture burst from her eyes and she fought back the tears, swallowed, choked on the impulse to give in to the unbidden anguish. She found herself taken back to a place she had long refused to recall. To a vicious summer followed by a bitingly cold winter, to a room too small for her and her babies, to loneliness and confusion, and then to the malicious hatred; hatred for being who she was: German. A single burning tear slipped, unseen, down her cheek.

Later, when the house slept, she threw off the bedcovers, let her feet find her slippers and tiptoed over to her dressing table. In the bottom drawer, tucked beneath her cardigans, was a brown envelope. She didn't look inside at her birth certificate, her papers. She slipped on her dressing gown, crept down to the kitchen. The fire in the Aga was still alight.

She opened the door to the fire box and shoved in the envelope.

Seeing the flames rear, the core of her felt cindered, as though she had erased her own existence.

1914

SINGAPORE

The *Kaga Maru* had only just docked in the port and already the derricks were in action, hoisting large wooden crates ashore in heavy nets. Below, men steadied the loads as they descended to the wharf. Others were waiting to ferry the cargo elsewhere. An officious-looking Englishman in a white suit marched up to a stevedore who might have been Chinese or Malay. There was a brief exchange and then the official, satisfied perhaps, crossed the wharf and entered the office building beside a warehouse.

Emma's gaze drifted. A tram had stopped at the far end of the wharf, as though awaiting the ship's passengers. A few gharries and rickshaws had drawn up. In front of all that activity, porters rushed up and down the gangway with luggage. The passengers, who were required to wait on deck until the porters had finished their task, crowded around, eager to disembark. Emma hung back, absorbing the scene, even as she was eager to leave the ship and the bustle of the port, eager to put distance between her and those funnels that had belched smoke the whole journey, infusing everywhere on board to a greater or lesser degree with the stink. And, above all, she was eager to find some relief from the heat.

The ankle-length skirt and cotton blouse she had on were much too much in the steamy afternoon air. The constant breeze upon the moving ship had provided a false sense of the climate and as she stood beside her husband, waiting to disembark, she felt warm trickles of perspiration descend from the pits of her arms. She held her elbows out a little from her body, hoping the moisture would not wet the fabric of her blouse and show.

Despite her discomfort, she grew fascinated by the people she saw down on the wharf, the funny conical hats, the oriental and Indian features of the men. But the waiting dragged on, and the heat and the stink took their toll, and as she lifted her gaze from the wharf and let it settle on the shabby-looking buildings and the flat, open fields beyond, she had no idea what could possibly attract anyone to Singapore. She had to suppose that, unlike her, many adored or thought they would adore the tropics. They were taken in by the romance of a luxurious, colonial lifestyle. When her colleagues at the nursing agency had discovered where she was headed, they were thrilled and envious and spoke of little else. All she had thought of then and could think of now, were the tropical diseases she would need to avoid and the loneliness she was sure to endure. She really couldn't fathom what sort of a life she would lead as Mrs Ernest Taylor, wife of an export agent, a nurse cooped up indoors fanning her face while her husband went to work. What would be expected of her?

She spotted movement among the passengers and a slow trickle headed down the gangway. Ernest began busying himself with their hand luggage as they inched forward. A man of average height, he was already portly and balding and, at the age of thirty-four, turning into something of a dandy. His face wore a permanent veneer of playful joviality, masking the steely resolve within, resolve only apparent about the eyes, which tended to penetrate and at times disconcert the unwary recipient of his gaze.

This current Ernest, all fuss and bonhomie, was a far cry from the man she had married. Awaiting his turn to walk down the gangway, he had regressed into a boy of about six. He had been so beside himself with enthusiasm ever since they left Southampton, there were times on the voyage Emma thought she had caught him bobbing in his seat.

His voyage had been markedly different from hers. She had felt heavy and ill the whole trip. The Bay of Biscay had been most unkind and the Indian Ocean little better. She had spent most of the six weeks in their cabin, lying down to ease her throbbing head and sitting up for as long as she could bear it, tatting to take her mind off the hideous sway, the lurching, the rolling. Through a conscious force of will she had managed to stave off being sick, but the awful headache never went away. All the while Ernest, decidedly indifferent to her malaise, had flitted about on deck, mingling with the others. He could not get past the fact they were travelling first class and was determined to make the most of every moment.

The cabin door burst open as she emerged from sleep. Ernest made to approach her bunk, staggering halfway and grabbing at nothing before lurching on and bending down to plant a sloppy kiss on her lips. His breath reeked of whisky. She pushed him away and he turned on the light.

'Ernest, you woke me,' she said, shielding her eyes from the sudden brightness.

'You were awake when I came in.'

She recalled faintly the giggling and whispering outside the cabin. Female voices, mainly.

'Emma,' he said, removing his coat, 'you missed an extraordinary night. You would have loved it. Miss Frobisher has a Ouija board!'

Her heart sank. Ouija was surely the devil's game. Contacting the spirits of the dead. Whatever was he getting himself into?

He sat down on the side of his bunk and leaned forward to untie his shoes. It proved an ordeal. When at last he had removed both shoes, he said, 'Have you ever...?' He paused to look at Emma. 'No, but you know how the game works. The letters, the upturned glass. We sneaked into the dining room after the waiters had finished setting out the breakfast cutlery.'

Emma made no effort to hold back a frown.

He eyed her for a brief moment as though slow to take in the meaning.

'Don't worry, we put it all back,' he said, as if the rearranged table settings were the cause of her annoyance. They both knew full well they were not.

He placed a hand on each knee, locked his elbows and sat up straight, grinning. 'You will never believe what happened. First the candle went out. Then the table rose and a strange voice that seemed to come from nowhere spoke in some ancient tongue. Then Miss Chance saw an apparition at the window and fainted.'

'Miss Chance!' Emma pictured the frail young thing, scarcely eighteen with a pale complexion.

'She's alright,' Ernest said. 'No harm done.'

'If you say so.'

She wasn't so sure. She turned over to face the wall, and waited for him to switch off the light, anticipating the snoring that would follow.

. . .

That poor Miss Chance. Summoning spirits was plainly evil and, as she watched the other passengers walk down the gangway, Miss Chance among them, Emma shuddered to think of the demons Ernest had let into his life, their lives.

They were among the last to disembark. Emma followed Ernest, relieved to be stepping onto land.

A gharry was to take them the rest of their journey. They were to spend a night at Raffles hotel while Ernest's predecessor vacated a bungalow on Orchard Road. Raffles could not be too far, she hoped. Feeling exhaustion setting in, the perspiration building on her brow, she suddenly craved the overnight destination. Inside must be cooler than this! Besides, she was excited to see the hotel. She had heard so much about it from Ernest and, of course, Raffles was well known.

They identified their luggage among the remaining trunks and Ernest, who could don the mantle of the Englishman-in-charge with what he considered to be remarkable aptitude, summoned two porters to follow. Satisfied they understood his commands, he marched off, all arrogant bluster.

With the porters trailing behind her, she followed this colonial version of her husband, who was preoccupied with pushing his way past the others as they milled about figuring out where they were headed. For Ernest, everyone was an obstacle and he all but barged past one man and his porter – who was hefting a suitcase into his rickshaw – and narrowly missed ramming into a couple with a baby a few paces on. Emma grew breathless as she struggled to keep up, feeling as though she ought to apologise for her husband's behaviour and refraining from doing so, except for the occasional apologetic look.

After much kerfuffle, Ernest located the gharry sent by the

hotel and ordered the porters – who wore bemused expressions on their faces – to take care as they loaded the luggage. She stepped up into the seat, relieved to be in a gharry drawn by a horse and not a rickshaw drawn by a sinewy Chinaman. Those men looked too small to pull the weight of the contraption, never mind whoever stepped aboard.

They were soon away from the commotion and the stink of the docks, and Emma settled back beneath the shade of the canopy, choosing at first to take little interest in her surroundings. They hadn't journeyed far, not much more than a mile, when Ernest, who was leaning forward in his seat, nudged her thigh and pointed enthusiastically down a side street.

'Down there is where I shall be working.'

Emma sat up straight and beheld two rows of Victorian buildings that looked very similar to those in the City of London and were a far cry from the dockland scene they had just left.

'Battery Road,' she said, reading a sign.

Taking in the scene, she imagined Ernest would feel right at home in Guthries' Singapore office. The branch had been in his sights ever since he started working for the trading company. Singapore, according to Ernest, was the real centre of operations and all of Guthries' key men back in London had spent time there.

They crossed a heavy iron bridge and grand municipal buildings set in lush green grounds filled the streetscape. Another block and the gharry came to a halt outside the hotel.

As Emma alighted, her earlier ambivalence to Singapore vanished. Before her was a magnificent building, with its rows of arched, multi-paned windows in wings angled like welcoming arms spread wide. What struck her even more were the doormen, regaled in smart black trousers below long white jackets trimmed with red and cinched at the waist by wide belts; jackets adorned with black sashes and braided epaulettes of vivid gold. Crisp white turbans completed the costume. No detail had been spared and, together with their smiling faces and gracious manner, the doormen left on Emma a deep impression.

The splendour continued through the marble foyer – a vast rectangular atrium flanked by rows of columns supporting the upper levels – and all the way up to their room on the second floor. An elegantly furnished room opening onto a deep veranda and, much to her blessed relief, there was a ceiling fan.

Setting down her handbag on the bedside table, the arduous journey and the sticky heat caught up with her in a sudden rush. She waited as the porters entered with their luggage and, once they'd gone, she lay down on the bed while Ernest fussed about inside his trunk. He soon found what he was looking for, a clean shirt that met with his requirements, and proceeded to change.

'I have a meeting with Mr Begg in the Long Bar,' he said with his back to her. 'You are welcome to attend.'

She hesitated for only a moment before deciding she could think of nothing worse than finding herself listening to business banter. Mr Begg was the general manager of the Singapore operations and she could picture in an instant the fawning Ernest would subject him to. Although she did understand and even sympathise with Ernest's enthusiasm. It was only after many years of striving to fulfil his ambitions through dogged hard work, a certain ruthless attitude when it came to getting ahead and a loyalty to the Lodge, that he had secured the position of export agent for Guthries' tin operations in Singapore. He would also be handling their cement and sandalwood trade.

Rubber was the trading firm's main export. Other agents worked in the tobacco trade, in sugar, flour, tea and coffee, or in whiskies, beers, wines and spirits. Even Jeyes fluid and Lipton's tea were represented. Whatever could be imported or exported, Guthries were in on it. Guthries, it seemed, were Singapore's version of the British East India Company and, just like Ernest, it was every young man's dream back in the London office to secure a position in Singapore.

Ernest had got lucky. The man who hired him was Scottish and had favoured a hard worker from a humble northern background. A pottery handler's son from Stoke-on-Trent, Ernest had fitted the bill.

She looked over at her husband, all nervous and proud as he straightened his shirt, and said, 'I think I will rest, if it is all the same to you.'

With a downward glance at her lying on the bed, he said, 'As you wish.'

And that was the last she recalled of her first day in Singapore. She awoke the next morning with Ernest snoring gently beside her and the ceiling fan whirring above. Feeling decidedly sticky, she slipped out of bed. A quick sort through her trunk and she found a fresh dress to put on and took herself to the bathroom.

She made the most of the running water and the deep and wide bath. As she reclined, submerged to her neck, and leaned her head against the rim, her eyes drifted to the elegant wash basin and the ornate mirror that was slowly steaming up. She gave herself permission to enjoy the luxury, the ample size of the room which was little short of palatial, and she breathed out a long sigh of contentment.

She wasn't to know it then, that this would be the last time she would use a flushing toilet for many months.

Ernest was still asleep when she exited the bathroom. Deciding the day had well and truly begun, she threw open the French doors and stepped outside. The same sticky heat greeted her and, after a brief look around, she withdrew, this time banging shut the doors.

Ernest stirred and squinted open his eyes. 'What time is it?' He answered his own question with a glance at his watch before throwing off the sheet and, wearing nothing but his pride, heading to the bathroom. An awkward atmosphere hung in the room when he came back. She took in his nakedness, all shiny and clean, as he ferreted about for fresh clothes. Evidently the heat had brought out another new Ernest and it was not one she found terribly attractive. Her upbringing had been too pious for that.

Dressed at last, he shot Emma a cautious look.

'Are you still in a mood?'

'Ernest, please. I am not in a mood, as you say. I have not *been* in a mood.'

'You've hardly spoken a word since we arrived. I call that a mood.'

She didn't want to argue. 'I am rather hungry,' she said, injecting some enthusiasm into her voice.

Breakfast was a solemn affair. Emma could summon no conversation and neither could her husband. Gone the chirrupy Ernest of the day before. If anyone was in a mood, it was him. Had his meeting with Mr Begg not met his expectations? Then again, Ernest was bleary-eyed and, she suspected, the worse for wear from drink.

She focussed on her food, content to work her way through the omelette on her plate and sip her coffee. The meal was over when she drew her knife and fork together, Ernest having eaten little. As a waiter collected their plates, Emma glanced around at the elegance of the surroundings, then at the other diners dotted about – women in loose dresses and men in white suits – tuning in to the hushed voices and soft chinks of cutlery. It was all so elegant and civilised. She hoped the bungalow and its locale would prove adequate. Soon to leave the luxurious confines of the hotel, she had to quell the apprehension building inside her.

They wandered into the main lobby and stood where their luggage had been deposited. Then a gharry pulled up outside, and Ernest oversaw the porters as though they had never before lifted a suitcase, and they were on their way to their bungalow.

The journey took them away from the port and the coastline and up the road beside Raffles; Bras Basah Road, she saw it was, wondering if she had pronounced that correctly in her mind. Ernest, seated to her left, while lacking the ebullience of the previous day, sat forward just the same, taking everything in.

She sat back and let her eyes absorb all that appeared on her right. She was anticipating dirty streets crowded with rundown shops in dilapidated shacks, but the grandiosity of the colonial settlement continued, with large buildings and parks lining the road. They passed a new construction and she saw dark-skinned men labouring outside, wearing nothing but baggy shorts and conical hats. They were the same conical hats she had seen at the port the day before. Coolies, she understood them to be. The semi-nakedness of the workers confronted her. She was used to London and Philadelphia where people went about fully dressed. She saw, too, the underlying inequality. Those Indian men were not only barely clad, they were skinny and poor. Noting the observation, she began to suspect there was another Singapore, distinct from the grandeur of Raffles and kept, as much as possible, hidden from the colonialists' view; one of deprivation and lack of basic services.

The realisation, formed out of her nurse's training, she would keep to herself. Ernest's eyes were configured differently. There was no point trying to make him see things her way. He wasn't capable.

She was confronted anew with the extreme inequality that was Singapore when they approached a man using a shoulder pole to carry large, open-topped buckets brimming with what she saw as they passed was night waste. The buckets swayed precariously. Where was he heading? Couldn't be too far and, as the city quickly gave way to fields of crops and orchards, she knew what that man was planning to do with the excrement and she blenched inwardly. It was a practice that could only lead to the very worst of diseases. All her training in hygiene, all her knowledge of sanitation and germ theory that had been drilled into her at the hospitals where she had trained and worked, came rushing to the forefront of her mind. Singapore descended further in her estimation with every turn of the gharry wheels.

Bras Basah Road soon turned into Orchard Road, and now large trees lined both sides of the wide track and the air smelled sweet and fresh and Emma faced a different Singapore again. Here, large bungalows nestled behind hedgerows. The roadside drains were deep – indicative of the monsoonal rains Singapore endured – and wooden decking straddled the ditches, enabling access to the dwellings. They journeyed another five minutes and then the gharry came to a halt outside a much smaller bungalow than those they had just passed.

'Here it is, here it is,' Ernest blustered, clamouring out of his seat.

Emma stepped down from the gharry and crossed the decking to enter the garden through a wooden gate, leaving Ernest to fuss with the luggage.

The bungalow, a square building fringed on all sides by a deep veranda, was set in a swathe of lawn and shrubbery. She could not see the side fences. She wandered up the narrow path to the front door, which was open.

Inside, off a long and wide corridor, large rooms with high

27

ceilings greeted her eye. The bungalow was furnished sparsely and elegantly and consisted of two big bedrooms, a drawing room and a dining room. She wandered through to the ample kitchen situated at the back of the house. Taking in the sink and the stove, she pictured herself cooking, but it was a moment too brief, for she turned and found herself introduced to, or rather she stumbled upon her servants – two diminutive women with kindly faces and subservient manners whom she presumed were to be her servants and who had walked up silently behind her. After drinking in the sight of the two women, she smiled awkwardly and introduced herself. Then she eased past them, thinking to wait for Ernest in the main bedroom, her mind in a flurry.

She closed the bedroom door and pressed her back up against it in sudden despair over what Ernest had brought her into – the steamy heat, the unsanitary conditions, the inevitable boredom – when her eyes were drawn to the dresser, where sat a fan, shiny and proud. She went over to switch it on, angling it in the direction of the bed. The breeze cooled her instantly and she sat down on the side of the bed, positioning herself to receive the full force of the fan's blast, and as she sat, she reflected on her new domestic situation.

A housemaid, she had anticipated. But two? That meant one would cook. And could they speak English? What on earth would she say to them if they couldn't? More's the point, what would she do with her time while Ernest was at work, when it was not her role to cook?

Her immediate thought was that she must give him a child. She knew he hankered to become a father. Perhaps if she did, his listless gaze would settle back on her. Three years of marriage and no conception had put a strain on their union. She carried in her heart a sense that she fell far short of his expectations, whatever they might be. She did know his interest in her had waned. Sitting on the edge of the bed with the fan's breeze blowing back her hair, she wanted to recapture the old times, when their love was young and fresh and he had shown her nothing but adoration and devotion. Back when her own heart was filled with love for him and not this creeping cynicism that threatened to become a fixture.

On a warm summer's evening seven years before, Emma, a blushing twenty-two-year-old, stood poised to enter the front door of 92 Hart Avenue. She was filled with misgivings. She had not visited Trenton, New Jersey, in a long time and the distance from her home in Philadelphia was further than she cared to travel. But her friend Clara, a fellow student at the Woman's Hospital of Philadelphia's School of Nursing, had insisted Emma accompany her, and she could hear laughter and lively banter above the music spilling out onto the street.

The door was ajar. 'Shall we?' Clara said and went in. Emma followed. The merriment was coming from the back of the house. Ten paces later and they entered a room filled with couples dancing. A gramophone in a corner of the room played a Scott Joplin record. Women giggled and laughed. Emma recoiled inside. She was tense, unsure of herself and dearly wanted to return to the safety of her home, to her embroidery, to the familiarity of her evening routine, but she smiled and decided to make the most of the situation, accepting the glass of punch thrust into her hand by a dapper young man in a suit.

'Allow me to introduce myself. I'm Ernest,' he said in a thick English accent, 'Ernest Taylor. Very pleased to make your acquaintance.'

His formal manner surprised her, then she saw he was fooling with her, pretending to be upper class.

'I'm Emma,' she said.

'Just Emma?'

'Emma Harms.'

'Well, Miss Harms, as you can hear, I'm not from these parts.'

'Are you here on business?'

'I'm visiting my sister. This is her party.'

Emma offered no reply. She glanced around for a woman who resembled Ernest but no one stood out as his sister.

'Have you come far?'

'Philadelphia.'

She sipped her punch, which she found sickly sweet and potent. The young man, Ernest, pinned her with his gaze.

'What is it you do in Philadelphia.'

'I'm training to be a nurse.'

'My word.' He laughed. 'Then will you take a look at my feet?'

'Your feet?'

He leaned forward to whisper in her ear.

'I have bunions, one on each foot, and I must say they are jolly painful.' He pulled back. 'It's why I don't dance.'

She had never met an Englishman before, not in the romantic sense, and when he went on to tell her he held a position as textiles manager, she was impressed. They spent the rest of the party huddled in a corner, talking. She found him ambitious and entertaining. He had a sparkling personality and in his company something in her sparked in response.

They arranged to meet again. And then again. In a few short weeks, he swept her off her feet and when he was due to return to England, he wanted to whisk her away then and there, but she thought of her parents and her training and remained steadfast. Nursing was her calling.

Philadelphia was a thriving city back then, largely off the back of the textiles industry and the sweatshops that mopped up cheap immigrant labour. Emma's father, a doctor by profession, had drilled into his offspring accounts of the appalling conditions, the shortened life expectancy, the diseases. Accounts that had inspired Emma's vocation.

She had waited years to become a nurse and she would not complete her training until the fall of 1910. Ernest was crestfallen when she told him, but she knew she had to make him, make both of them be patient.

'I'll wait for you,' he said, going down on bended knee and clasping her hand in his. 'You have stolen my heart, Miss Emma Harms, and I will wait and come back for you. I promise.'

He was true to his word. Three whole years of letters, assignations and encouragement, of total devotion and lovesickness, and all the while she kept her aching heart a secret from her parents, who were German migrants. Not only German; things might have been different if that was all they were. They were dyed-in-the-wool Mennonites.

The only member of her family she confided in was her younger brother George. Her older brother Herman was too preoccupied with his studies. He had chosen to follow their father into medicine. She was closest to George in age and in temperament and he stood by her decision, encouraging her to follow her heart. She wasn't to know he was planning to follow his, all the way back to Germany.

Her family had migrated to America from Germany's Eastern Friesland in 1890, when Emma was five and George three, leaving her elder sister Karin – who was married – behind and joining three uncles on her father's side. Diedrich, Karl and Wolfgang Harms were farmers who had sold up and joined the Mennonite exodus of previous years, tired of the persecution over their choice of faith and optimistic of a better life. Uncle Karl had settled in Kansas and Uncle Diedrich in Nebraska and Uncle Wolfgang had gone to Canada, but

Emma's father had chosen to put down roots in Philadelphia where he thought his children would have better prospects. He held high aspirations for all of his offspring.

While other Mennonites brought their customs and built their churches and retained their way of life, her father was a touch more flexible, except when it came to marriage. They were all expected to keep the faith by marrying into it, just as Karin had.

Emma knew her parents, who had not lost their German ways or their faith, would disapprove of her choice of mate, for Ernest was not a Mennonite or even an Anabaptist. In fact, he had no meaningful faith at all, which meant marriage, as far as her parents were concerned, was out of the question. Yet she loved him. She loved that he loved her. They were well-matched, she thought, both hardworking with aspirations. Ernest brought out the best in her, brought her out of herself. Besides, she loved his sense of adventure, his dreams and plans, his sparkle and especially his wit. Nonetheless, she wavered. It was only when he returned to visit his sister in Trenton a few years later, pleased as punch that he had just been made assistant manager at Guthries' London office, that she went against her parents' wishes and agreed to marry him.

They married in a New York registry office and viewed the steamship to Liverpool as their honeymoon. After a brief visit to introduce her to his brother Edwin and his older sister Sarah – both living in Stoke-on-Trent with large families, and neither displaying the warmth or conviviality of his sister Hannah – they travelled to London and arrived at the small Lambeth flat he was renting. One day later, without providing his wife with an opportunity to adjust to her new surroundings, Ernest was back at his desk at Guthries. She didn't hold it against him at the time. It was only when reflecting back that she saw the neglect.

The office was situated on Whittington Avenue right beside Leadenhall market, a central location right in the heart of the city. She visited a few times in those early days of their marriage, meeting Ernest on his lunchbreak. She had a marvellous time soaking up the atmosphere and she soon found she enjoyed London immensely, with all its cobbled lanes and bridges and funny little pubs and decorative shop windows. One of her favourite pastimes back then was gazing in shop windows.

Before long, spending too many hours at home in a small and dreary flat, Emma grew bored and listless. One day, she enrolled at a local nursing agency which, much to her surprise, approved of her training at the reputable Woman's Hospital of Philadelphia, the agency manager having heard of the institution, which had been founded back in 1861 by physician and Quaker Ann Preston. It was something Emma's father had informed her of when she'd told him of her wish to become a nurse, pressing home the good works of those of faith.

In London and married, Emma hadn't needed to work and, in another profession, she may well have been denied the chance, but over dinner that night she insisted to an irritated Ernest that she would go batty without it, and he relented.

Three years went by. They were pleasant years, happy years filled with work and optimism. She didn't notice Ernest's fading passion for her. She didn't notice because all he ever talked about was Guthries and her mind was occupied with her own work. Yes, she was happy, yet she had broken with her faith and deep inside she found herself adrift. When Ernest was out with his work colleagues or entertaining a client, she would attend the services of this and that church, slipping into the back pew to worship. None of the various denominations she tried satisfied her. There always seemed something missing, but she never wanted to be too far from God and any church was of great comfort. She once even masqueraded as Catholic – not that anyone knew – so she could enjoy the fine church interior during Mass.

Where were the churches up this end of Singapore? There had to be one, at least. The colonialists would not establish themselves in a faraway place and not build a single church, surely? She regretted not inquiring at the hotel, for she had no idea when she would next have a chance to ask someone, and she did not relish the trip back to the vicinity of Raffles – alone in a gharry – where she was sure she might have glimpsed a cathedral.

Ernest's heavy footsteps on the wooden floors jolted her from her reverie. She was loath to stand up and move away from the cooling air of the fan, but she needed to instruct her husband as to where to deposit their things. As she re-entered the hot, still air, she became acutely aware that dissatisfaction had moved into that bungalow on Orchard Road, like an unwelcome lodger snapping at her heels as she left the bedroom.

The driver had deposited most of the luggage in the hall, evidently unwilling to take it further. The task was left to Ernest, who huffed and puffed, perspiration dripping from his brow as he dragged one of the largest trunks down the hall.

'Bring it in here,' Emma said, squeezing past to fetch a lighter trunk.

Between them, they ferried the luggage where it needed to go. The effort proved taxing. Ernest disappeared into the lounge to catch his breath, leaving Emma with the unpacking. Thinking she might as well get it over and done with, she went slowly from drawer to drawer and from wardrobe to closet with armfuls of this and that, all of it from Ernest's trunk, striving to keep herself as comfortable as she could in the heat. She had soon had enough, and joined Ernest in the living room, eyeing him reclining on a sofa, a desk fan on the console table angled his way. He acknowledged her entry with a lacklustre smile.

'Some tea would be nice.'

'I'll go and make some.'

'We have servants.'

Seeing Ernest was not about to stand, Emma went to the kitchen. She found the cook preparing food. Strange, leafy vegetables covered one end of the small table. There was the smell of onion frying. And garlic, she thought. Spices that she could not place. A large pie was cooling on a wire rack. She glanced back down the hall and then out the kitchen window. The maid was nowhere to be seen.

'Ernest wishes some tea,' she said to the cook, not sure if the woman – Chinese, Malay, Emma couldn't tell – spoke English. 'I can make it,' she added. 'Since you're busy.'

'Go sit,' the woman said. 'I get tea.'

Not relishing Ernest's company, Emma returned to the bedroom and began unpacking her clothes, item by item, assessing, sorting, and realising as she did, she had little suitable clothing for the climate. The fabric was either much too thick and heavy, or had too many layers. She had brought everything with her, even coats. They had left their Lambeth flat for good and there was no telling when or even if they would return to England. She could not send or store the clothes anywhere and she would not part with the little she had.

She returned most of her apparel to the trunk. Despite the fan angled her way, she was perspiring again. She went to the bathroom to splash her face. Running water, at least, but she knew better than to drink it. She wouldn't so much as wet a toothbrush.

The lavatory, to her dismay, was a pit toilet situated not outside, as was customary in England, but incorporated into the house. Access was off the hall a door down from the bathroom.

One lift of the lid was enough to turn her stomach. Beside the wooden seat she noticed a pail of sawdust and a metal scoop. It had been a long time since she had used a pit toilet. She had no choice or her bladder would burst. It seemed to her as she sat on the wooden seat that life had sunk as low as it could go and when she left the little room, she made certain the door was closed behind her.

After washing her hands, she thought tea must be ready and joined Ernest, still lounging in the living room. She wondered if he was still nursing his hangover.

'I had no idea we were having servants,' she said reproachfully, sitting down in an armchair annoyed to be receiving none of the fan's air.

'The previous tenant offered to pass them on.'

'You might have mentioned it.'

'I forgot. Aren't you pleased?'

She had to concede she was. The thought of cooking in this foreign clime was daunting, although it would have been an activity and an adventure.

Tea arrived. The cook set down the tray. She was about to pour when Emma said, 'Thank you, I'll do that.'

Ernest sat up. She joined him on the sofa to pour.

'How did you find Mr Beggs?' she asked lightly, handing him a cup of generously sweetened tea and deciding to remain where she was, now in the fan's reach.

Ernest gave his tea a stir and took a mouthful before replying.

'He's rather grand and most helpful,' he said, depositing cup and saucer on the arm of the sofa. 'I'm flattered he took the trouble of meeting me himself. He might just as well have sent his staff. He said the London office had spoken highly of me.'

'That's marvellous.'

'Indeed, although it does put me under rather a lot of pressure.'

'I suppose it does.'

She knew instantly this meant long hours at the office and a wave of apprehension rose up in her again. How ever was she going to cope here?

A silence descended as she sipped her tea.

He gulped down the rest of his and said, 'I think I'll take a bath.'

'Now?'

'Why ever not?' The indignation in his voice as he exited the room left her disconcerted.

Yes, why not? If they were to have any marital contentment in Singapore, she would have to accommodate his wishes.

She stayed where she was, drinking her tea as she took in the shuttered windows and the painting of an oriental boat in a gold frame hanging above the buffet. No fireplace. Of course, no fireplace.

He reappeared about half an hour later wearing nothing but a sarong.

Her jaw fell open, and he was instantly defensive.

'Beggs gave it to me. Said I'd need it. All the men... What are you staring at me like that for?'

It was his lily-white skin, the flaccid flesh, the bulge of the stomach, the sloping shoulders, and all capped off by a balding head. Standing there in broad daylight in clothing scarcely fit for the bedroom, all her harboured doubts crowded her mind and she questioned what she had seen in him seven years before. Had she been blinded by his charisma? Although he was thinner back then and had more hair, and besides, it wasn't so much his appearance that bothered her, she told herself, but rather his decision to flaunt his almost naked body in the middle of the day with other women in the house.

SETTLING IN

The following morning, Ernest went to work, leaving Emma to spend the day unpacking and arranging the rest of their things. She took her time, avoiding exertion, but by lunchtime she was fanning herself and staring at walls, bored. After eating the sandwiches the cook – whose name, Emma discovered, was Chun – had prepared, Emma wandered outside to inspect the pretty bushes in the garden. Some were in flower. She had never seen such flowers, so large and colourful and scented. She had just strolled over to a bush in full bloom when a very English-sounding voice called out, 'Yoo-hoo,' taking her by surprise.

A woman appeared in a gap in the dense foliage separating the two properties.

'Hello.' She beamed at Emma. 'Welcome to Orchard Road.' She had a strong, loud and distinctly plummy voice typical of the British upper classes, and she continued in something of a gush. 'You must be the new neighbour. I must say I'm delighted to find another Englishwoman in the street.' She reached forward and held out her hand. 'The name's Dottie. Which I probably am, but you will just have to make your own mind up about that. And you are?'

'Emma.' She shook the woman's hand. 'Emma Taylor.'

'Your husband a Guthries' man?'

Emma nodded, holding the older woman's gaze. She was tall, thin and fashionable. Emma felt diminutive in her presence.

'We won't be seeing too much of him, then. How are you settling in? Have everything you need?'

'I think so. I really have no idea.'

'Early days. You'll soon find your feet.' Dottie paused, her mouth falling open. 'But you are not English at all, are you, darling. You're American. How fascinating.' She clapped together her hands. 'Now, I want to know everything about you.'

The woman grinned. Emma shrank back inwardly. No answer formed in her mind, but Dottie didn't seem to need one.

'I tell you what. I have nothing on this afternoon and I'm at a loose end. Would you be a dear and keep me company? We'll have tiffin.'

'What time will that be?'

'Right this minute. How does that sound?'

She thought better of saying she had just eaten. Besides, she was curious to hear what Dottie had to say about Singapore.

'There's a larger gap in the herbage, just along a stretch,' Dottie said, with a tilt of her head.

Emma went in the direction indicated and found herself squeezing sideways between two large bushes. Once safely on the other side, she took in Dottie's garden – larger and lusher and more stylish than her own – and Dottie's bungalow, which seemed enormous by comparison.

'Have you lived here long?' Emma said, following Dottie through the garden.

'Too long and not long enough, depending on who you ask.' Dottie threw back her head and laughed. Emma laughed with her without knowing why. 'I will answer you properly. We have been in Singapore for a decade and in this house for six years. My husband, Edgar, works for the administration.'

They crossed a deep veranda filled with wicker furniture and entered a spacious sitting room adorned with various oriental vases, rugs and paintings. Plus, the all-important fans. There was a delicately scented aroma Emma couldn't place. She spied a vase of orchids and presumed they were the source. She went to admire them.

'Aren't they amazing!' Dottie said, approaching her from behind. 'They grow everything around here. Spices, fruit, cocoa. But I wouldn't go wandering off anywhere. There are tigers.'

'Tigers?' Emma repeated with alarm.

'One or two. They wander in from the jungle. Can be a bit bothersome, so do keep a watchful eye, especially when in the garden.'

'I will,' she said, thinking she might not even venture more than a few paces outside.

Dottie went off to another part of the house and when she returned, a maid appeared behind her carrying a tray of iced tea and small cakes which she left on an ornate coffee table before hurrying away.

The two women sat down, Dottie on one sofa, Emma on the other. As Dottie attended to the tray, Emma observed her host. Dottie seemed a confident woman, at ease with herself. She wore her hair pinned back, revealing a long, sculpted face with inquiring eyes and a generous mouth. She had on a light-weight linen dress that hung from the shoulders, a dress that, now she was seated, only reached her mid-calf. The dress had a low neckline and her legs were bare, as were her feet. Her apparel, or the lack thereof, would have been scandalous back home, but Emma could see it was pragmatic for the tropics. She saw she had much adapting ahead of her.

Ice chinked as Dottie handed her a tall glass of tea along with a small cake on a plate. Emma balanced the plate on her knee and took a sip of the tea and found it sweet and refreshing. The cake looked light and airy and she took a small bite to be polite, grateful as Dottie took command of the conversation. Emma soon found herself relaxing in her company, more than happy to let her new acquaintance detail the trials and tribulations of living in Singapore.

The rapid expansion, the number of young men pouring into the Malay Straits to work in rubber and tin, the lack of entertainment – no cinema, no theatre, no libraries – the gambling, drinking and debauchery that went on, the reliance on clubs, especially the Ladies Lawn Tennis Club – perhaps Emma would like to join? – the melting pot of cultures, everyone from Japanese, Chinese, Indian, Belgian, Dutch, German and British, and of course Malay.

'You can spot the Eurasians,' Dottie said with a mild scoff. 'They're quite obvious.'

What could she possibly have against Eurasians? Emma took a gulp of her tea to mask her unease. She never liked it when others singled out ethnicities.

'You do get used to the heat,' Dottie said, having evidently covered everything else.

'At least there's that,' Emma said, trying to assimilate this new impression of Singapore.

Dottie hesitated, momentarily lost in thought, then she stood abruptly as though, having made up her mind about something, she'd become resolute about it.

'Excuse me for a moment,' she said and left the room.

Emma heard doors and drawers banging shut. Dottie returned minutes later, laden with clothes.

'These should all fit,' she said, slinging her bundle on the back of the sofa she'd been sitting on.

'Fit who?'

'Why, you, of course.'

'I couldn't!' Emma said, taken aback.

'You must. You'll die wearing that.' She gestured at Emma's dress, which had begun to feel like a fur coat. 'Besides, all these dresses are much too short for me.' She smoothed an appreciative hand down the dress nearest to her. 'They're new. Never worn, in fact.'

'But...'

'No buts.'

'Then, thank you.'

'You can thank my new dressmaker for her miscalculation of my height.'

They both laughed and Emma flushed, secretly coveting the new apparel with something like desperation as perspiration trickled down her back.

'We'll have an outing one day,' Dottie said, resuming her seat. 'I'll take you to Raffles Place.'

'Raffle's place?'

'It's a square off Battery Road. There are two good department stores there, John Little and Spicer & Robinson.'

Dottie's suggestion brought Ernest to the fore, and Emma thought back to when he had pointed out Battery Road. She was about to ask Dottie if there was a church nearby before changing her mind.

'Do you miss your family?' she said instead, thinking ten years a long time to be far away from loved ones.

'Heavens, no!' Dottie said quickly. 'They are my one single motive for staying.'

Emma found her reaction shocking, perhaps a touch dismissive, even harsh. Whatever had Dottie's parents done to deserve such a response? Brothers? Sisters? She didn't like to pry, so she said nothing.

'What about yours?' Dottie said with interest. 'Do you miss them at all?'

'I do. I haven't seen any of them for three years. Not since I married Ernest and moved with him to England.'

She knew even as she spoke that she should not have said all that. She should have made some flippant remark as Dottie had done and deflected the conversation elsewhere. Instead, she had flung open the door on her private life, a door Dottie determined to march right through.

'What part of America are you from?'

'Philadelphia.'

'Sounds fascinating. Will you go back?'

'I hope so.'

'You must.' She eyed Emma quizzically as she sipped her tea. 'Brothers? Sisters?'

Emma stiffened.

'Two brothers,' she said, omitting her sister. It was an instinctual response she'd acquired from her childhood growing up in Philadelphia against a backdrop of hardened anti-German sentiment among the locals. If she'd mentioned her sister to her schoolfriends, she would have had to reveal Karin lived in Germany or lie. Easier to lie by omission and deny her existence.

'And where are they?' Dottie said, pursuing her inquiry.

'Herman is still living at home. He's studying to be a doctor.'

'A doctor! You must be proud.'

'I am.'

Emma hoped Dottie would move on to another topic but no, she was nosy and tenacious, qualities Emma realised she might already have taken in had she been more observant. But she was too nervous and unsure of herself, too on edge.

'And the other one?' Dottie said. 'You said you had two.'

Emma thought quickly. George had returned to Germany to work for an uncle in Hannover, a watchmaker. There was no point mentioning her German background, not to a woman she had only just met, a bored woman who no doubt loved to gossip. It was bad enough to be interrogated over being American.

'George? He is working in an uncle's business.'

'What sort of business?'

'Watchmaking.'

Dottie looked at her expectantly.

'George has always been fascinated by watches, and clocks. The mechanics of them. All those fiddly bits and pieces.'

'My, you do have interesting siblings,' Dottie said with what appeared to be genuine interest. 'And where does your brother George do that?'

A doorbell rang and Emma was saved from further probing as a look of uncertainty appeared in Dottie's face.

'You must tell me all about them next time,' she said, regaining her composure and smoothing down her dress as she stood.

Emma stood, too. Dottie steered her in the direction of the back veranda. Emma heard a voice, male, coming from deep inside the house. Dottie's gaze did not waver.

'You must drop by again tomorrow, Emma dearest.'

'I wouldn't want to put you to any trouble.'

'No trouble. Besides, what on earth will you do with your

day otherwise? There is simply nothing to do here but partake in each other's company, you will find.'

Emma soon discovered, much to her chagrin, that Dottie was right. Worse, she found all the European expatriates residing on Orchard Road to be languid hedonists who liked nothing more than to lounge about sipping tea or cocktails on each other's verandas. Everything was too much effort in the tropics, so for the most part they did nothing other than put on airs and while away the time. The men, who far outnumbered the women, invariably had jobs, but their wives, if they had wives, invariably did not. Their only interest, as far as Emma could tell, was gossip.

It took Emma no time at all to ascertain religion played no part in the lives of the European community in Singapore, except for the very few missionary types who were there to save the souls of the natives, and in the absence of the mores and strictures of a solid faith in church and God, there was an atmosphere of looseness in the camaraderie, especially amongst the men, and Ernest absorbed it all in a single breath. As the days turned into weeks, he spent less and less time at home, arriving late in the evenings and finding every reason to be out on weekends. It was as though she did not exist. When he was at home, he would waft around in nothing but that sarong, which he wore like a second skin, and try to flirt with the maid, who bowed her head, embarrassed. Emma did her best to ignore him.

One morning in May – a Friday, a month into their stay – they were seated in the dining room at either end of the long table, Emma watching as Ernest read the newspaper and wolfed down his breakfast with all the manners of a hog. He really couldn't wait to get out of her sight since he paid her no attention whatsoever. What other conclusion could she draw? He set down his spoon and folded the newspaper in half and only then, after harbouring the invitation she had received the previous afternoon, did she summon the will to mention it.

'Dottie has invited us to the Teutonia Club.'

He looked at her strangely, as though she had taken leave of her senses.

'What for?' he said. 'We're not German.'

She winced inwardly. Even Ernest, her own husband, had no idea of her true place of birth. She had become accustomed to hiding the truth after enduring the playground taunts and the bullying when they had settled in Philadelphia, which precipitated a change of primary school and an altered identity. A small lie she ground into her soul, for she shied from confrontation, never one to retaliate. She had always been mild-mannered and restrained. The most Ernest knew was her German parentage and his remark annoyed her, for the subtext was transparent. Why cast aspersions on another nationality?

'You don't have to be German to go there,' she said. 'Any-way, they are putting on a concert. Beethoven, I think. It's tonight.'

'Beethoven?' he said doubtfully. 'And you wish to go?'

'It would make a nice change. And Dottie is eager for you to meet Edgar. Your paths never seem to cross and this would be a good opportunity. Edgar is in the administration here.'

'I am well aware of what Edgar does.'

Did he have to be so pompous? He never used to be pompous. She was about to give up when a thoughtful look appeared in his face.

'Who else is going?'

Emma thought back to the names Dottie had mentioned. 'Mr Maddox and his wife, Eve.'

'Maddox? I met a Maddox at the Lodge.'

'The Lodge? I had no idea the Freemasons had a Lodge in Singapore.'

'You needn't sound so surprised. Where there are British businessmen, there are Lodges. The Freemasons were hardly going to overlook Singapore. The Lodge, I might add, is a magnificent building not far from Guthries.'

Figures, she thought.

'And you've been?'

'Of course I've been. Beggs invited me to a meeting.' He paused, a self-interested look appearing in his face. 'What time does the concert start?'

'Seven, I believe she said.'

'Seven?'

'We are to meet at Dottie's for drinks at six. Will that be alright?'

'It will have to be, I suppose. But it does mean I shall need to leave work earlier than normal.'

'I am sure Guthries can do without you for an hour.'

'Very well. Six it is.'

Their mutual reserve in each other's company had become habitual, yet the atmosphere that morning was especially strained. She felt she had well and truly lost her husband. Lost him to his new-found love of Singapore, to his work, to whatever he got up to after work, at the Lodge and wherever else he went. Her own dissatisfaction with the Orient seemed to feed in him not sympathy or compassion, but an equal if not stronger dissatisfaction with her. As though she had failed him. If only she would become pregnant. Surely a child would bind them and heal the rift that grew wider by the day?

Ernest arrived home promptly on six. Emma had already put on a sailor blouse and grey skirt, an outfit much heavier than the dresses Dottie had given her, yet more formal and, she thought, more appropriate for a concert. She was sitting primly at the edge of an armchair in the living room, and she turned to observe him standing in the doorway in his newly purchased white linen suit, noting the fabric, a trifle crumpled about the elbows and crotch.

She was about to alert him to the condition of his outfit when he said, 'Best get going then,' evidently feeling no need to change.

Five minutes after he had entered the house, they were making their way next door via the street.

Edgar, an imposing man with an equally imposing coat-hanger moustache, greeted them each in turn and ushered them inside, where a party of eight were having drinks, the men on one side of the room, the women on the other.

Ernest's gaze gravitated to the women as he allowed Edgar to steer him in the direction of the drinks table, leaving Emma to her own devices.

'Dottie's over there,' was all Edgar said as he walked away.

Emma took a cocktail glass from the tray the maid proffered and drifted over to the sofas, where Dottie and the other women were gathered.

Dottie had her back to the room and Emma was unsure she had seen her come in. Not wanting to interrupt, Emma stood and listened as Dottie related her latest encounter with a tiger. Noticing her new arrival, Dottie paused mid-flow to welcome Emma, who greeted each woman in turn.

Formalities dispensed with, Dottie went on, and Emma eyed the women as she listened. She had only met Cynthia once, as she had only just returned from a trip to Hong Kong. She was a diminutive woman in every respect, save for her eyes, which were large and brown and rendered all the more striking set in her small, round face. Emma was yet to assess her nature, but the woman seemed placid and kind enough. And inordinately attentive, Emma thought, watching Cynthia hang on Dottie's every word. In marked contrast to Lizbeth standing beside her, whose sharp blue eyes darted around beneath her thick fair hair, drinking in every nuance in those in her purview. Lizbeth and her husband were from Hamburg and they had a bungalow in Scotts Road. Gustav was a banker and long-standing member of the Teutonia Club. The evening was his idea. Emma found Lizbeth an assertive woman, full of beans. And she had quickly found Lizbeth and Dottie were almost inseparable. Even now, as Dottie continued relating her tale and Lizbeth appeared disinterested and impatient for her to finish, Emma knew that was only because, like her, Lizbeth had heard the story before. And the tale really wasn't that gripping.

Emma found it surprising that no one made to interrupt. Then again, there was little space in Dottie's narration to interrupt. She scarcely seemed to take a breath. She was up to the part when the tiger took a slow step forward, its head protruding through the foliage at the rear of the garden, reaching, staring, preparing to pounce.

'Oh, my word,' Cynthia uttered, and momentarily drew attention away from Dottie, who paused for a microsecond before resuming.

On the other side of Dottie was Eve, who took a large sip of her drink. She was a big-boned woman, rather stocky and plain, and she had a strong, almost formidable presence. Eve was listening to Dottie with what Emma surmised to be forced patience, since her mind was usually filled with staunch opinions which she took pains to share, every chance she had.

Dottie, Cynthia, Lizbeth and Eve – these were Emma's friends and neighbours, her new coterie, the women she shared her days with and in whose company, she was learning to settle into her expatriate life in Singapore.

The maid continued to circulate around the room with trays of nibbles and drinks. Emma stole a glance at the men milling about over by the drinks table. Ernest looked right at home chatting merrily to Robert Maddox who matched his wife Eve in height and build. Robert ran a competing merchant company with offices in Battery Road. Lizbeth's husband Gustav had a scholarly look about him, with his goatee beard and round glasses, although he hadn't a scholarly bone in his body. He was a banker. And he was engaged in what appeared to be a meaningful conversation with Edgar. Which left Cynthia's husband Ian, a financier and by far the most handsome of the men, hovering with little interest in either of the two conversations going on beside him, as far as Emma could tell. Then, no doubt feeling a female gaze from across the room, he caught Emma's eye and gave her a cheeky wink. Embarrassed, she looked away.

The women gathered around Dottie carried on listening. Emma hovered, sipping her cocktail, her attention waning. She had already heard the tale twice. As they finished their drinks, Dottie reached the climax – when she was saved from imminent attack by the heroic efforts of an Indian guard who happened by up Orchard Road, heard the screams, saw the commotion, raced down the side of the house and fired his rifle. There were gasps of relief and a sudden burst of chatter among the women, and the next moment Edgar announced it was time to leave.

The Teutonia Club was a short distance up Scotts Road and they were piling out of their motor cars – Edgar's and Ian's – in a matter of minutes. The five couples walked into the club as a group and, in the middle of the cluster, Emma felt cosseted and privileged, and a wave of wellbeing swept through her. She wished every evening could be as fine and convivial, even as she knew it was the novelty that made the experience special.

Entering the grand concert room – already full and rich with German voices – her euphoria gave way to nostalgia for a homeland she could scarcely recall and a deep longing for her brother George as she imagined his head bowed over the innards of a watch somewhere in Hannover.

The emotions faded as fast as they came, as she continued to be swept along by the moment. They took seats in one of the middle rows, and Emma found herself sandwiched between Ernest on one side and Dottie on the other. They had only just managed to settle themselves when the pianist shifted his stool a touch closer to the piano and played a single note. In response, a hush descended.

Soon, the room was filled with music. Emma was not a classical music lover – she preferred ragtime – and she had no deep idea of what she was listening to, but it was impossible not to be swept away by what she heard. For the first time since their arrival in Singapore, she felt content and at peace, her heart rising and falling as the music rose and fell, and she ebbed and flowed on a pleasant tide of aural beauty.

During the intermission, everyone flocked to the bar where waiters served trays of drinks. Emma took a glass of champagne, although she didn't feel she required the bubbles or the intoxication. She found herself near Gustav, who was chatting intently to a tall, bearded man Emma later discovered to be Herr Weber, the chief chemist running the Medical Hall, a German-owned dispensary near Battery Road. It seemed half the men in the room were influential German businessmen, in Singapore for the same reasons as the British.

Not confident enough to break into the two men's conversation, Emma sipped her champagne and looked around for the others. She soon saw Dottie and went and stood at the edge of her group. Dottie had taken up the centre as was her wont, throwing her head back periodically and laughing gaily. Lizbeth laughed along with her, her gaze darting across to her husband. Emma hovered, feeling awkward, then went to find a place to deposit her empty glass. A bell rang and she was jostled by the crowd keen to resume their seats. When she at last had a chance to rid herself of her glass, she found herself again standing near Gustav and his friend. They were speaking in German and she couldn't help but overhear.

'I shouldn't worry,' Gustav said. 'The British are fools.'

'But right under their noses.'

'Don't get paranoid now. There's too much to lose.'

As soon as she was able, Emma moved away, disturbed by what she had overheard. Whatever those two were talking about sounded like a secret plot. She put on a pleasant smile and then she saw Ernest and her face fell. He was downing a cocktail – his second, possibly his third – and he was about to take another when a second bell rang and she grabbed him by the elbow and steered him back to the auditorium.

The musical performances were again superb, the music exhilarating and timeless. Emma sat for the most part lost in the sound and steadfastly ignoring her somewhat sozzled husband beside her.

The concert was over all too soon and the audience, clearly as pleased as she, was quick to rise in a standing ovation. Even Ernest, not a classical music lover in the slightest, rose in applause. Overall, it had been a perfect evening and Emma left the club a touch euphoric. She looked forward to another social occasion when they would all attend a similar event. Singapore took on a slightly better hue.

As they were making their way to their motor cars, Ernest stopped abruptly and caught her arm and pulled her towards him. Lizbeth was the first to notice. The others turned as well.

Once he had a full audience, he said in a loud voice, 'Have I told you already how ravishing you look tonight, dear Emma?'

He leaned forward, cupped her face in his hands and planted a kiss squarely on her mouth. Was he that drunk? She took a step backwards, embarrassed in front of the others. He then drew himself up straight and gestured with a sweeping arm.

'My beautiful wife,' he said and he offered her a bow.

When he straightened again, his face wore a cheeky grin, and there was that sparkle in his eye that had dimmed these last months, whenever his gaze settled on her. The others seemed amused and he made a show of wrapping her arm in his and walking on. In an instant, she knew why he had made such a display, like a strutting peacock. It was to impress not her but their friends. She felt cheapened and disgusted.

His amorous mood did not wane when they arrived home that night and she was forced to change her attitude; pleased, privately, for one cannot make a baby alone. If it took a drunken Ernest to find her attractive, then so be it.

Ernest was back to his usual self the next morning. Emma grew accustomed to his new Singaporean persona and his long absences from Orchard Road. Despite her frequent visits to Dottie's, or perhaps because of them, ennui set in. Dottie, Lizbeth, Eve and Cynthia formed a unit of four, and they had allowed in a fifth, Emma, but she sensed her membership to their clique was provisional, as though none of them had quite made up their mind about her.

She became increasingly aware she needed to find an occupation. She missed nursing. She was twenty-nine and had worked or trained her whole adult life, and she resented having to stop. She mentioned her wish to her new friends at tea one afternoon and after the anticipated gasps – Cynthia could not imagine why anyone would wish to work if they didn't have to, a sentiment Eve and Lizbeth shared – Dottie voiced her approval. In the days that followed, she put Emma in touch with Mr Farquhar, a doctor at the Government Infectious Diseases Hospital on Moulmein Road.

A conversation, a letter of interest and an interview later, and Emma found herself on a quarantine ward for expatriates who, for various reasons, had picked up one of the awful diseases that abounded throughout Singapore. She was told when she started that the hospital received numerous patients with malaria and pneumonia, some with smallpox or tuberculosis, and even the odd case of the plague. Then there was the rather large number of sufferers of venereal diseases. They had their own ward. But by far the highest number of patients presented with cholera – the epidemic went on and on – and with dysentery and typhoid and hookworm disease. All of these illnesses were caused by poor sanitation, and Emma soon found everyone at the hospital agreed that the practice of using untreated night waste as fertilizer on food crops had to stop, but there was no way of persuading the administration.

Ever since she had arrived in Singapore, whenever she used the lavatory in her bungalow on Orchard Road, her stomach turned over. The night waste was collected weekly, and on those days before the collector was due, she did her best to hold her breath until she could escape the confines of the little room. The thought that what she and Ernest had voided ended up dug into the soil of nearby farms to feed crops, seemed to her abhorrent in the extreme. Her new position at the hospital reinforced her view.

The authorities were not ignorant of the problem – how could they be when sanitation and sewerage had been a major concern of municipal governments for decades? – but they were unwilling to take action. A sewerage system had been installed in the heart of Singapore a few years before, but it was inadequate. It was Dr Farquhar himself who informed Emma one afternoon on his rounds, that Chinese syndicates ran the night-waste business and they were not about to relinquish such a lucrative enterprise, not when Singapore was expanding rapidly and there was a lot of money to be made. There were moves afoot to at least have the waste processed at treatment plants before it was used on soil, but the rate of change to any new system would be slow.

Meanwhile, for the poor patients suffering on her quarantine ward, treatments were few. Much of her work involved rehydration and tending to the various sanitary needs. When a patient was close to death, she would sit at their bedside, fully attired in a long gown and mask, and offer words of comfort and prayer.

She held fast to the importance of supporting souls as they migrated through death to wherever they were heading on the other side. Her Mennonite upbringing had led her to adopt the view that after death, the soul sleeps and loses self-awareness, but ever since the night she saw her grandfather standing in her bedroom doorway, only to discover the next morning that he had passed away the previous afternoon, she believed in the enduring nature of the soul. She was convinced that when someone died, their spiritual essence lived on. For her, of utmost importance was supporting a smooth transition with as little fear and discomfort as possible. Trauma at the point of death seemed to cause souls to linger. She wasn't sure why and she'd never voiced her view. She carried in her heart the conviction that it was her duty on earth to bring peace to those in need and there was no greater need than someone dying.

If death could be prevented, all the better. Emma was a Nightingale nurse through and through, having absorbed as paramount the importance of sanitation and scrupulous hygiene. At the hospital, she brought all her training to bear on the situation on her ward and oversaw the improvement of some patients, and the loss of others. In all, it was rewarding work, albeit often harrowing. She didn't like to see the emaciated bodies, the hollow eyes, the pleading looks, the desperation and the sense of fatalism among patients and staff alike. What she did enjoy was the knowledge that she was contributing in a meaningful way to the Singapore community. She felt useful and needed.

She had worked at the hospital a whole week before she broke the news to Ernest.

'Whatever will the others think?' he said, eyeing her uniform neatly folded at the other end of the dining table. They had just finished dinner and she had brought in the crisp white dress and cape to broach the news.

'Who?' she said, placing a protective hand on her uniform as she ran through all the people who might criticise her decision. No one sprang to mind.

'The neighbours, for a start.'

'The neighbours? It was Dottie who put me onto Dr Farquhar.'

'They will think we are hard up,' he said, answering his own question. 'They will think I have a low-paid position and cannot support my wife.'

'That's ludicrous,' she said, angered by his self-centred reaction, his hypocrisy. 'What do you care? You, who swans around the house in a sarong. I hardly call that keeping up appearances.'

'That's different.'

'How so?'

He offered no response. She might have left it there. She might have let him stew on the news, but she was too rankled and for once determined to stand up for herself. She locked gazes with him and said, 'You had no problem with me working in Lambeth.'

'No one knew us there. And you were doing agency work. Tending to the needs of frail old birds stuck at home.' She was sure she saw a sneer in his face as he said that.

'I am a trained nurse,' she said between gritted teeth.

'A fulltime nurse in a hospital for infectious diseases is a different kettle of fish.'

'I'm doing something valuable and important, Ernest.'

'And I'm not, I suppose.' Now it was his turn to flare.

'I didn't say that.'

'I'll have you know an export agent is a very important position.'

'Yes, Ernest,' she murmured, deflated.

'One that comes with certain expectations.'

'Expectations?'

'That my wife is amply cared for, *at home*.'

'If you cared for me at all, you would be pleased,' she snapped.

She left him there, dumbfounded, and went to the bathroom to splash her face. In the small mirror above the basin, the woman staring back at her seemed almost foreign, indomitable. Yet she was shaking.

THE TEUTONIA CLUB

Emma's journey to and from the hospital took her up Scotts Road and past the Teutonia Club. Every time she glimpsed the fine colonial building with its single turret and fancy façade, she was reminded of the concert, of Ernest's unexpected and somewhat grotesque display of affection, and also of her heritage, of her extended family back in Germany and, above all, of her younger brother George. She thought of him with much affection, and as she did, she pictured him bent over the internal mechanism of a watch.

He had been a sensitive boy back home in Philadelphia and was bullied ruthlessly at school as a result. He grew into a quiet young man, withdrawn and wise beyond his years. She hadn't seen him since she left for London. Tired of the way Germans were treated, he migrated to Germany a year later. She wrote to him often, although even when she was still in London he had rarely answered. When he had, he'd written pages and pages of reflections on how he found life in their homeland, the people, the politics. Since she moved to Singapore, she had not received a single word from him and she worried after him and hoped all was well. Perhaps he had met someone, a demure young woman who would suit his needs. Emma wished that was it, that he had fallen in love and hadn't the time to write and tell her, his devoted sister.

Life at Orchard Road was as humdrum as ever. One day, after Ernest had set off for work, she found Chun sitting at the kitchen table. She had her back to Emma and her head was bowed. She appeared engrossed in some activity and Emma didn't like to disturb her, but she was curious. When she crept round the corner of the table and peered down at the contents of Chun's lap, the tiny woman started, embarrassed and gushed a string of hurried and almost incomprehensible apologies – from what Emma could gather, whatever Chun was making was for her daughter's upcoming wedding.

'It's alright,' Emma said, hoping to reassure her, but it was no use. Chun stood and tried to ferret away the small wooden frame. Emma recognised the loom straight away when a shuttle clattered to the floor and Chun reached down to retrieve it. 'Please,' Emma said and held out her hand, using her position of authority and not wanting to cause Chun any further distress all at once.

Instantly submissive, Chun handed her the loom. Emma studied closely the weave of fine coloured silk, delicate and exquisite – it was a bird and some flowers – and she could see Chun had almost finished the pattern. There were bobby pins dotted in the weave, presumably to hold the pattern in place, and there was not one shuttle, but three, resembling little canoes, each containing a different colour of silk thread. Emma marvelled over the handicraft, the obvious complexity and skill, and as she handed the loom back to her worried servant she said, 'Chun, will you teach me how to do this?'

'You want learn kesi?' She sounded doubtful.

'Please,' was all Emma could think of to say.

'It is very hard.'

'I can see that it is.'

'You need good eyes.'

'I have good eyes.'

Chun didn't seem convinced.

'I'll pay you for the materials and for your time.'

'You already pay me for my time.'

'Then I'll pay you for the materials.'

They agreed on an amount and Emma doubled it. Emma felt honoured. Whatever she paid Chun would never be enough to equal the skill she had agreed to pass on.

The following day, Chun arrived with a small loom, three spools of silk thread in three canoe shuttles, a wooden-handled brush and a small tin of bobby pins. The loom already had an outline of a design on the warp. Emma gazed in awe at the makings of her new and time-consuming project, but she had to wait until Ernest had left for work and Chun had finished her chores before they could begin.

Chun proved an excellent teacher and Emma learned fast. She embraced the meticulousness, the repetitiveness, the array of techniques. Above all, she enjoyed watching the small blocks of colour ever so slowly form petals and wings. Whenever she had nothing else to do, she would sit in the kitchen with Chun and take up her little loom. In the evenings before Ernest returned home, she would weave some more, although she found the light too weak and her eyes quickly tired, so she read or embroidered instead.

Dottie provided a distraction one Saturday when she invited Emma to accompany her and Lizbeth to Raffles Place. Ever since her arrival in Singapore, Emma had been avoiding travelling into the city centre. She had enough to adjust to with her new life, her neighbours and her employment, or so she'd thought. She did enjoy shopping, but she would never have ventured to Raffle's Place unaccompanied. It wasn't that she feared for her safety. It was the confusion, the hubbub, the foreignness and the intense tropical heat, all of which was sure to overwhelm her. Ernest might have taken her, but he was not a shopper and besides, he was always busy doing something else.

The three women went by gharry. They were seated in a row with Dottie and Emma on the ends, squashing up against Lizbeth in the middle.

The journey into the city felt markedly different from the one she'd taken out to Orchard Road. Back then, all was unfamiliar. This time, she viewed her surroundings differently. Beneath her gaze, the tree-lined road gave way to an urban streetscape lined with grandiose municipal buildings. Emma averted her gaze as they neared the construction site she had seen that first time, lest she witness more semi-naked men. Lizbeth was sitting quietly while Dottie provided Emma with a brief commentary on the schools and the other fine buildings they passed, and the churches which Emma had missed seeing on her way to the bungalow. Dottie pointed out the Masonic Hall, too, and Emma noted the building's classical features, all columns and arches arranged in perfect symmetry, the impressive size and central location, and therefore the prominence of Freemasonry in Singapore. In a few short miles, Dottie had given Emma a welcome overview of the city and she began to familiarise herself, take an interest, even enjoy her surroundings.

They crossed a short bridge, all stout with chunky arches, and carried on some distance before turning left and carrying on down the road. Dottie leaned forward to talk to the driver but thought better of it and sat back.

'He's gone too far,' she said to Lizbeth. 'We should have turned off at the last intersection.'

There was a brief pause in which Emma succumbed to rising unease.

She began to relax when Lizbeth said to Dottie, 'You fret too much. Besides, I think the road might have been busy.' Then she caught a glimpse of Dottie's expression before she turned her face away and the unease returned.

Another few blocks and, just as Dottie announced they had almost arrived at their destination, the gharry came to a sudden halt at an intersection and Emma found herself staring down a side street at the poverty and dilapidation she had anticipated all along was lurking in the city. It was a confronting sight, and she suddenly wished they could turn around and head back to the safety and comfort of Orchard Road. Neglect was evident in the rundown shophouses, the people in shabby clothing, Chinese-looking people too poor for shoes. Deep drains edging the wide and muddy roads. Narrow verandas sheltering shop entrances. She saw men cooking in wide, flat pans. Others standing around or leaning on posts. Aromatic smells invaded the air but the stench of poverty rose above it, the heat intensifying the reek of human waste. Emma fished a scented handkerchief out of her purse and held it to her nose. The heat, the ever-present tropical heat that caused Emma perpetual discomfort, seemed to intensify in the squalor.

'My dear, as you can see, Chinatown is not for us,' Lizbeth said, addressing Emma in a mockingly dramatic tone. 'The area is filled with gambling dens, secret societies and houses of ill-repute.'

'It's a frightful place and I wish we didn't have to drive past it. I think the authorities should clean the place up,' Dottie said, screwing up her face. 'Especially being as it is so close to town.'

Lizbeth laughed. 'I agree. But no one is going to listen to the likes of little old us.'

They were moving again. Another two hundred yards and the gharry turned left into a side street and pulled up in a large square framed by tall buildings. The centre of the square was given over to parking, comprising a mix of motor vehicles, rickshaws and gharries. Men in white suits ambled about. Even here, in the heart of metropolitan Singapore, a wizened man with a shoulder pole hefted away the night waste. Emma averted her gaze.

The women alighted and crossed the macadam and entered the John Little department store. Emma enjoyed the cooler air and she soon welcomed the array of goods on display at every turn. How marvellous it was to see familiar items. There was a grocery department, a section devoted to furniture, another to millinery, others to stationary, books and clocks, and then moved on to menswear – thankfully not a sarong in sight – and to the all-important womenswear. Dottie and Lizbeth knew exactly where to go and Emma followed, taking it all in.

They stopped at the haberdashery department and browsed the bolts of fabric, Dottie insisting Emma needed silk and linen and the finest of cotton if she was to survive in a climate that was always hot and humid.

'The weather never changes here,' Lizbeth said, casting a shrewd eye over the dress Emma had on. It was Dottie's. 'Even when it rains, it doesn't cool down.'

Unsure if Lizbeth knew the original owner of the dress, Emma diverted her attention back to the fabrics. She had a watchful eye on the prices and erred on the side of frugality, although she was equally mindful of not appearing to scrimp, especially with Dottie cooing and Lizbeth tutting over her shoulder. She made her selection and then they went and browsed the clothing. With Dottie and Lizbeth both focussed on helping Emma choose the best possible cut and cloth, she was unable to satisfy her own instinct for a bargain. Instead, after what felt like hours of discussion, she came away with two readymade dresses, a skirt and two blouses, enough fabric for two more outfits and ten spools of silk thread for use in tapestry. Lizbeth bought five yards of an expensive silk, along with some matching ribbon and Dottie bought a hat.

'We'll save Robinsons for another day,' she said, helping Emma carry her purchases.

They took tea in the refreshments area over by the furniture department. As they sipped tea in porcelain cups and nibbled dainty cakes, Emma listened to Dottie and Lizbeth's chitchat without taking much interest. Before heading back to Orchard Road, she summoned the courage to ask about churches in Singapore.

Both women turned to her at once. Their faces wore identical expressions, part disbelief, part disdain. Emma felt the heat rising in her cheeks.

'What sort of religious are you? Catholic?' Lizbeth asked.

'Of course she isn't Catholic.'

'Nothing wrong with being Catholic.'

'St Andrew's would probably do her, don't you think, Lizbeth?'

'We're not churchgoers, I'm afraid.'

'Tell you what. We'll drive by St Andrew's on the way home. At least then, you'll know where to find it.'

Emma wished she'd kept her mouth shut, although she was grateful when they took a detour past the church, which turned out to be a cathedral, and she found herself in awe of the building's stature and vowed to attend a service at the earliest opportunity. She might not be keen to venture into the city for shopping, but nothing would stop her attending church.

Despite the awkward moments, the outing proved agreeable and for the first time, Emma felt comfortable in Singapore. The British colonialists had clearly ensured their every need was being met, Emma thought, and the ease of living was obvious, just so long as one was able to blinker the eye to the conditions of the natives and the various other impoverished communities, whoever they might be.

The weeks slipped by. Emma settled into the rhythm of work, enjoying the sense of independence and the collegiality of the hospital staff. At home in Orchard Road, she took pleasure in creating her new dresses in the evenings when she was home alone, and when she was home alone in the daytime she worked on her tapestry. As soon as she completed the simple bird and flower design, Chun set her up with a new and larger loom and a more complex scene: two birds sitting on the boughs of a tree in blossom. The moment Emma saw the design, she knew it would take her many, many long hours to complete. She found she adored making tapestries. Whenever she wove the delicate silk threads, she slipped into a state of peace. Nothing troubled her. Not even the heat. She was lost to herself and at one with her craft. With a shuttle in her hand, she never once thought of Ernest.

An uncertain calm had descended on the Taylor marriage. Every now and then, Ernest would mutter remarks about what pestilence she might be bringing home with her from the hospital, but otherwise he tolerated her decision. Her first shopping expedition had pleased him enormously, much to her surprise, and towards the end of each week he told her to go into town again, although he never offered to go with her. She did go out on shopping expeditions, on Saturday mornings whenever Dottie and Lizbeth were free. They explored all the stores in Raffles Place before venturing further afield on the search for comfortable and cool shoes for Emma to wear in the house. No matter how hot her feet were, no matter how tight her shoes felt, Emma would never, not even when home alone, walk around in bare feet. Seeing she was stubborn, Dottie and Lizbeth – who both traipsed about barefoot indoors – had taken it upon themselves to do something for "poor Emma's feet". Thus far, they'd had no luck, but they had a pleasurable time trying.

On weekdays when Emma passed the Teutonia club, she thought of George. Fleeting thoughts laced with affection. She wondered what Germany was like, what her other relatives were doing, her sister Karin and her family. Emma spoke German very well – her parents had been keen for their children to recall their native tongue and they had spoken German at home as her mother found English difficult. Sometimes, when she spoke to Lizbeth, she felt an urge to break out in their shared language, but she never did. It never seemed appropriate and would have excluded Dottie who didn't even know of Emma's heritage – none of her new friends did – and Emma had no idea if Lizbeth would even have welcomed the gesture.

The last Monday in June, Ernest arrived home unexpectedly early. He greeted Emma in a cordial fashion and deposited the newspaper on the console table in the living room before heading to the bedroom to change into his customary sarong. Emma had arrived home an hour before and was sitting comfortably in one of her new dresses of lightweight muslin and lace. She knew the moment Ernest returned he would want his paper, but she was bored with her embroidery, what with the needle forever sliding through her fingers, and she was keen for a different distraction. Her day had been gruelling after a patient with cholera had died and she needed to keep her mind busy, lest it drift back to the last moments of his suffering.

She set aside the needlework and fetched the paper. The moment her eyes took in the details of the main article, she wished she had persisted with her needlework. On the front page, the headline announced Archduke Franz Ferdinand and his wife had been assassinated in Sarajevo and martial law had been declared in the city in response. The journalist included a quote from Sir Thomas Barclay to reassure the paper's readers the killings would most likely not provoke war in Central Europe. She did not share his confidence. What would Sir Thomas Barclay know? He was a politician and politicians said whatever they felt like. War in Central Europe? Between Austria and Serbia, surely? Nowhere else? Not Germany? She had no idea. She had not been following the news and she did not have a head for politics or speculation. She pushed aside her fears, refused to think about what may never be, yet every time she passed by the Teutonia Club from then on, her affectionate thoughts for George shaded into concern.

July proved a fretful month. Ernest was having difficulties managing his workload, which he said increased by the day, and he arrived home later each evening. A growing unease permeated the atmosphere at Dottie's on the weekends when Emma, and on occasion also a weary and distracted Ernest, joined the neighbours for tiffin. As the month drew to an end and the newspapers filled with talk of ultimatums and mediation, everyone could see that Europe was spoiling for war.

One Saturday afternoon, finding herself home alone as ever, not even her tapestry could still her restless mind and Emma popped round to Dottie's, braving the garden and emerging through the gap in the bushes to find Lizbeth, Cynthia and Eve lounging in the wicker chairs on the veranda. After the usual hellos and how-are-yous, she followed Dottie as she made her way into the living room to fetch another glass.

Once they were out of the line of sight of the others, Emma drew near.

'Will there be a war, do you think?' she whispered, the question that had been brewing in her mind for days finally spilling from her lips.

'I expect there will,' Dottie said sagely. 'But don't you worry. Edgar says we will be as safe as houses here, and I believe him.'

Emma thought Dottie was probably right. She was a sensible and pragmatic woman, more intelligent and more worldly than she gave herself credit for. Yet Emma drew no comfort from her reassurances. It wasn't here she was worried about.

At the end of the month, as nations declared war on each other one by one until finally, on the sixth of August, all the major players were at war and the alliances decided, she was beside herself with fear. What would become of George, a young man in Hannover, a pacifist by faith, but nevertheless fit for war? She had no choice but to keep those concerns to herself. Now that Britain was at war with Germany, she would become persona non grata in an instant if anyone discovered her true identity. After all, she was German in every respect. She had an American accent and she was a British subject by marriage, but after migrating to America as a small child she had never thought to get naturalised. There had seemed no point. She told herself that, as a British subject, she should be safe. Even so, she hid her German papers in the bottom of her trunk.

She felt for Lizbeth and Gustav, although neither appeared the least bit concerned. Perhaps they should have been. No one seemed to know what would become of all the Germans living in Singapore and it put everyone in an odd position as the

British got along best, out of all the various ethnic groups in Singapore, with the Germans.

She discovered their fate ahead of Ernest, ahead of her British neighbours she thought, and certainly ahead of most of Singapore when, on her way home from work, her gharry came to a sudden halt outside the Teutonia Club. There was much commotion in Scotts Road that afternoon and several motor cars were making their way into the club grounds. It took Emma some minutes to realise the cars were official, and there were military men in uniforms standing at the club entrance. A cluster of civilians milled about outside, under the watchful eye of the guards. One by one, the civilians were ushered inside. When she recognised Lizbeth and Gustav among them, a sick feeling welled in her belly. The internment continued, the cars filing in until eventually there was a gap in the stream of motor cars and she was on her way in her gharry.

The moment she arrived home, she deposited her uniform in her bedroom and rushed over to Dottie's, not even bothering to scan the garden for intruding tigers as she hurried through the gap in the fence.

'It's Lizbeth and Gustav,' she said breathlessly to a puzzled Dottie who was seated in her favourite wicker chair.

Dottie stood up languidly and led Emma inside. When she was sure there were no servants around, she said, 'Whatever's going on?'

Emma detailed in short sentences the scene up Scotts Road.

'Oh, that.'

Emma stared into Dottie's nonplussed face.

'You knew?'

Dottie touched Emma's arm with a reassuring hand.

'Edgar has inside knowledge of most things. I shouldn't worry. From what he says, things won't be too bad. They are allowed to take their servants with them. They've been told they can operate their bank accounts, buy goods and send messages. That much we know. Edgar has already spoken to those in command and we are planning to visit in a few days.'

'They can receive visitors?'

'Oh, yes. I was thinking of taking some flowers. Poor Lizbeth, though. I'm sure they'll be comfortable enough, but being Lizbeth, she will feel rather cooped up in there, I imagine.'

Emma absorbed the information, point by point, and relief rushed through her. She had grown fond of Lizbeth and her sardonic wit, her self-assurance and her disdain for pessimism. Lizbeth could be counted on to make the best of any situation and being interned in the Teutonia Club didn't sound all that bad.

Despite the German internment, the war felt far away and Dottie proved accurate in surmising Singapore would not be affected, at least not directly. Edgar complained of the lack of staff after the civil service lost forty-five young men who had left to enlist. 'Fancy themselves bloody heroes, the fools,' he would grumble. Dottie – who made no bones about her dislike of Edgar's expanding paunch – thought it would do her husband good to work a bit harder. At Guthries, the employment situation was worse. Rubber and tin estates had lost most of their staff as young British men enlisted to do their duty to their country and others took their wives and children back to England.

Cynthia's husband Ian complained he wanted to join them but was too old. He joined the Volunteer defence force instead, as did Edgar and Eve's husband Robert. The three men pressured Ernest to do the same, but he said he would be of little use on account of his bunions. They were quite large, Emma knew, and painful, and each big toe was almost crossing over the next, but he really didn't need to remove his shoes in front of the others just to make his point. But he did, and Ian and Edgar stared down at his crippled feet one afternoon at Dottie's while they were having tiffin and extended their sympathies. Ernest was duly exonerated from all responsibility in the war effort.

To his credit, at Guthries, to make up for the loss of staff, Ernest worked harder than ever. He had become rather enthusiastic, too, for a war was sure to be good for business, and it affected his mood profoundly. Emma found she had the old Ernest back, the ebullient, joyous Ernest full of little jokes and witticisms. The Ernest who knew how to make her laugh. Although his good spirits seemed to be at the expense of the rest of the world and he could be astonishingly insensitive about it.

'Just what the world needs,' he said one time over breakfast, 'a darn good war.'

Emma brought her teacup to her lips to mask her displeasure. For her, war was abhorrent. She had been reared on values of peace and adhered to the view that there really could be no justification for armed conflict.

In what should have been autumn but wasn't in the tropics where the seasons didn't exist, the Germans interned at the Teutonia Club were moved to Tanglin, where they were forced to forego their sanctuary in a grand hotel for a hospital ward in a military barracks.

For Lizbeth and the other internees, the move reinforced the reality of the war and that they were, in no uncertain terms, prisoners. Emma's immediate reaction when she heard the news from Dottie was selfish, she knew, but the strain of passing the Teutonia Club twice each weekday had become too much, especially since seeing the guards outside brought to the forefront of her mind her concern not only for the internees and for her beloved brother George but also for herself. It would be better for her emotional wellbeing if she could keep her worries from bubbling up each day, and without those guards posted outside the hotel as a constant reminder of what lay at the bottom of her trunk, she felt a little better.

For everyone other than the German internees, the war remained distant, although an atmosphere of anxious concern hung in the air like fog. The closest the fighting got to Singapore was when the *Emden*, a German raider masquerading as a British ship, stole into harbour and fired on a Russian cruiser. Emma followed the story in the daily newspaper Ernest brought home from work, her interest aroused because Emden was also a town very close to where she was born. The Russian cruiser had sunk in fifteen minutes. Over a hundred men had died. The *Emden* then sank a French destroyer before disappearing out to sea. Emma couldn't help but feel relieved when the *Emden* itself was later run aground, even though she was not sure which side of the war she should be on, or even if she was able to take a side.

Things were not so uneventful over in Europe. Hopes that the war would be over by Christmas were dashed when battles continued on the Western Front. Every day, the newspaper reported more death and destruction, and in so many different places it was impossible to hold the events inside the mind all at once. All Emma could do was pray, and so she prayed and prayed. She prayed for an end to the war and she prayed for all those who had perished or were injured, and their loved ones on either side.

Perhaps God would intervene and put a stop to so much senseless killing.

Perhaps God would intervene and spare George.

She felt powerless, just as she felt powerless on the quarantine ward at the hospital. She could soothe, but she could not cure.

At work one afternoon, Dr Farquhar came into the ward and Emma joined him on his rounds, together with the matron and another nurse. They paused at the end of each bed to discuss the patient's progress. Sometimes Dr Farquhar asked a question which Emma found she could answer. Otherwise, she just listened impassively. It was part of the routine of hospital nursing, as familiar to Emma as eating bread, and she performed the ritual in much the same manner as she always did, respectful and engaged, her attention unwavering.

Which was why, when they had seen the last man on the ward and Dr Farquhar drew Emma aside, he took her off-guard. She had no idea the worry and tension she held deep inside were showing on her face, no idea her emotional fatigue was visible to the discerning eye.

He suggested she take some time off but she refused.

'But you look done in,' he said.

Then matron was soon standing by his side. In cahoots, there was no doubt about it.

'We all need a rest from this ward at times,' she said sympathetically. 'It's nothing to be ashamed of.'

'I'm fine,' Emma said in her defence. But she agreed the quarantine ward was proving rather taxing. Perhaps there would be less emotional strain in the venereal diseases ward under Dr Huang? It was Dr Farquhar's suggestion. He made the arrangements and she transferred the next day.

The other nurses on the venereal diseases ward were pleasant company and Emma soon fitted in. She found Dr Huang to be an erudite specialist who liked to show off his extensive knowledge. But not with arrogance. On his rounds, she enjoyed his banter in his heavily accented English. He had a wry sense of humour, too, which he no doubt needed considering his specialism, and it proved infectious.

The suffering of the patients for the most part was less severe and the deaths not as commonplace, but Emma had to draw on all her resolve not to judge the patients, for impropriety was rife in Singapore and, despite the war, the illicit brothels continued to thrive. When she observed the cankers, the lesions and the sores, she had little sympathy, and she all but rolled her eyes inwardly whenever her patients roared in agony while voiding their bladders.

It was here that she encountered her most challenging patient, a Mr Frobisher from Kent. Mr Frobisher – he wanted her to call him Frank but she refused – was in the late stage of syphilis. He had difficulty coordinating his movements and was half blind. He would have been a dashing young man in his day and was still something of a rake. Yet he was losing his mind and suffered bouts of delirium. Dr Huang had also diagnosed a weakening of the heart and it wouldn't be long, everyone thought, before Mr Frobisher passed on.

The other nurses whispered to Emma the day she started on the ward to watch out for the dying patient, but the instant he saw her fresh face, he homed in and made Emma his fantasy sweetheart. She couldn't help but be amused by his assignations, the way he would call out to her across the ward in his lucid moments, hand on heart and insist she attended to his needs. She had no idea if it was entirely fakery.

One day, when he was short of breath after a seizure, she sat by his bedside and put a soothing hand on the sheet covering his arm and left it there. She closed her eyes and prayed inwardly. She kept still, leaving her hand on his arm and as she sat, she noticed his breathing steady and he drifted into slumber. After a short while, she removed her hand and left his bedside. She thought no more of it as she carried on with her tasks.

At the end of her shift, the matron beckoned her aside. She thought she must have done something wrong and her mind hurried back over her day, but the matron only smiled and said, 'You have a gift, Emma Taylor.'

'A gift? I don't understand.'

'I saw you with Mr Frobisher.'

Emma felt the colour rising in her cheeks. Despite the warmth in her smile and her words of praise, Emma still felt the matron was about to remonstrate her.

Instead, she gazed at her intently. 'You are a healer.'

'A healer?'

'I've seen it once before. You guard your gift, Emma. It's God-given.'

She meant it.

Emma found out the next day Mr Frobisher had died peacefully that night. It was the best anyone on the ward could have hoped for.

Now that she worked on the venereal diseases ward, at home, Ernest was less disparaging of her desire to work, relieved as he was that she was no longer at risk of infecting herself and those around her, mainly him, with a deadly disease, although he refused to pass comment on her patients.

The end of that year passed without bonhomie. It was as though the expatriates of Singapore felt too conscious of the war that raged far beyond the shores of the Orient to celebrate Christmas and the New Year. Happiness had been put on hold.

The one highlight for Emma was attending church.

St Andrew's Cathedral held a sombre Christmas Eve service, but it was enough for her to sit in the nave beneath the towering vaulted ceiling beholding the impressive stained-glass window behind the altar. The acoustics made the voices of the choir soar and as she sang the hymns, she forgot where she was and her heart filled with childhood Christmases, with presents and special cookies and Christmas Stollen. She hankered for those times when her family were all together back in Germany, although her memories were hazy. It was just a feeling she had. A feeling of Christmas, of belonging. The dim days of the season shading fast into long cold nights. Snow. How could she not hanker after snow.

Ernest, who was standing beside her pretending to sing, dropped his hymn book and she was catapulted out of her nostalgia and plonked back into steamy Singapore with something of a thump.

She enjoyed an altogether different experience of her German heritage one Saturday in early January. Emma was home alone when there was a loud hammering on the front door. Emma found Dottie standing on the front porch. She looked desperate.

'You must come with me to the barracks to visit poor Lizbeth. Do say you will.'

'When?'

'Now.'

Dottie eyed her neighbour expectantly and, feeling she had not been given much choice in the face of Dottie's determined expression, Emma reluctantly agreed. She didn't even have an excuse. Ernest was having lunch with his Lodge cronies at the cricket club and Emma had not been invited. Besides, the Germans had been interned for five long months and reports from Dottie on Lizbeth's wellbeing were not good.

'Meet me out the front in, what, fifteen?' Dottie said, looking Emma up and down.

'Very well.'

Satisfied, Dottie headed off through the front garden, leaving Emma to rush to her bedroom to change into a smarter dress.

Emma had rarely accompanied Dottie on these visits and not once since the internees were moved to Tanglin. Her work at the hospital provided the excuse. She wanted to support her new friend, of course she did, but she found the confrontation with her own German identity overwhelming. And, she couldn't go empty-handed. Whatever could she gift? She knew Dottie would have organised a hamper. She ran through options in her mind as her eyes darted about. Nothing second-hand would do. Something homemade? In the living room, her gaze landed on her first tapestry, the only tapestry she had created so far – the tree with birds and blossom looked set to keep her occupied for at least a year – and it was with a pang of regret that she picked it up and wrapped it in paper and popped it in her bag. Still, she knew Ernest wouldn't miss it. She'd shown him her first effort with much pride over dinner one time and his gaze had scarcely paused to admire the fine detail.

An hour later, they set off in Dottie's gharry laden with gifts of food and flowers. Dottie had even thought to buy their friend some lipstick. 'She'll have run out, I imagine.'

Emma offered no reply. The last thing she could have imagined wanting if she were interned was lipstick.

The town quickly gave way to trees and open fields. They bumped their way up Dempsey Hill and before long, the gharry came to a halt outside the barracks. The two women alighted, Emma ferrying down to Dottie the boxes and bags, before stepping down to take her share.

'You really are a treasure.'

Emma felt more like a packhorse. She struggled to find

anything positive to say so she kept quiet. Dottie told the driver to wait and they headed off with their cargo.

As they approached the compound, a cluster of large colonial buildings with enormous roofs greeted Emma's eye, buildings that were fringed with verandas supported by stout, square posts. A few more paces carrying her heavy load and Emma coveted the shade. The barracks had been given over to a military hospital, with one whole building devoted to skin and venereal diseases among the troops. Dr Huang had told Emma all about it – how Tanglin received one half of the problem and the infectious diseases hospital the other, while most of the carriers, prostitutes of all nationalities, never crossed the threshold of medical care.

They approached a guard leaning against the wall beside an entrance door, looking as though he hadn't a care in the world. He took in their white English faces and their packages and shooed them on inside, to where the German internees were housed all together in one wing. Upon entering, Emma saw immediately that the internees' belongings were much reduced, and she took in at a glance the miserable faces, the despondency, the boredom, and the resilience in those determined to make the best of things. Some were gathered around a bed, playing cards. Others were gossiping, one or two reading a book or a magazine. The atmosphere was sombre, and no one spoke loudly, but Emma understood the voices she did hear. Curious as she was to listen in, she feigned ignorance, maintaining a deadpan expression.

Lizbeth and Gustav were among the more privileged and had been given a private room – a nurse's staffroom, Emma thought upon entry – as had a few of the other wealthier, socially prominent couples. Everyone else had to make do with the conditions on the open ward. No doubt it was a source of some resentment.

Seeing her friends arrive, Lizbeth rushed forward and gave Dottie a lingering hug. Emma hung back as Gustav exited the room, accompanied by the man he'd been talking to at the concert.

'Herr Weber is not best pleased.' Lizbeth laughed as she closed the door on the men.

'I'm sure no one is pleased, not in here,' said Dottie. 'Him more than most. He'd had a lot invested in a little business venture and it looks like his plans are scuppered. But if you want my opinion, Gustav is too loyal to the wrong people.'

Emma struggled to feel any sympathy for Herr Weber. All his sort seemed to care about was the security of their own profits and investments, not the poor, suffering souls required to fight on the front lines. She recalled that earlier furtive exchange at the Teutonia Club, when Gustav had cautioned Herr Weber not to be paranoid. Those two had seemed shifty then and Emma couldn't help deciding they were just as shifty now.

She was soon brought back to the present by her arms, which had started complaining about the weight of Dottie's gifts.

'We brought you these,' Dottie said, depositing her portion of the load on the end of the bed. Emma quickly did the same, then retrieved her own gift from her handbag.

Lizbeth scanned the boxes and bags with interest.

'Thank you,' she said.

'I brought you this,' Emma said, proffering the tapestry.

Lizbeth's face lit with puzzlement and delight as she opened the paper and beheld the tapestry, Emma cringing inwardly as her own eyes landed on all the little flaws. It was, after all, her first attempt.

'You made this?' she said, lifting her gaze to Emma's face.

'I did,' Emma said shyly.

'Then, thank you. Homemade gifts are always the best.'

Lizbeth set the tapestry down on her pillow. Momentary joy gave way to angst as she turned to her friends.

Dottie searched her face. 'Are you really alright?'

Lizbeth shrugged. 'What to do. Gustav says we'll be deported to Australia soon enough.'

'No!'

'Herr Weber says we must be grateful we're being treated so well.' There was a tinge of sarcasm in her voice.

'Will Gustav be alright?'

Lizbeth's eyes darted to Emma. 'Would you be a love and fetch me some water?' She handed her a jug. 'It's down at the other end.'

Taking her cue, Emma wandered down the ward and, seeing no sign of fresh water, she pushed through the double doors and entered a short corridor. She found herself beside a small janitor's room. There was a storeroom opposite and the door was ajar. Hearing voices, she pulled back a fraction before she was seen. The conversation going on inside that storeroom was, of course, in German and something about the voices, furtive and hurried, made her hold her breath, her hearing sharp.

'Lauterbach, are you sure this is going to work?'

'They already despise the British. They only need a nudge.'

'The tunnel isn't ready.'

'We probably won't need it.'

'Then how will we escape?'

'Leave it to me.'

Lauterbach? The name rang a bell but she couldn't think why.

She heard movement inside the room, footsteps. Before the men exited, she hurried on by and pushed through another set of double doors. A large bucket of water sat on a table further on. She rushed over, then feigned nonchalance as she filled the jug, the men filing past behind her. As she made her way back to the ward, she glanced through the window to see a group of Germans, no doubt Lauterbach and his men, chatting and laughing with two Indian soldiers who were meant to be guarding the hospital wing.

MUTINY

One afternoon in early February, Emma arrived home from a tedious shift at the hospital to find Chun busy in the kitchen and the maid pottering in the garden. After welcoming her employer with a dazzling smile and offers of tea and cake – Emma declined both as she had only just had a cup and a biscuit in the nurses' station – Chun directed her to the two letters on the table in the hall. Not anticipating post, Emma had walked right past them.

Post?

She forced herself through her usual routine, depositing her handbag and her uniform in the bedroom, splashing her face with water in the bathroom and then heading to the living room, collecting the letters on her way by. She switched on the fan and directed the breeze at her favourite chair. Ernest would not be home for a few hours at least. She settled back and studied the envelopes in her hand.

The first was from her parents, date-stamped Philadelphia, the envelope all new and crisp. The other was from Germany, date-stamped August 1914 and much the worse for wear. Its envelope had been slit open and resealed at least twice by the look of it. Emma was surprised the letter had even made it to Singapore, given the war.

She opened the letter from her parents first. It was written by her father in German in neat, compact cursive. He said he was thinking of retiring or at least spending more time at home. Her mother was sixty-five. She had a heart condition and was finding it harder to manage the household. Her brother Herman was soon to qualify as a doctor and already talking of becoming a surgeon. That would please her father enormously. Her parents had managed to retain one of their offspring while the other three were scattered to the winds, but it appeared her brother was more than making up for the absence of her, Karin and George. Odd that there was no mention of her other siblings in the letter, and her father did not ask her how she was faring. No mention of Ernest either, but that was to be expected.

She put the letter back in the envelope and set it down in her lap. The larger part of her did not want to open the other envelope. She held it in her hands as her heart filled with dread. Eventually, after persuading herself that George was alright, that he'd done the right thing, that he'd taken a stand, that he'd become a conscientious objector, she extracted the letter. The news was not what she had hoped for.

She hadn't fully comprehended the magnitude of the war or the formalities of conscription. She could have had no idea that a young man of twenty in Germany would already have been drafted for at least two years of military service and that same young man would now be required to fight for his country. George had left America in 1908. Now he was twenty-six, no doubt still a spindly and delicate man, slight of build and entirely unsuited for battle. He explained he would rather fight than languish in prison as a conscientious objector. Don't worry about me, he said, and she worried all the more, tracing her fingertips over his writing, feeling the impressions the pen nib had made on the paper, hoping to absorb a trace of him through her skin as her eyes brimmed with tears.

Did their parents know? In an effort to quell her anguish she replied to her father, deciding she must break the news she knew he must hear, although it felt like a betrayal of confidence. Their father would as soon cast adrift any son of his who took up arms. George knew that. She was certain he was telling her in private. Filial loyalty won out and she tore up the page and began again, this time outlining her life in Singapore, the poor sanitation, her adventures with Dottie, the heat.

By the time Ernest came home, barging through the front door and causing it to swing open and hit the wall with a sharp crack, Emma had sealed the envelope on her letter to her father and tucked the one from George in her trunk. Footsteps came down the hall, heavy and irregular. He was intoxicated again. She thought she could smell his breath even before his corpulent visage appeared in the doorway. He steadied himself against the doorjamb and arranged his face into a playful smile, the effort contorting his features. She looked up at him, her gaze sliding away as contempt reared inside. He was grotesque. In that moment, she could not understand what had possessed her to marry a man as self-indulgent and as base as he. A man with stuck-on graces. A man bent on flirting with pretty young women and rising up the social ladder. A man conveniently placed outside the war effort by a matter of months due to their departure for Singapore – his bunions placing him outside even voluntary service – and there stood her drunken husband protected from all danger, all that would or already had befallen her brother, indeed befallen any good and loyal man called to do his duty by his country.

'Don't I get a greeting, dear wife?' he slurred. 'A kiss would be nice.'

'Chun will have dinner on the table soon,' was the best she could offer in reply.

'Fobbing me off again, are we, Emma?' There was a tinge of hurt in his tone.

'Now is hardly the time.'

'For what? I only wanted a kiss.'

He lumbered into the room, bent over her and cupped her face in his hands and planted his slobbering lips on hers.

'Must you?' she said, pushing him away.

'Very well.' Now he sounded curt. 'I shall take a bath.'

He reappeared half an hour later, barefoot and garbed in his sarong.

The following Monday was the Chinese New Year and she had taken a day off, not that she was involved in the celebrations. Dottie and Cynthia had been invited by one of their rich Chinese acquaintances to attend a garden party they were hosting at their large residence in Bukit Timah, a suburb past Tanglin. Emma had not been invited. Neither Edgar nor Ian had wanted to mingle with their Chinese counterparts – they maintained a boorish stance towards any and all non-Europeans and, now that the war was on, Germans were unacceptable, too – and they had chosen instead to spend the day watching cricket at the Singapore Cricket Club. They had taken Ernest with them after he had declined an invitation to attend a party hosted by some work colleagues at their home in Pasir Penang. Emma was surprised by his decision, until she discovered the men were relatively new members of staff holding lowly positions in the company hierarchy. Clearly nothing to be gained there for Ernest. And clearly, the thought of being with his wife on a public holiday did not cross his mind, although he had extended her an invitation to the cricket club, and she had, as he knew she would, declined.

Seated in the living room, Emma grew listless. Orchard Road was uncommonly quiet for a weekday and her shoulders were tense after the hours she'd already spent bent over her silk tapestry. She was finding the first cluster of the cherry blossoms a challenge. Each object was separated by a thin border of silver thread, which added to the intricacy. She began to feel constrained by the design Chun had given her. The fan whirred, blowing cooling air on her face but her hands were hot, the palms a touch damp and the shuttles stuck to her fingers. Ten months in Singapore and she still had not acclimatised to the heat.

The afternoon ticked by as though time itself felt idle. The house was too still. Chun had the day off, as did the maid. Emma couldn't rouse herself to go to the kitchen for refreshments, but her thirst grew, as did her hunger and finally she stood up.

She was on her way back to the living room with a glass of tea julep and two biscuits on a plate when a sudden bang in the distance caused her to stop in her tracks. She listened. There it was again, and again, irregular explosions, like fire crackers maybe.

Or gunfire.

She tuned in to the direction of the source and thought the noises came from the west, from the vicinity of the Tanglin Barracks about a mile away. Her mind leaped back with sudden alarm to that last time Dottie and she had visited Lizbeth, to the conversation she had overheard, to Lauterbach and his devious plot, and she wondered if the German prisoners of war had broken out of the hospital and the Indian guards had opened fire. Should she have told someone what she had overheard that day?

The explosive sounds abated and she dismissed her thoughts as fearful nonsense borne of an idle mind and resumed her armchair with her julep and her biscuits, keen to finish a section of the flower pattern she was working on.

Around four in the afternoon, the front door burst open and a very hot and sweaty Ernest rushed into the living room. He was breathless, gasping as though he had just run up the entire length of Orchard Road.

'The match over already?' Emma asked. She observed him for a moment and added, 'Why don't you sit down and stop panting.'

He waved his hands about, beckoning her to come. He was frantic.

'There's trouble at the barracks,' he said at last.

Alarm shot through her. Lauterbach! Picturing Lizbeth's body prostrate on the ground as she attempted to flee, Emma feared the worst.

'Have the Germans broken out?' she said.

'No, no. Well, I don't know. Probably. It's the Indians. The guards.'

Concern gave way to relief. 'Calm down, Ernest. Your words will come out all the better if you catch your breath.'

'There isn't time, Emma. The 5th Light Infantry have gone berserk.'

'Berserk? Whatever do you mean?' In his exasperated state, she was struggling to take him seriously.

'It's a mutiny,' he cried. He sounded almost childish. 'Hundreds of sepoys are on the rampage.'

'Sepoys? Who are these men?'

'Just about the only bloody army the British left to protect Singapore, other than the volunteers. I've come to collect you.'

'I'm not going out there in the streets! We will be safer indoors.'

'I wish it were true. Reports are coming in that the mutineers are killing every European they clap eyes on. They are going from house to house. It's a massacre.'

It was the way he said the last word that convinced her he wasn't exaggerating and she needed no further persuasion. She stood and grabbed her purse. 'Where will we go?'

'Not sure. Into town and then we'll have to find somewhere where it's safe. Guthries, maybe. Or the Lodge.'

After a frantic dash in the motor car Edgar had insisted Ernest drive, and which had accounted for much of Ernest's fluster on entering the house since he had little experience behind the wheel, they stopped first here, then there, asking whoever looked official in the city streets where best to go, and ended up back at the cricket club.

The building, with its solid walls and imposing pillars, looked capable of fending off the most vicious attack, but as more women and children arrived, hurrying in with looks of terror on their faces, and as reports of more and more killings came in with them, it became apparent, to Emma at least, that an evacuation from Singapore would soon be called for. The new arrivals hurried through to join the others huddling at the back of the large reception room. Emma chose to stay near the main doors of the wood-panelled entrance hall in case she could be of some use. Ernest was forced to stay with her.

An officer rushed in with more news, hurrying past the Taylors and coming to an abrupt halt before the official-looking men milling nearby.

'The mutiny has spread to Alexandra Barracks,' he

announced to those within earshot. 'Commander's shot down, other officers narrowly escaping with their lives.'

'Good lord!'

Mouths fell open, faces looked stricken.

'It gets worse. Major Galway and Captain Izard of the Royal Artillery have been murdered at Sepoy Lines. And a doctor has been shot dead in his car.'

'It's a mutiny, right enough.'

The other officers, along with various civilian men who had put themselves in charge, Edgar among them, quickly gathered into a huddle to devise a plan of action. Emma watched, wishing to be included in her capacity as a nurse, but her gender precluded any involvement in decision-making. There was much arguing among the men and then nodding and toing and froing.

Minutes passed like days. Then Edgar broke away from the group and approached Emma and Ernest.

'I'm ferrying passengers. Emma, come along.'

Ernest made to step forward before realising, with an alarmed glance at his wife, that he would be required to stay behind. This time, bunions would serve as no excuse for cowardice, Emma thought as she walked away. Although her footsteps were not without compassion for her husband, who appeared completely out of his depth.

After a short but cramped ride, the women crammed into Edgar's car decanted and joined the small group already gathered on St Johnson's Pier. Emma knew no one there. Children were crying and clinging to their mothers. Women consoled each other. More motor cars pulled up and more women and children arrived.

With a rising sense of her own standing as a health professional, Emma went and stood near a staunch and proud-looking man in a uniform who was clearly in charge. Without further ado, she announced she was a nurse, should anyone need her help.

'Thank you, madam,' he said, scarcely taking her in.

'May I ask,' she said, persistent. 'I heard the shooting at home. Has there been a raid on Tanglin Barracks?'

'That is correct, madam.'

'I'm Mrs Taylor,' she said. Keen to make an impression, she proffered her hand.

'Major Thompson,' he said, giving her a brief handshake. 'Now, if you'll excuse me.'

She hesitated, choosing her words with care. 'Wait. Please, Major. And what of the Germans?'

'The Germans are fine. Liberated, in fact. The sepoys drove them all out of the barracks and then shot at the personnel.'

She maintained her composure. 'Any casualties?'

'At this stage, no. Although there is no telling what will happen in the next hours. The nurses and doctors at the barracks chose to stay where they were and tend the wounded.'

'Unlike the guards, I suppose.'

'The guards scattered.'

Seeing he was again about to walk away, the urge to confide grew strong and she overrode her reticence at revealing her German identity in the telling.

'Major Thompson, I should tell you I believe some Germans there were plotting.'

'I beg your pardon, Mrs...'

'Taylor.'

'Mrs Taylor, as you can see, I'm rather busy.'

'I think it's important you hear what I have to say. Please.'

He sighed. She gave him the briefest account of what she had overheard the previous month, hoping to avoid the obvious question that might have played in the major's mind – just how was it she knew the German language so well? He listened with forced interest until she mentioned Lauterbach. The expression on his face changed in an instant.

'They could speak Hindustani, too,' she went on, realising the veracity of what she said as she spoke. 'I saw them later, chatting with the guards.'

'The scheming rat,' he muttered under his breath.

She had no idea what use the information would be, but she had lightened her conscience in the telling.

There was the sound of gunfire in the distance.

'Thank you, Mrs Taylor.' The major turned to speak to another officer who had rushed over, and she peeled away and joined the throng of distressed women and children.

The next thing she knew, she was being herded onto a launch, crammed in with the other evacuees in the rapidly falling darkness. As the boat pulled away from the pier, the darkness grew thicker, broken only by the lights of a steamship out in the harbour. No one spoke. A child cried. Another whimpered. Emma clung to the railing as the launch listed to the right and the crush of bodies pressed against her.

The discomfort was soon over, and the launch pulled up beside the ship and, one by one, they were ferried off, made to scramble up a rope ladder to the main deck. The rise and fall of a light swell made the initial rungs of the ladder precarious and Emma was grateful for the two men guiding her way. As she neared the top and the launch felt far below, her palms began to sweat and she gripped the ladder all the tighter, taking no comfort in the presence of the woman below or above her.

On deck, Emma soon found the SS *Ipoh* had no means of coping with the new passengers. A kindly crew member announced he was giving up his cabin for the children and the captain, a gracious and obliging man, instantly offered his for those women who wanted to remain inside. Emma chose a recliner that had been put out on deck along with some mattresses and, after accepting a bowl of chicken stew and a hunk of torn bread, she spent the night staring back at the lights of Singapore, anxious for news, picturing a frantic Ernest dashing about, doing nothing except avoiding the danger.

The mood was tense. Everyone had loved ones on shore. No one would sleep that night, of that she was sure, yet neither of the women seated to either side of her seemed predisposed to converse. On her left, a young woman sat hunched, clutching her knees and periodically burying her face in her clothes, and on her right a prim-looking woman in her thirties kept looking around nervously as though hoping to glimpse a friend or a loved one.

'It'll be alright,' Emma said.

'Will it?'

Emma sighed inwardly. She had no idea how many of the women knew each other, but she knew none of them and now, it seemed, was not the time to strike up conversations.

Emma wondered what had become of Dottie and Cynthia. Neither of them had made it aboard the SS *Ipoh*. As for Lizbeth, Emma hoped that if the Germans had escaped through that tunnel, they were on their way to Malay.

And then there was Ernest, her husband, the reason for her presence in Singapore, a man she was less devoted to than she should have been. She prayed for him nonetheless.

Morning brought rising heat and fresh misery. The women started complaining about the food and the facilities. They were feeling uncomfortable in sweat-laden clothes, and irritations rose over petty concerns coupled with anxieties over husbands and fathers and sons. Emma found herself offering words of consolation and praying for a quick resolution. She refrained from announcing she was a nurse for fear of being confronted with a deluge of minor complaints she had no means to fix.

Later that first day, word came through that the mutineers had attacked a house in Pasir Panjang. Little more was said. The news left the women in dismal spirits. Everyone was thinking the same. If one had been attacked, what of all the others? Would the military personnel manage to quell the mutiny? It was the question nobody dared ask aloud. Emma could only hope Ernest was managing to stay safe.

They were kept on board for three long and fretful days. Arrangements were made for the women to wash, but they had no choice but to put on the same perspiration-laden clothes. Some of the older women attempted to take command of the dire situation and rouse some cheer with a sing-along, but there was little participation. With so much despondency, during the evening of the second day Emma reluctantly made it known to the captain that she was a nurse, should anyone need assistance, but no one did.

On the fourth day, spirits rose at the sight of a launch approaching, and when the vessel pulled up alongside the ship a cheer broke out among the women and the decanting began in earnest. The cheer proved short-lived. A sea breeze had whipped up the waters of the bay and the launch lurched and rolled and bucked its way back to the pier. After clinging to the railing watching the woman beside her turn pale, Emma was relieved to reach dry ground.

There was much commotion on the quayside as women arrived from other launches. Overhearing the chatter going on all around her, Emma discovered she had fared better than most. The women arriving from the SS *Nile* did nothing but complain about conditions on board. To quash the discontent, one of the officers in charge of the horde of disgruntled women said sternly that they should all be thanking their lucky stars, because many women and children never made it onto either ship and had been crowded instead into the city's gaol cells with all the firing going on right outside. His words had the desired effect and the women were chastened.

Emma noticed a group of women gathered around a uniformed man who was attempting to raise his voice above the hubbub and barrage of questions as everyone wanted to know what had happened. Eventually, someone brought a crate and the officer stood head and shoulders above his audience and was able to announce in a reassuring tone that many of the mutineers had been rounded up and imprisoned, all ninety-nine of them.

'Ninety-nine!'

The number was repeated amid gasps of horror.

Others, the officer said, had escaped to Johore.

'What have you done with the captives?' a woman shouted.

Emma recognised her voice. It was Eve. She was standing towards the back, hands on hips, face defiant.

The horde was quick to repeat the question with cries of, I hope they're shot! And, String 'em up!

'Those captured have been put in gaol,' the officer said.

'Not the same gaol those poor women and children were herded into,' Eve yelled.

'The women and children have been relocated elsewhere,' the officer said roundly, somewhat alarmed at the vicious indignation building before him, largely thanks to Eve. 'Now, move along.'

Emma was one of the first to head off. She fought her way through the throng and, not waiting for a motor car, she hurried to the nearest gharry. An obliging-looking local helped her up to the seat. She sat back, pleased to be getting away from the port. She said a short prayer of thanks as the gharry journeyed through the streets of the city and then on up Orchard Road.

She arrived home to find a maudlin Ernest prostrate on the sofa in front of the fan, a glass of whisky in one hand and a handkerchief in the other. The full extent of his experience of the mutiny was brought home to her when he looked up, his face filled with sadness, and said, 'Thank goodness you're back.'

'Whatever's the matter with you, Ernest?' she answered, dismayed by his attitude. 'I thought you would be relieved, if not pleased to see me.' Overjoyed would have been too much to hope for.

'I am, dear heart. But Guthries have lost three men. MacGilvray, Dunn and Butterworth were shot dead in the garden of their bungalow.'

'The fighting in Pasir Panjang?"

'You knew?'

'Only that there had been another massacre. Was this the party you decided not to attend?'

'The very same.'

'I'm sorry, Ernest.'

'I didn't know them that well. They were newcomers.'

'Even so.'

'It was a close shave, Emma. I would have been killed.'

She eyed him with a measure of derision. All he cared about was himself. Him, her husband, lying on the sofa in his sarong, supping whisky and feigning remorse when the truth was, he had no doubt contrived various ways to escape all the drama and mayhem and stay right away from any danger. Even as she had the thoughts, she censured herself. It wasn't Christian or wifely to harbour such opinions, even of Ernest. After all, she had no idea if her suppositions were unfounded. Although she had to admit the chances were slim.

Over the next few days, the newspaper was full of the news of the mutiny and it was all anyone talked of, at work and at Dottie's. Forty-four Europeans had been shot, many harmless victims. The worst tragedy was the shooting of a pair of newly-weds. News emerged that the Germans had contrived the mutiny by playing on the Indian Pathans' discontent, the result of anti-British propaganda coming through from India. Lauterbach and his crew convinced the guards up at Tanglin barracks that since Turkey had come out against the Allies, the British would be sending them off to fight, and they would be forced into battle against their own fellow Muslims. It was a false rumour, but it had the desired effect. Lauterbach had also led the mutineers to believe they would escape on the *Emden* and reach safety in the State of Johore. The mutineers had no idea the *Emden* had already been run aground. Meanwhile, the plotters had dug a tunnel at Tanglin barracks and when the chaos erupted, they hid. Six were recaptured but ten, including Lauterbach, escaped by boat to the Dutch East Indies. Emma had been right to suspect Lauterbach, but she said nothing of her prior knowledge, not to Dottie or even to Ernest. If she did, she would most likely be quizzed as to how she knew the German language so well.

Two weeks later, Emma awoke, cooking in a tangle of nightgown and sheet. Ernest had an arm over her. She gently removed it and eased herself out of bed and went to the bathroom. She felt suddenly nauseous and thought she might be sick, but the feeling soon passed. In the kitchen, she found Chun preparing breakfast. The smell of frying eggs caused the bilious feeling to return and Emma about-faced and ran to the bathroom, where she was sick in the sink.

She washed her face and gazed in the mirror, counting back the days. There could be no doubt about it. She was pregnant. She stood there staring at her careworn face, lost in thought, wondering at her future.

Her reverie was disturbed by movement in the hall. Ernest appeared and came up behind her and grabbed her by the waist. She gave a small start. Then he wrapped his arms around her and kissed her ear. She ought to have swung round and hugged him back, beamed into his face her own radiance, her glow from within, knowing she had at last conceived his child. But she could bring herself to do none of that, not yet, not when she had yet to come to terms with the realisation. Too quickly, the knowledge of the pregnancy came with the sickening thought that she harboured a deep ambivalence towards her husband, an ambivalence that grew larger by the day. She would never have permitted herself thoughts of leaving him, but even if she had, they were now dashed. Carrying his child, she was trapped. As soon as he knew, as soon as it was impossible to hide the bump, she would have to give up her work at the hospital and occupy herself at home. She gave Ernest a soft, almost coy smile as she disentangled herself from his embrace.

It was well into May before all the court martial trials were over and thirty-seven mutineers were condemned to be shot in batches by a firing squad. The ringleaders were to be publicly executed, something Emma found abhorrent. More abhorrent still was Ernest's decision to attend.

'I owe it to my colleagues,' he said the day of the executions, pulling on his jacket.

'You said you hardly knew them,' Emma said indignantly.

'That's not the point.'

'It's a grotesque spectacle, Ernest. I cannot think you would choose to be there. Especially when...' She caught herself mid-flow.

'Especially when what?'

Emma hesitated. There would be no hiding the bump for much longer and perhaps, just perhaps the knowledge would change his mind.

'I'm pregnant.'

His mouth fell open.

'And you choose to tell me now!'

'That is no way to display your joy.'

He rushed towards her and reached for her hands.

'I am pleased. Of course I am. More than pleased. Overjoyed in fact, but I am heading out the door, as you can see.'

'And you won't change your mind?' she said, dismayed.

'I told you, I owe it to those men.'

He hurried from the room. The front door clunked shut and a dull weight of anguish settled deep inside her.

She spent the next two hours trying her best not to think of the spectacle.

Two hours bent over her silk tapestry.

Two hours pushing Ernest's recalcitrance from her mind.

Two hours and he returned with a bunch of flowers.

She offered him a smile of gratitude. Maybe he wasn't so selfish after all.

He spoiled the moment when he said, 'It was very well done.'

She instantly cupped her ears with her hands to make it plain to him she did not want to hear anything about it. She was not sure she would be able to account for her actions if her husband persisted with a recount of the event. He respected her wishes and took himself off down the hall, returning in his customary sarong.

After the executions, life in Singapore returned to normal and it was as though the war was no longer happening. Except that it was, and she read about the trenches and the battles and the loss of life in the newspaper every day, and she thought of George and no word came.

No word would come, she knew that, for how would he

have managed to have a letter sent to her when he was fighting for the other side.

Bored and hot and more uncomfortable by the day, the only respite for Emma came six months into her pregnancy when Dottie insisted she take her and an enthusiastic Cynthia to the Indian quarter in the motor car. It was Cynthia's idea. They had still not managed to find Emma comfortable summer shoes.

'Your feet will only swell and swell and there will be no respite until you pop,' Cynthia had said the previous Sunday afternoon. 'You need a pair of jutties.' She showed Emma an image of a pair of decorative and flimsy-looking slippers in a magazine. Emma looked askance. 'I'll manage with what I have,' she said.

'You're already bursting out of your Mary Janes, Emma!' Dottie said, bending down and examining Emma's feet. 'The strap is on the last buckle hole.'

Cynthia stabbed a finger at the magazine on her lap. 'And the jutties will be comfortable and cool.'

'Where will I wear them?'

'At home around the house.'

'Or here at mine,' Dottie said.

Cynthia gave Emma a sympathetic look. 'You won't be going anywhere else, now, will you.'

Except to the Indian quarter, it seemed. She had acquiesced and that Saturday morning, seated in the front of Dottie's motor car, Emma took in the ramshackle shophouses as they ventured up Serangoon Road, heading to where Cynthia had suggested they might find Emma a pair of these simple, exotic shoes.

In the car, Dottie was in a patriotic mood. She had grasped the idea of fundraising for the war effort with both hands after she heard Mrs Lee, wife of a Chinese millionaire, along with the wife of Dr Huang, were running fêtes in aid of the British

Red Cross and had raised a substantial amount from the Chinese community. Cynthia joined in the discussion with much enthusiasm. By the time they reached the shoe shop, Dottie and Cynthia had decided to put on an amateur-dramatic performance in Singapore's Victoria Theatre in December.

'We'll put Eve in charge of the tickets.'

'Perfect!'

It would be, Emma thought, considering Eve. In the aftermath of the mutiny, Eve had volunteered for the Red Cross in an administrative capacity. Emma thought her well-suited for the role. She waited for them to assign her a role as well, but they didn't. There were some advantages to being pregnant.

The shoe shop Cynthia had singled out was more of an emporium. The air inside was infused with sweet incense and filling the space was an array of brightly coloured scarves, saris, jewellery, brass ornaments and shoes. If they were to be called "shoes".

Dottie and Cynthia handled the situation, sitting Emma down on a stool deep inside the shop, removing her Mary Jane's that really were too tight, and slipping on her feet several pairs of jutties until they had the right fit. Dottie paid and Emma came away with six pairs.

'They wear out fast, Emma,' said Cynthia, the expert on jutties.

On the way back, Dottie took a small detour and pulled up in Race Course Road on the pretext of adjusting her mirror. They were outside a terrace of shops and small businesses, only the building right beside them was neither of those things. Instead, a small sign announced the Theosophical Society Lodge.

Emma had never heard of such a lodge.

With her hands on the steering wheel, Dottie turned and began without preface to confide in Cynthia, and, by virtue of her presence, Emma, some personal difficulties she had been having with Edgar.

'Does he know about Bob?' Cynthia breathed, scarcely loud enough for Emma to hear.

'Absolutely not.'

Dottie's eyes darted to Emma on the back seat, and she was reminded of the arrival of a man at Dottie's that first time they'd met, and how Dottie had shunted her out through the back garden. It came as a shock to realise Dottie might be having an affair.

Dottie continued with her confidences, choosing to detail a horrible row she'd had with Edgar the previous night. Cynthia listened, responding in all the right places and relating, once Dottie had said all, her own discontent with Ian. A discussion on the foibles of their husbands ensued. At first, Emma shut her ears, not wanting to know the details, sordid or otherwise, but she soon paid attention as she realised she was not the only discontented wife in Singapore. And listening to the shortcomings of Edgar and Ian and all that Dottie and Cynthia were forced to put up with, she told herself she ought to be grateful to have a husband who provided for her, who was never mean and never admonished her or fiercely controlled her and certainly had never raised a fist to her. Even so, Emma remained discreet, saying nothing and keeping her gaze firmly on the view through the window of the strange-sounding lodge. Eventually, she asked if either of them knew what the place was.

'Aren't they a bit like the Freemasons?' Dottie said, somewhat taken aback by the non sequitur. 'Cynthia, you would know.'

'They hold strange beliefs. Something to do with the Spiritualists.'

'Aren't they into séances?' Dottie said.

'The Spiritualists, yes. I think the Theosophists have taken things in another direction.'

'Sounds creepy and weird.'

'Nothing for you there, Emma,' Cynthia said, peering out the passenger side window.

Emma couldn't have agreed more.

1939

COTTENHAM HOUSE

Observing Adela as she slumbered, the gentle labour of her breath, her precious copy of *The Picture of Dorian Gray* on the table at her bedside, and then the totality of this lavishly decorated room, Emma pictured the cosseted life of indulgence and merriment her patient had led and recalled her stories of the pre-Raphaelite circle's gatherings at Babbacombe Cliff. She could almost hear her talk of those rarefied ideas – mystical, complex, esoteric – that Emma doubted Adela had ever truly comprehended. Adela seemed to Emma the type to dally at the edges of knowing, there just for the fun of it, and, above all, for the difference from all she had grown up with in the Victorian era. She decided the only thing Adela really ever knew about the Theosophical Society was that it existed and was populated with interesting people.

Perhaps her assessment was too dismissive and inconsiderate and, for all Emma knew, Adela might have studied the teachings or at the very least familiarised herself with the basic tenets, just as Emma had, long after her time in Singapore was over, when she found herself in London, in Wimbledon, and a new phase of her life had begun.

Her musings were disturbed by a light knock and an opening door as Susan appeared to relieve Emma of her duties. After a brief handover, Emma retired to her room, crowded now as memories scurried in behind her.

She sat down in her armchair and drew closer her upright tapestry loom resting on a table on casters. The tapestry was an ambitious project requiring all her skill. The scene was side-on, and the only section of her design that could be considered simple was the pale fawn sky. The rest, the quaint country cottage with its picket fence, the shrubbery and garden beds, required all of her patience and precision. She drew the shuttle through a few strands of warp comprising the tiny porch and ran pinched fingers lightly down the fine wool. As she wove, her mind drifted back to Singapore, to that last year, her first of motherhood, when she found she had no time at all for her silk tapestry and had put away the loom with the work only one quarter complete, the silk spools sitting in their canoe shuttles obscuring the image.

What became of those jutties? She wore three pairs out, but one of the other pairs she had never worn. She was sure she had packed them when they left Singapore. Did she have them in Japan? She couldn't recall. Her life back then was a blur to her now and besides, the whereabouts of a pair of shoes was not something she would readily commit to memory. She scarcely recalled the birth of her first daughter other than her anxiety that she might inadvertently yell out in German and reveal her true identity – she hadn't – and the tribulations of early moth- erhood in the tropics, the hot and clammy flesh, the nappies and baby cries. During her last year of tropical heat, she scarcely left the bungalow. That much she did recall. Even the steamship that took them to San Francisco was a hazy recollection.

Gladys had been a good baby, she did remember that, but all babies cried and all babies crawled and toddled and caused a nuisance and she needed eyes and ears everywhere and never had any idea of Ernest's whereabouts at any given moment, other than noting that when he had been present, he showed his daughter nothing but unconditional kindness and complete adoration. They shared the same large, smoky-blue eyes and when Gladys's didn't turn brown, he was over the moon. From the day she arrived in the world, he was a changed man. He became attentive and focussed on family matters, concerned for the welfare of his child and, by extension, his wife. Back then, Emma had even begun to wonder if she had been wrong about him, misjudged his behaviour, her prejudices skewed by the infernal heat and humidity, when really, he was just an ordinary man with ambitions and a great love of children.

Emma threaded her shuttle through a few strands of the warp one last time and got ready for bed. Looking back, she knew she had much to be grateful for. She, a humble nurse from Philadelphia, whisked away by the love of her life and taken on a grand adventure halfway around the world to live a charmed existence in a British colony as the wife of a successful export agent. Mother of a beautiful girl, a pretty baby now grown into a fine young woman of twenty-four, engaged to be married to a clerk in the civil service. And her sister Irene now married and heavy with child. She must visit them soon. She might have seen Irene the next morning, but her ankles had swollen, she'd said on the telephone, and she declined Emma's invitation to go shopping in Wimbledon for Christmas.

Morning came, and not a chink of light breached the blackout curtains. Emma turned onto her back and folded her hands across her abdomen beneath the sheets. All was quiet in the house. No sounds came from outside. No shouts, no gunfire. She had started to wonder if the war would ever come to Britain. Perhaps her prayers would be answered and the fighting would be over soon and she would be rid of this anxious knot in her abdomen.

The anxious knot told her otherwise. In some ways, news of bombs and gunfire would be a relief from grim anticipation as England lived out a false normality, a normality filled with trepidation, foreboding an invisible shadow over the sun. The Germans were tenacious, everyone said, an organised and determined race. She supposed she had to agree. She had no doubt about Hitler's capabilities. That he was a dangerous maniac she also didn't doubt. And her people had fallen for his bluster – at least, all those attending his rallies. There would be exceptions, many, many exceptions. Those like her. Those able to see with the mind's eye beyond the outward appearance and into the face of darkness.

She found it ironic, this war unfolding not far from Britain's shores, yet as distant for her now as the last war was in Singapore, the mutiny the one exception.

Despite the internment of the Germans, back then there had been little anti-German sentiment among the British expatriates; at least, not that she saw. That form of hatred made its ugly appearance in her life much later, and she feared a repetition; feared it all the more, believing she couldn't claim she was a British subject when her husband had died. She wasn't certain that he had, but she certainly wasn't about to make enquiries. As a widow – and surely, she was a widow – she was German, that was all she knew, and she would never want her national identity known. Not after witnessing what Lizbeth went through at the Teutonia Club and then at the Tanglin barracks, after which she was shipped to Australia to endure heaven knew what hardship. Had she taken Emma's tapestry with her? She had no idea. Lizbeth never did write to her. And she had never written to Lizbeth. That was Dottie's role. Dottie kept in touch for many years, but Emma never heard from her any more, either.

Even with the gnawing fear a fixture in her belly, she regretted setting fire to the only evidence she had of her German heritage, among her papers that last letter George had sent before he went to war in 1914. It had been a keepsake and a great comfort to her through the years. For a long time, she had carried it with her in her purse. Couldn't she have found somewhere to put it where it would never be discovered? A single tear prickled her cheeks as she pictured his boyish face and conjured those last words he wrote. Her brave George.

She told herself she did the right thing. It was only paper. Better to incinerate her past than have to deal with the persecution that would follow if it was discovered.

She thought of Adela in the next room, Jewish by birth and not by faith. Had she guessed the true identity of her beloved nurse? Emma suspected she had. Adela was shrewd. Emma was sure she would say nothing. Yet as she turned on her side and considered getting up, that old apprehension stirred again and she lay there for a while longer, frozen.

The bus from Cottenham House took Emma up Worple Road and she was in the heart of Wimbledon in under ten minutes. Gladys, all bundled up in a thick coat, hat and scarf, was waiting outside the bank. It was Saturday, and the church in Queen's Road was having a jumble sale. Emma thought to visit there first to see what they had in the way of baby clothes. After that, they could pop into Woolworths and browse the bargains. She saw Gladys crossing the street to join her. Once on the pavement, she skirted a huddle of gossiping women and then offered her mother a smile. Emma greeted her daughter warmly, looking up into her made-up face, those smoky-blue eyes shaped like her father's, the full and determined lips, the straight, no-nonsense nose. It was a face that brooked no challenge; not a soft face or a kind face, but neither cruel or harsh and most definitely appealing. It was just that Emma couldn't help but notice a stern set developing in her daughter's features with every passing year, a certain inflexibility, or perhaps it was guardedness, Emma couldn't decide.

Gladys hovered, and Emma suggested they head off down the street.

'How's Irene?' she asked.

'Tired,' Gladys said with a dismissive sigh. 'Does nothing but sit around with her feet up.'

Emma smiled. 'Just wait until it's your turn.'

'I am not looking forward to it, I assure you.'

Emma believed her. She knew her daughter only too well. Gladys was engaged for the third time now and it had not escaped Emma's notice that each fiancé had offered greater financial security and status. The latest, Tom, worked in Cable and Wireless and had much ambition, according to Gladys.

'I thought we were shopping for Christmas,' Gladys said, looking askance as Emma halted outside the church.

'A jumble sale never hurts and baby clothes never wear out,' Emma said, making her way inside with an ambivalent Gladys on her tail.

They rummaged through the apparel on the tables in the hall, Gladys with little interest, Emma with fixed attention. She had a certain flare for finding quality in amongst the tired and the drab. After a short while, Gladys hung back and left her mother to it. In half an hour, Emma came away with a string bag crammed with cardigans, booties, bibs and jumpsuits, all in white or purple or green, the whole lot for less than a shilling.

In Woolworths, Gladys took an interest in the sweets and little else. Emma wondered if her own frugality had rubbed off on her daughter rather too strongly. To shop for a bargain was one thing, to be miserly another – although Gladys could be extravagant on occasion and it didn't do to be harsh. Out of the two daughters, Gladys was the cautious one, reserved, steady. Emma didn't need to worry about her. It was Irene she kept her eye on; Irene whom she sensed would have a hard road ahead. Her choice of husband, Emma couldn't fault, especially as his name was George, but then again, it was impossible to see what was going on inside a marriage and Irene, she knew all too well, was headstrong.

With Gladys trailing her around, she bought small Christmas gifts for her daughters and everyone at Cotteham House, including Adela. As she left the store, she cast her eye around, taking in the few men hovering at the entrance and wondering, as she always did, if one day Ernest would appear and prove wrong her assumption that he was dead. It was impossible to know. He had left one day eleven years before and never came back. Set sail from Southampton bound for Australia. That was the last she saw of him.

With two young girls to care for back then, she was hardly going to admit she had been abandoned. And besides, she had no idea if that was the case. No word of Ernest had come her way since. Missing, presumed dead, wasn't that what they said? Lost in battle, lost at sea; lost. Well, he was lost, lost to her after he sailed off and never came back. Hardly a heroic loss, either, or even tragic, as far as she was aware. Just lost, to Australia. She imagined him as she so often did, lazing on a veranda in the heat and the scorching sun, watching a kangaroo, perhaps, or shooing away a fly. Then, just as she always did, she told herself he was dead. He had to be dead because he had never been in touch and he adored his daughters and would never abandon them. Something tragic simply had to have occurred and that was that.

She took Gladys to a nice tea room on the corner, claimed her favourite table by the window and, after placing an order of tea and a small cake each, she made small talk with her somewhat moody daughter.

Gladys had little to say and Emma was left carrying the conversation. She related stories of Cottenham House, of Miss Schuster and the other members of the household, but Gladys showed only polite interest, so she gave up. When the tea and cake arrived, Emma found herself remarking on flavour, on texture, on the strength of the brew, and Gladys politely agreed. Emma began to despair. The outing was meant to be a pleasant affair. Her daughter was distracted, that much Emma could see, and she was wondering what could possibly be the matter when suddenly Gladys said without any preface, 'Who will give me away?'

Emma was quick to note the tone of despondency and caught her daughter's gaze.

'You've set a wedding date?'

'I was just wondering what you think. With no father to walk me down the aisle, the wedding won't feel right.' There was more than a tinge of reproach in her remark and Emma was hurt by it.

'Irene didn't mind.'

'I am not Irene.'

Emma sighed inwardly. What could she possibly say in response? There were no uncles to fulfil the role. Perhaps a male parishioner at the church would perform the duty? Gladys wouldn't hear of it. Defeated, Emma drank her tea in several quick gulps and informed her daughter that she wished to catch the next bus back to Cottenham House. 'Before it gets dark.'

'It won't be dark for ages.'

'I am sure you and Tom will think of something.'

Back at Cottenham House, Emma entered the hall loaded up with her purchases and, before she had a chance to catch her breath, Mr Holt, dutifully closing the front door, informed her that Adela had been asking for her all morning.

Emma filled with concern. 'Is something wrong?' she said, narrowly avoiding dropping one of her bags as she rushed for the stairs.

'I think not, Mrs Taylor. It appears she cannot do without you, even for a few short hours.'

There was a soft chuckle in his voice. Then Mrs Stoker appeared, beckoning Emma to the kitchen.

'You might as well have a full stomach before you go up,' she said, inviting Emma to sit down at the head of the large table.

Emma deposited her purchases beside the dresser before taking up her seat. 'I hope you can tell me what is going on,' she said, nonplussed.

Mrs Stoker busied about behind her.

'Miss Schuster has a bee in her bonnet, right enough. She's been fretting all morning, ringing that bell. Had Mr Holt up and down those stairs so many times.'

'Where's Mrs Davies.'

'Out. Relatives, she said. Her sister. And I told Mr Holt not to wake Susan. Anyway, it's you Miss Schuster is demanding. So much for a day off! Sounds to me like you'll need plenty of energy to see you through the afternoon.'

She set down a plate of steak and kidney pie, potatoes and peas. Emma was relieved it was only a tiny cake she'd consumed at the tea rooms as she picked up her knife and fork.

She ate slowly at first but, finding herself unexpectedly hungry and, despite Mrs Stoker's reassurances, rushed, she quickened her pace. Mrs Stoker watched on, satisfied when the plate was empty.

After a visit to her bedroom to deposit her purchases, she entered Adela's room, steeling herself for the inevitable warm and stuffy air. Time and again she tried to convince Adela a little fresh air would do her the world of good, but Adela wouldn't hear of it.

'There you are, at last!' Adela said with a broad and relieved smile. 'Where have you been?'

'Wimbledon, to do some shopping.' There was no point reminding Miss Schuster of her day off.

'And you have done your shopping now?'

'I have.'

'Then sit yourself down. I have something to tell you. Or rather, show you.'

Emma obliged and it was then Emma noticed Adela was clutching some letters.

'Has there been some post?'

'Not at all. These are old letters, Emma dear. And I had completely forgotten about them until today. We can thank Miss Hint for that. She was cleaning out the bottom drawer of my dressing table and oh, look what she found!' Adela waved the letters in Emma's direction.

'Who are they from?'

'Oscar! My dear, dear Oscar. Oh, do read them to me, dear Emma, and we can discuss them. I want you to know all about my Oscar and now we have the perfect starting place.'

Emma thought she already knew quite enough about the Irish poet as she stood and walked around the bed to collect the letters. When she got there, Adela's hand relaxed by her side in a sudden shift of focus. Emma left the letters in Adela's light grasp and returned to her seat.

'I was young back then,' Adela said wistfully, her gaze fixed on the ceiling. 'And fresh, my dear. In the sense of being new at things.' She paused, her mind drifting. 'He told me a delightful tale of a nurse, once. Have I told you?'

'I don't think you have,' Emma lied.

'This nurse was nothing like you. He had her killing the man she was nursing. Have you ever imagined doing that?' She was quick to shoot Emma an appraising look. 'I presume some patients can be quite obnoxious. You must have had your share.'

'Once or twice,' Emma said, recalling the venereal diseases ward in Singapore.

'He couldn't write, you know, poor Oscar,' Adela said, her mind wandering off again. 'Not in prison. I tried so hard to encourage him.'

'I should imagine he was too unhappy.'

'He was. But his writing would have saved him. I am sure of it.'

Emma didn't speak.

'His writing is electrifying, don't you think?' Adela sighed. 'Perfection. He is a genius who can only be admired. I say "*is*" advisedly.'

'I understand.'

'What an honour it is to have known him.'

'I can only imagine, Miss Schuster.'

'Adela, please.'

She reached for Emma's hand. Emma obliged.

'Poor Oscar. He came to such a terrible end. And for what? He had done nothing wrong, the poor, poor man. Greek love, they call it. Do you know about such things?'

Again, there was that shrewd, penetrating gaze. Emma couldn't help but feel awkward.

'I am afraid I do not.'

'There are some matters, my dear Emma, where society

and the law have it all wrong. There, I just had to say it. Quite, quite wrong. Oh...'

Adela caught her breath in a moment of sudden pain, then slumped back, taking shallow breaths.

'Please, Adela, you must not excite yourself.'

Emma reached for her patient's wrist to check her pulse. Adela was quiet for a while. When she spoke again, the topic was the same.

'I have only ever known Oscar to be entirely good, Emma, and exceptionally kind. He displayed such courtesy. Manners are so important. You do agree with me?'

'I do,' she said. 'Now, let me tuck you in.'

'He told me stories... oh, such stories.'

'He did,' Emma murmured.

'He was in every respect superior. Superior to me, superior to everyone. Will you read some more Oscar for me, Emma dear?'

'Of course.'

Emma checked the time and administered Adela's medicine and settled her down. The letters slid off the bed, and she retrieved them. Seeing Adela quieten and drift into slumber, she scanned the contents of the letter on top of the pile, not wanting to be nosy but unable to resist. She knew that when Adela was young, she had spent the winters in Torquay, where she often visited Babbacombe Cliff to attend Lady Georgina Mount Temple's pre-Raphaelite circle. She hadn't known, because Adela was light on facts, that Oscar went to join his wife, Constance, at Babbacombe Cliff for the first time in the December of 1892. It seemed from his letter they rented the house off Georgina for several months.

Emma read on with furtive interest. It turned out Wilde had the lease for a few months while Constance went away with her aunt to the continent, to Italy. This was when Adela and Oscar must have first met and, left alone together, their friendship blossomed. Although the new friends were not entirely alone. At that time, according to the next passage of the same letter, Oscar was entertaining Bosie. Adela often referred to Bosie by his full name of Lord Alfred Douglas, which made him sound mature. From what Emma could make out in the letter, Bosie was only just an adult.

Oscar's remarks seemed to Emma suddenly too private. She folded the letter and put it, along with the others, on Adela's bedside table and returned to her chair, opening the copy of *Dorian Gray* at the introduction, keen to check on the facts. She discovered Oscar was nearly forty when he had met and entertained Bosie. That was quite an age gap. Oscar was almost double Bosie's age. Something in Emma recoiled as the disparity seeped into her awareness. She had no difficulty accommodating the homosexuality itself; she was a Spiritualist and a free thinker, after all. It was the age difference that affronted her, the age difference and the betrayal, and she couldn't override her indignation. She admonished herself, a quiet voice within whispering the source of her reaction. She read on. Bosie's tutor Campbell Dodgson was also in attendance at Babbacombe Cliff at this time, and Oscar, while entertaining his friends, was also writing *A Woman of No Importance*.

Emma thought again of Oscar's wife.

Poor Constance. For how long was she aware of her husband's sexuality, his infidelity? Emma had no idea. From Adela's own account, she was never that close to Constance. Emma couldn't recall her ever mentioning Oscar's wife other than to dismiss her. Emma recollected the little Adela did know through the spiritual circles in which she moved. Constance was a free thinker and rational dresser, conveying an outlook not dissimilar to her own. Emma had always admired a practical, sensible woman, and could only commend those female forerunners who transformed women's apparel for the better in decrying corsets and layers of restricting clothes and introducing free-flowing skirts and even bloomers. Constance's interests were broad, too, much broader than her own, and they included theosophy. She had even joined the Hermetic Order of the Golden Dawn. For Emma, those interests were a step too far. All her life, she had kept away from those less Christian occult interests. For her, the need for a more traditional interpretation of the Christian faith had always been paramount. Theosophy offered a rather peculiar stance on the meaning of Christ and the Gospels, and the Golden Dawn seemed to Emma far removed from Christianity and, if anything, tinged with darkness.

Her curiosity wouldn't be stilled. She watched Adela, noted her rhythmic breathing and, without wasting a moment, she tiptoed around the bed and extracted another letter from the pile. This time a letter not addressed to Adela but to someone else, a name Emma couldn't make out. How did Adela end up with this letter? Emma wondered if she should read it. Then again, Adela had already given her permission. Bolstered, she scanned the sentences. She was immediately affronted by the first sentence of the second paragraph and wished she had left well alone. Cats are killed by their curiosity, she reminded herself. She had no truck with a man who chose to be physically repelled by the condition of his wife's body after pregnancy. She would rather not have been privy to the confidence that Oscar spoke of so bluntly and plainly. He plummeted in her estimation in the imagining. Oscar's wife could hardly help what had happened to her body. Worse, was Oscar implying that his wife's supposedly disfigured body drove him to have sexual relations with his own gender? Emma was appalled.

How could she continue to read his work and accommodate Adela's ceaseless praise in the light of this new knowledge?

Men and their idealised view of beauty! It was contemptible!

Her affiliation sat more firmly with Constance than ever.

She hurried around the bed and put the letter back in the pile, relieved to have been confronted by the revelations in the absence of Adela's watchful gaze.

Adela stirred but didn't wake. Back in her seat, Emma tuned in to the rhythm of her breathing, letting her gaze wander around the bedroom as her mind noted the disparities between her own humble existence and that of her patient.

She tried to picture Oscar Wilde, his charisma, his charm, and the special bond he had with Adela. Imagined their social milieu filled with artists, poets, actresses and also with aristocrats and government ministers. Even Haile Selassie visited the Schusters. Adela and her mother hosted lavish garden parties featuring open-air performances and musical soirees at Cannizaro House. Emma had walked past Cannizaro House many times. The mansion lay to the northeast of Cottenham House and beyond its gardens were large parklands, including Wimbledon Common and Richmond Park, stretching in a wide arc all the way to Kingston-upon-Thames and Hampton Court Palace. Not far for the wealthy to travel to each other's abodes. Not that the many wealthy residents of old Wimbledon had to travel far, either, Emma supposed. Eagle House and Gothic House were also nearby. As was the old Theosophical Society Lodge. Spirituality for the well-heeled, Emma surmised. She had sat by the bedside of many an old and wealthy soul in the Wimbledon area, a number of them proclaimed Theosophists who, in their lucid moments, were wont to take her to task over her Spiritualist beliefs.

The two belief systems were at odds, she knew, and she had

never been persuaded to venture beyond her own conviction that it was the safe passage of departed souls that mattered and their eventual destination with Christ and God, and not as the Theosophists had it. For them, evolution spanned aeons and souls reincarnated over and again, bound in mortal existence through the strictures of their own karma. She didn't want to have to think about anything more than this life, lived in a Christian way, which for her had always meant a life of healing.

She offered Adela a silent prayer, waiting a little longer by her bedside as the wintry sun faded. A soft knock, and Miss Hint appeared to see to the fire. She brought with her the smell of roasting meat wafting up from downstairs. Mrs Stoker was a marvel in the kitchen and Emma enjoyed the communal meals. Miss Hint was soon finished and departed with a polite nod and a smile.

Emma had not until now accepted a live-in position. Her daughters had always needed her more. Looking around the opulent room, she smiled to herself. Her, a humble nurse, good enough for the local aristocracy, more than good enough, even at times demanded, and here she was, employed not as a servant but as a companion. Her, unassuming Emma, living amongst the sort of society Ernest so coveted, the sort of society he hoped to mingle with on ships, in hotels, at clubs and especially at the Lodge.

Back when she was first married, it took Emma a long time to realise what drove Ernest, and just how dogged was his purpose. She was never included in his ambitions or his confidences. She wondered now why he chose to exclude her. She could converse with anyone. She was then, as now, a prized companion. True, she had never put on false airs, and she was not given to gossip or frivolity, yet Dottie took to her, as had Cynthia and Lizbeth. And she had had no trouble making new friends in Japan. Familiar feelings of hurt stirred within her, shading into the realisation that Ernest's choice never to include his wife in his affairs was all part of his slow and steady rejection of her as anything other than the potential, and then the real, mother of his children.

Had it never occurred to him that he might have fared better in his campaign to climb the social ladder had he included her, instead of treating her as a social liability? Although she suspected there was more to it than that. 'I cannot announce to these people that my wife is employed as a common nurse,' he was fond of saying. That was an excuse. He had acted as though he were ashamed of her, but really, he was ashamed of himself, of his own humble roots – he, the son of a man who made pot handles his whole life in Stoke-on-Trent, something she had to wheedle out of him. Perhaps Ernest had never trusted her to keep his past hidden, while he swanned about, all stuck-on charm, all smiles and laughter and gaiety for the world at large, full of his funny little ways. People found him endearingly fastidious, almost comical, and yet she came to know him to be a supreme actor playing the self he had created. He might as well have learned all of his tricks from Oscar Wilde, swallowed whole his plays.

'You must tell me all about your life, Emma. Did you have anyone in it like my Oscar?'

Emma gave a little start. As she emerged from her slumber, it was as though Adela had been reading her mind.

'No, not at all, I am sorry to say,' she said quickly, vowing never again to dwell on Ernest in Adela's proximity, even when she was sleeping.

1917

KOBE

The *Nippon Maru* put in to Kobe harbour one cold January morning and its passengers were greeted with a blast of icy air from the snow-capped mountains that rose up sharply behind the town. Emma shifted her gaze from those towering peaks to the foreground, taking in the long row of staunch-looking colonial buildings that spoke of European wealth. Ignoring the usual bustle on the pier below, she let her attention come to rest on a few fishing boats moored to the west and bobbing lazily. A familiar port smell reached her nose, but there was no undertow of drains and sewage. Kobe, indeed what she had seen of Japan so far – the ship had already put in at Yokohama – seemed to her more sedate and orderly than Singapore, and at once more foreign and strange. Singapore was, after all, a British colony. Japan was anything but.

She was on the main deck, waiting to disembark. With a heft of her arm, she repositioned Gladys, propped on her hip. At fifteen months, she was getting heavy. Standing by her side, Ernest was in an informative mood. She wondered if his remarks were intended for her or for those who stood nearby.

She humoured him regardless. She'd taken an accommodating stance on his foibles ever since that episode in Dottie's car when her friends made shocking revelations about the state of their marriages.

Continuing in the same raised voice, Ernest said the waterfront settlement – known as the "bund" – was a Japanese concession allowing foreign merchants to establish their businesses. 'They call them "hongs" here,' he added.

'Hongs?'

'You'll get used to it.' He patted her arm and grinned at her and then gave Gladys a little pinch through her clothes. 'Ready for your next adventure?'

Emma wasn't sure which of them he was addressing.

'The history here is fascinating, Emma,' he went on. 'Did you know foreign residents used to be exempt from Japanese laws and governed themselves through a municipal council?'

Of course she didn't know.

'Used to be?'

'The concession ended in 1899.'

'Why?'

'A matter of size. The settlement began bursting at the seams. That was when other parts of Kobe were opened up to foreigners.'

'And you know all this because?'

'The chaps back in the San Francisco office.'

She again scanned what she could see of the hinterland, the mountains so close, the near absence of anything that could be called a city.

'And where were the Japanese living all this time?'

'Not on the bund, I assure you. That was the whole point of the concession. Never the twain, so to speak.'

'In the back streets, then.' Emma shot him a cool look, picturing the segregation of Singapore, the poverty she had seen in Chinatown and in the Indian quarter up Serangoon Road. 'They must have had servants,' she said. 'The British always have servants.'

'Naturally. Still do. Plenty of Japanese and Chinese to choose from.'

He sounded pompous and was undoubtedly proud of the British presence on the Japanese islands, another outpost for the purposes of trade in an empire circling the globe, him, a humble pottery handler's son. Whereas Emma saw the bund as an imposition. And once the hinterland had been opened up to foreigners and the infiltration continued, she could only imagine the dismay in the hearts of the locals, their resentment, forced as they were to tolerate the strange, white interlopers.

In the light of Ernest's explanation, Emma felt uneasy, sensing already that she would be living amongst a resentful Japanese population. Progress is progress, Ernest was so fond of telling her. She was not convinced it was all for the good.

For the foreign traders, Kobe was a major gateway into Asia. Back in Singapore, Guthries had had their eye on their Kobe branch as the war progressed and demand for Japanese goods exploded. When he was asked to take up the post of export manager at the Kobe office, Ernest had agreed without even telling her. Apparently, he had assumed she would be pleased since she so despised the heat. He saw the posting as a promotion, despite the fact that his job title would remain the same, and he had been wild with enthusiasm ever since they had left the tropics. His enthusiasm was not infectious. He was only thinking about himself, his career, climbing the promotional ladder as far as those in charge would allow. Emma felt yanked along for the ride, thrust once more into a world of men, young men busy importing this and exporting that. She did not need to know the particular details of the Kobe bund to picture the free and easy lifestyle, the alcohol, the clubs. Although at least this time, in the cool Kobe climate, Ernest would not be lounging about the house in a sarong.

Her mind grew so crowded with misgivings as they waited to disembark that she felt no compulsion to step ashore, even though dry land was always welcome after a long spell at sea.

Crossing the Pacific, the only land between the two continents were the tiny islands of Hawaii, where they were required to change ship, an ordeal of over nine hours in the sweltering tropical heat. She hadn't taken much notice of the islands, ignoring the fuss others made as the verdant green and the mountains came into view, but as ever, when she did look around at the port she was not impressed. Neither had she taken any interest in cold and dreary Yokohama.

She wanted to feel optimistic. She told herself she ought to be counting her blessings. How many nurses from Philadelphia got to travel first class and live in foreign climes? Few, and on that count alone she was privileged. It was simply that she feared Kobe offered her nothing. From what she could see and what she had been told, it was an enclave on a small parcel of land sandwiched between the sea and the imposing mountains; inhospitable and not at all a British colony with all of the structures of its own administration and society. The prejudice fixed in her mind and filled her with dread.

The other passengers were growing restless. Several had managed to make it ashore before disembarkation was delayed when a man with a large trunk that he insisted on carrying got jammed halfway down the gangway. Hearing the American accents of the couple standing behind her, she succumbed to a twinge of nostalgia. Memories of the long train journey across America with Gladys on her lap flitted into her mind. She missed her parents and her brother Herman, her visit last November all too brief. She had no idea when she would have the chance to see them again.

. . .

When they had arrived in America last November, she'd left Ernest at the modest Stewart Hotel in Geary Street, while he familiarised himself with the San Francisco office and learned all he could about Kobe from the export agent who had just returned from his stint in Japan. It wasn't to Philadelphia she was headed. Her parents, sensing America's entry into the war, had moved to Canada to join her Uncle Wolfgang who had a farm there. Herman would be exempt from conscription as long as he worked on the farm. That seemed to be the root of the decision. Ernest had insisted she travel first class, as the regular class of train passengers had to sit on slatted wooden seats. Her ticket was something she was forced to be grateful for, since the journey had taken five whole days.

When she arrived in Montréal, she received an unexpectedly cool reception and then spent the whole of her two weeks' stay in her parents' small house in Pointe Claire explaining that she would indeed be bringing up her daughter to be a good Christian. But not a Mennonite, was their united complaint, and she was forced to remain silent, for an explanation seemed pointless. There were no Mennonite churches in Singapore and she very much doubted there would be any in Kobe. Outside of a small sprinkle of American states, the Mennonite faith was practically nowhere to be found unless you happened to reside in Prussia. She could hear her parents' response were she to voice the blunt truth. If that's the case, then you should live where there *are* churches, and not swan off to heathen lands.

Herman, who was living on Uncle Wolfgang's farm, came in to Montréal to visit one Sunday afternoon and that was all she saw of him. He, too, seemed remote and ambivalent towards her, although she sensed a little awkwardness, too, as though he was uncomfortable with the attitude he had been required to adopt. They barely exchanged a word. Seeing his sullen face made her ache all the more for George. Her dear, beloved brother who always paid her attention and offered kind words. Why couldn't it have been Herman who left for Germany and George who stayed behind? Why was it that the only family member she felt close to had chosen to depart to a country now at war with her own? There seemed no justice in the cards she had been dealt. Only this perpetual heartache, this missing.

In Montréal, she felt nothing but disappointment in her family's attitude. She'd been ostracised. That much was plain. She had thought the five years since she'd last seen them ample time for them to have mellowed. They hadn't, but they had aged. Her father was now entirely grey at sixty-nine, and her mother, although two years younger, was showing her age much more than her husband in the lines on her face. They were old in their minds and their hearts as well as their bodies. Her mother was having problems with breathlessness and she confessed she often felt faint. Her heart. She carries the burden of missing her children, her father would say. It was a pointed remark. The war cast a shadow over the welfare of Karin and George, but it was Emma who should have stayed to make up for the absence of her siblings. Somehow, her parents made even her mother's poor health Emma's fault.

To them, their youngest daughter had committed a betrayal of monumental proportions. After all, Karin might have stayed in Germany but she had remained loyal to the faith. Emma had not only abandoned her family, she'd walked out on the congregation, too. She was acutely aware of that and it was a painful recognition. After all their people had suffered, loyalty was required of each and every Mennonite, according to her father. The flock must adhere to the old customs or the faith would dissolve, and all the persecution and the struggle and the diasporas would have been for nothing.

After a dismal two weeks aided and abetted by the weather, Emma was relieved to board the train heading west. On the long journey back to San Francisco, despite the strained relations, she vowed to keep her family in her heart, write to them, hope for their forgiveness one day. She felt saddened, too, not to be spending Christmas with them, but the passage to Kobe would take almost four weeks and Ernest was due to take up his new position before the end of January.

Passengers on the gangway broke into a raucous cheer. The gangway was free at last. Emma's mood lifted a little as she shuffled forward in the queue. Perhaps she was mistaken in all of her misgivings and Kobe would offer up some pleasant surprises.

Down on the pier they were met by a runner from the hotel, who loaded their luggage into a pony cart. They soon left the port and headed north along the waterfront. They arrived at their destination a few minutes later, having traversed a distance easily walkable, even with a baby on the hip.

Ernest had booked a room at the Oriental Hotel, Kobe's version of Raffles, although, looking up at the façade, Emma saw it was not quite as grand. It was a four-storey building, and as they passed the façade facing the waterfront, she took in the corners fashioned as towers, with a portico inset between, and she felt tucked between the covers of a Kipling novel. The main entrance was around the corner where many rickshaws were lined up against the wall.

Leaving Ernest to deal with the luggage, Emma climbed the long flight of stairs to the entrance, passing between a pair of sturdy columns. Her mood improved when she entered the vast, marbled foyer. Taking in the stairs rising to either side of a central area furnished with cane chairs and decorated with numerous potted plants dotted around, she breathed an inward sigh. This time, unlike her one night at Raffles, she was determined to stay awake and enjoy the experience. She would become acculturated as much as it was possible to achieve in the hours ahead, before she found herself thrust into domesticity somewhere else with a foreign servant her only companion, forced to fend for herself and while away her days when Ernest was at work.

Their room was on the third floor and enjoyed a sweeping view of the harbour. The furnishings were stylish, the bed comfortable and every detail had been thought of. After the confines of the ship, Emma enjoyed the high ceiling, the sense of space, the stillness and obvious luxury. The moment the porter exited the room she extracted a fresh nappy from a holdall and laid Gladys down on a towel on the bed. Ernest stood by the window with his back to her. Not once in Gladys's short life had he changed a nappy – he wouldn't know how – but he was good with his child, adoring and attentive, when he was around.

The task complete, she let Gladys roll over and slide off the bed and toddle about.

'I almost forgot,' Ernest said, turning as he reached into his pocket. 'This came for you.'

He proffered a letter. It was from Dottie.

Under her husband's watchful gaze, Emma levered open the envelope and unfolded the thin pages. Her surroundings, even the presence of Ernest, receded from her awareness as she pored over the words.

They'd put on another fundraiser for the war effort. Eve proved marvellous in her administrative role and Cynthia had discovered a talent for creating backdrops and costumery.

Although it pained Dottie to say it, they struggled to outdo Mrs Lee. The Chinese community of Singapore were not only wealthy but generous with it, unlike some of the British she could mention.

Edgar was having heart trouble. Dottie suspected he'd developed too close an alliance with Gustav, whose dealings with Herr Weber were nothing short of shifty. Emma recalled the conversation she'd overheard in the Teutonia Club. Some deal going on right under the noses of the British. Had Edgar been involved in that as well? Dottie's letter confirmed it. Dottie said she couldn't reveal too much but it served Edgar right if he thought to use his position in the administration to smooth the way for whatever Weber had going on the side, a scheme that could have had grave implications for the British, indeed the whole of Singapore. Weber's company had been forced into liquidation, but if the truth came out, Edgar was finished. It would be rather hard to explain how they now drove a Rolls Royce.

Emma read between the lines. The German-run dispensaries in Singapore had been resisting regulation by the Poisons Ordinance and the Deleterious Drugs Ordinance which sought to curb the dispensing of opium and morphine. As a banker, Gustav must have had a financial interest and Edgar would no doubt have been asked to turn a blind eye.

There was no news of Lizbeth, and Emma surmised there wouldn't be until the war ended. Reading over the chitchat that comprised the rest of Dottie's letter, Emma found herself missing Singapore, or at least Orchard Road, a place she never in her wildest dreams thought she would miss.

'Any news?' Ernest said, bringing her back to the reality of Kobe with a bit of a jolt.

'Not really. Eve's twisted her ankle and Edgar's been having health issues.'

'He should lay off the whisky.'

They both laughed.

Emma reached down and unbuckled her shoes and sat up on the bed. Ernest joined her, turning on his side and idly stroking her forearm. She remained motionless, yet she still felt in motion after a month at sea. She yawned. 'Forty winks', she murmured, her eyes heavy. Seeing her exhaustion, Ernest rolled over, leaped off the bed, steered Gladys over to the other side of the room and kept her entertained.

The afternoon faded and it was soon dark outside. Emerging from half-sleep, Emma wondered what plans Ernest had made for himself and where that left her and Gladys.

Much to her surprise, Ernest was in a generous mood. There was to be no meeting with his Guthries' associates in the hotel bar. Instead, the family enjoyed a sumptuous dinner of the famous Kobe beef before retiring to their room, where Emma settled Gladys into her cot.

Emma had not been anticipating anything other than sleep, but Ernest had other ideas. He'd had an amorous glint in his eye ever since they arrived at the hotel, no doubt fortified by the bottle of red wine he'd quaffed over dinner, less the small glass she had consumed. He approached her, cupped her face in his hands and kissed her gently on her lips.

She yielded, accommodating his needs as she always did, with little thought of her own.

The next day, Ernest arranged for a pony cart to take them to their accommodation near the foreign enclave of Kitano, a suburb – although she would scarcely have called it that – of steep and narrow streets tucked up hard against the mountain-side about a mile inland from the bund. They passed huddles of low shophouses, not unlike those she had seen in Singapore, save for their terracotta-tiled roofs. The people looked different here and wore long, grey or black dresses with loose sleeves, cinched at the waist with wide, coloured bands, and the women appeared fond of umbrellas. The oriental feel, so different from anything Emma had seen before even in Singapore, had its charm, and she hoped she would find a way to fit into life in Kobe, or at least in Kitano. Whatever lay ahead for her, she knew she needed to give it time.

As the narrow streets steepened further, they turned into a narrow lane and the cart pulled up outside a small, terraced house with wide eaves and a pitched roof. Emma looked around. Uphill, the Kitano district carried on reaching up, a thin band of streets and houses stretching towards the base of the mountains. The immediate area appeared pleasant enough, if cramped, and she could see the foothills were not quite as steep as those they had left behind in San Francisco. The only greenery to greet the eye was in the spaces between the buildings, where she glimpsed the fields beyond the city.

Inside the house, she was approached cautiously by a tiny Chinese woman who Ernest had hired through Guthries. Perhaps, as in Singapore, she came with the house. Squeezing past the servant who appeared in no hurry to step aside, Emma walked around the interconnected rooms on the ground floor and found the house airy and spacious. There was a view out onto the lane from the kitchen window. Upstairs were the bedrooms and at the rear, accessed through large, sliding doors in the living room, was a walled garden filled with plants. Her spirits lifted the moment she made the discovery. The sliding doors were multi-paned, the glass opaque, which she thought rather odd and very much a pity since she would have enjoyed being able to see the garden from inside. The furnishings were strange, too. In the centre of the living room, positioned on floor mats, was a low table surrounded by low chairs she came to know as *zaisu*. The Japanese, she thought, all but ate on the floor. She was relieved the room also contained a large, Western-style couch and two armchairs, even if they did look out of place. In all, the house was pleasing and had a calm, soothing atmosphere. She thought she would be at peace here.

Behind her, Gladys started whining. As though on cue, Ernest said, 'Can you see to her?'

He promptly put her down and headed outside to deal with the luggage.

Finding herself unexpectedly free in the open space of the living room, Gladys ran around, circling the table and chairs, until her foot caught the leg of one the two armchairs and she landed flat on her face and the screaming began. Reaching down to offer solace, Emma felt her domestic reality crowd in on her with a curdling sense of disquietude. She shooed away the unease. Told herself she needed to be valiant. Reprimanded herself for giving into her fears. She would be fine. She was a capable woman with a toddler to look after. She had a more than adequate husband and she was amply provided for. She needed to simply keep busy and think positively, put on a sunny hat and count her blessings.

The rest of that day she spent unpacking and arranging their things. Ernest kept Gladys entertained, and the servant, Yu Yan, who functioned as both cook and maid, prepared their lunch and supper. Before she left – presumably to attend to similar chores at her own home – she beckoned Emma into the kitchen and proceeded to issue instructions. Emma stood in the doorway bemused, listening hard to Yu Yan's broken English. Making out little, she was forced to rely on hand gestures when it came to reheating the dishes and the location of plates and wondered if it were possible to learn a little Chinese.

She found her new servant to be an excellent cook. That evening, Ernest devoured his serving of Yu Yan's beef casserole with fluffy dumplings, patting his stomach when he his plate was clean.

'I think we'll all be much happier here, don't you?'

He reached over and ruffled his daughter's hair. Gladys giggled and gazed up at her father with her blue eyes wide as saucers.

'I'm sure we will be, Ernest,' Emma said reassuringly.

But by the end of the second day, in the absence of Ernest who had gone to the office, Emma discovered Yu Yan to be a very bossy matriarch who considered white people incapable of doing anything in the correct manner, least of all looking after a toddler. Owing to the language barrier, there seemed no point trying to explain she was an experienced nurse perfectly capable of rearing a child. Even if she had managed to communicate her profession, it would have made no difference. Yu Yan had already determined that when it came to childrearing she was the boss, an attitude no doubt reinforced by Gladys's wild behaviour and ensuing screams after her fall on their arrival.

Yu Yan was a mature woman, wiry, with delicate hands, a few wrinkles about the eyes and wisps of grey in her tied-back hair, and Emma thought she was probably a grandmother. It was Yu Yan's way with everything, or else. Emma didn't know whether to laugh at the absurdity or scream in exasperation. She couldn't pick Gladys up or put her down, let alone feed or change her, without Yu Yan appearing in a doorway or hovering over her shoulder, often with a kitchen utensil in hand which she would use as a pointer, no matter if it were a spoon or a spatula or a knife, and issue directives.

Ernest saw none of this. Yu Yan arrived as he was leaving the house in the morning and she was gone before he came home at night. Emma tried to explain one time and his response was to guffaw and then lecture her gently on the inappropriateness of her reaction.

'You really should see the funny side.'

He was right, and mostly she did. And she appreciated the presence of Yu Yan in the house, of course she did.

She never brought the matter up with him again.

Ernest spent the working week and sometimes Saturdays down on the bund, busy sourcing nuts and bolts and all manner of hardware items manufactured in Japan and exporting them to Singapore or to wherever they were needed. As Japan profited from the war, so did Guthries. Business was booming and as the weeks shaded into months, Guthries stole Ernest just as the firm had in Singapore, leaving Emma to fend for herself at home with Gladys and the indomitable Yu Yan.

Whenever there was an opportunity, Emma retreated to the little courtyard garden and tended the plants, tip-pruning and pulling out the occasional weed. There were early signs of spring with bulbs thrusting their leaves up through the soil. It was still too cold to be outside for long and she could only potter about when Gladys was having a nap, but the garden quickly proved Emma's favourite part of the house.

In the warmth and the quiet of the living room, she would extract her loom from its wooden box and attempt a few more rows of her silk tapestry. Progress was slow but she took pride in the work, although the calm that had descended on her in Singapore whenever she set to work was patchy and short-lived, as part of her remained attuned to her sleeping daughter and another part of her to Yu Yan. The knowledge that she would have to pack the loom away at any moment instilled tension in what should have been serenity.

There was nothing much to draw her beyond the confines of the house but as the days grew longer, she began to feel cooped up and the overbearing presence of Yu Yan became stifling. Every morning, she donned a coat, hat and scarf, bundled Gladys into warm clothes and popped her into the new wicker pram they'd purchased in San Francisco. Whatever the weather, she went out for a stroll, doing her best to get used to the vicinity, the people, the shops.

Eager to learn, she educated herself as much as she could about Kobe, reading the English-language newspaper from cover to cover. Her daily walks provided their own education. She saw with her own eyes and smelled through her nose that Kobe had the same issues with sanitation and therefore infectious diseases – cholera, dysentery, typhoid – as Singapore. Through the newspaper, she also discovered Kobe housed a large number of prostitutes. She didn't think there were any in her neighbourhood, at least none soliciting on street corners. All she saw were shoppers and shopkeepers and everyone but her looked Japanese and none of them were at all friendly. Indeed, some appeared suspicious, even openly hostile, the way their eyes would follow her, dark eyes in deadpan faces. In all, it was a strange, alienating experience and she had to summon all her resolve to persist with her walks. In those first few months, indeed during her whole stay in Kobe, she learned scarcely a word of Japanese and the Japanese, in their turn, appeared to know not a word of English.

One morning over breakfast she asked Ernest – who'd overslept and was busy shovelling toast and jam into his mouth and slurping his tea – how he managed to broker export deals without a word of the native tongue.

'Guthries employ Chinese interpreters,' he said between mouthfuls. 'They send them up from Hong Kong.'

That explained it. No one associated with the bund, it would seem, bothered to learn Japanese beyond the obvious *konnichiwa*, the all-purpose greeting.

After seeing Ernest off for work and finding herself bored with keeping Gladys entertained, Emma decided to venture further afield. Yu Yan had arrived that morning in a bad mood about something or other. At first, Emma suspected her husband had upset her, but then she caught Yu Yan rubbing her hip and decided she was in some amount of pain. Whatever the cause, Emma wanted to escape the crashing of pots and pans and muttered curses for as long as possible. She put Gladys in the pram, determined to push her up to Kitano where there were more British and American residents. Surely, if she wandered around long enough, she would meet another aimless, listless expatriate wife with a baby or a child.

At first, she was able to push the pram with ease despite the incline, and she began to feel optimistic. She made a right-hand turn at the next intersection and headed along for a stretch, putting a bounce in her step. But as she turned into the next lane and began to push the pram up the hill, she started to feel breathless. Before long, she was panting. The incline grew steeper and the further she went, the more often she had to pause intermittently to catch her breath. About halfway, she gave up and turned around, pulling back on the pram to stop it careening down the hill.

She had no idea where all the expatriate women congregated but it was not out in the near-deserted streets of Kitano or down where she was in Yamamoto-dori. They must have tea parties, just like Dottie, but she was not about to start knocking on doors to find out and besides, having a toddler precluded her from such activities.

Once on the flat, she walked home as slowly as she could.

It was with a moment's hesitation that she opened the front door, only to find Yu Yan in better spirits. She came rushing into the hall, reached for Gladys in the pram and lifted her up with a big grin on her face. She dodged past Emma and hurried back to the kitchen, cooing. Emma followed, nonplussed, entering the kitchen just as Yu Yan was popping a portion of cake in Gladys's mouth. Gladys chewed, eyes wide with wonder. Emma watched on and smiled. She thought of her own mother, who was nothing like Yu Yan and would never have fussed and mithered and indulged in the way this small, ageing Chinese servant did. Servant? Emma could hardly bring herself to think that way about this kind, if domineering, woman. She wasn't a companion, either, and didn't seem interested in making small talk with her employer. When it came to Gladys, the lines of demarcation between master and servant were blurred, but in her dealings with Emma, Yu Yan had a strong sense of her place.

Seeing the delight Yu Yan was taking in Gladys, Emma took advantage of her freedom to compose a letter to Dottie. To start with, seated in the courtyard with the blank paper resting on a book, the words flowed easily enough as she responded to all that Dottie had described in hers. It was when she tried to describe Japan, Kobe, the bund, Yamamoto-dori, that the words faltered in her mind. She described the little garden she enjoyed instead, the cherry tree in full bloom, the scattering of petals like pink confetti. She strove to be positive, upbeat, not wanting to convey doom and gloom. Goodness, there was enough of that around without her adding to it. She said Ernest was a marvellous father, which was true, and she provided an endearing portrait of Yu Yan, who was growing on her, despite it all. She signed off, urging Dottie to reply soon. She folded the pages and slipped them in an envelope, her duty done. As she wrote the address on the front, she vowed to scour the streets of Kobe until she found herself another Dottie. A friend, that's what she needed; a warm and loyal female friend.

That evening over dinner, she considered asking Ernest if he had met any men with wives at Guthries, that perhaps they could all have dinner together one time, but again she thought of Gladys and who they would find to look after her even for a few hours. She wouldn't dare ask Yu Yan. Deflated, she shuffled her food around with her fork, resigned to her fate.

Oblivious to her loneliness, Ernest polished off the last morsel of stew on his plate, drew together his cutlery and pressed his fingertips down on the table, leaning forward and holding her gaze.

'Cheer up, pumpkin. Might never happen.'

'Ernest, I...'

'You'll be pleased to learn I have been invited to join the Kobe Club.'

He was beaming, eyes alight, and she could feel the pride in him. It was Singapore, all over again.

'What do they do?' she said cautiously, hoping women had a place at this club.

'The usual. It's an exclusive gentlemen's club.'

She might have known.

'Only for British businessmen,' he added with an air of triumph.

'I see.'

'Don't sound like that. I have to establish my... our... respectability and joining the club is the only way to do it.'

Ever the social climber. She should have left it there. She'd shown her displeasure and he'd reacted defensively. What was the point in continuing when it would only add fuel to her own hollow existence, the magnitude of which, until that moment, she hadn't fully embraced. But she couldn't restrain herself. It wasn't jealousy motivating her. It was desperation.

'You have the Lodge. Isn't that enough?' she snapped.

Now he was indignant. 'Not if I want to get on. Besides, my membership has been proposed and approved. I can hardly back out of it.'

'I shall never see you, then.' Tears welled.

Seeing her distress, he modified his manner. 'Of course you shall.'

'I suppose they don't ever invite their wives to anything?'

'No one has a wife here, Emma. Or only a very few, at Guthries at any rate.'

He might have told her that before she agreed to come here. He must have known. Not that she would have refused. How could she? She was his wife.

'Then what am I to do while you are out all day and most of the evening?' she almost shrieked.

'You have Gladys. Surely that's enough?'

And Yu Yan, she thought to herself.

She wanted to throttle him. Instead, she took her plate to the kitchen sink and stared out the window at the wall across the street.

The following morning, after Ernest had left for work, she arranged her time around Yu Yan's movements and Gladys's needs, snatching whatever free moments she had to embroider or make lace and read yesterday's *Japan Daily* which Ernest brought home with him after work.

She read the headline article three times, puzzled Ernest hadn't mentioned that the United States had joined the war. Then again, he'd been too full of the Kobe Club. And she supposed to him, the matter was of little consequence. To her it was. Her immediate thought was Herman, although he was safely tucked away on their uncle's farm in Canada. Her parents had been right to move from Philadelphia.

The news cemented her loneliness, arousing a deep yearning for Philadelphia or London, places where she could be useful. She was homesick for nowhere, anywhere but here. She had to remind herself she had no home in Philadelphia. She had lost all contact with her school and nursing friends. She had to face facts. She had no one to go back to other than her parents in Montréal, who didn't seem to want to know her and wouldn't take kindly to her turning up with Gladys. She was trapped, an alien in an alien land. The cultural isolation was rapidly becoming extreme. With the war showing no sign of ending, the only other Germans in Japan were languishing in prisoner of war camps dotted around the islands and, in her maudlin state, she felt for those prisoners, too, incarcerated like her. In a rebellious moment, she felt like announcing her true national status and joining them.

In the days that followed, she kept forcing herself out of the tiny house for fresh air and exercise and to while away the hours. She took in the same shops and the same stony faces, breathed in the same strange, fishy smells and pondered what the neighbourhood really thought of this foreign woman with her baby in a pram. And when Gladys was napping, Emma sat in the garden in the cool spring air, allowing the beauty of the falling cherry blossom to work its way into her soul. Cherry blossom bursting with colour and life. The blossoms of her tapestry, contained in silver thread in small clusters, paled in comparison to the riot of petals on the courtyard tree. Although she admitted to herself it was a wise move on Chun's part to issue her with a simple, stylised version. She would never have coped with creating a tapestry out of the real thing.

The tapestry only kept her occupied in short bursts when Gladys slumbered. While she watched over her daughter in her waking hours, boredom drove her to read every page of the *Japan Daily*. She'd even taken to reading the obituaries. It was there, in the next column, that she found an announcement from the Kobe Ladies Benevolent Society. They were holding a charity bazaar at the All Saints' Church the following Saturday. The All Saints' Church? Where was that? She hoped to persuade Ernest to take her but if he refused, wherever it was, she would go alone.

With no idea where in Kobe the church was situated, she felt frustrated and on tenterhooks the whole afternoon, impa-

tient for Ernest to return home. The moment she heard the
front door open, she rushed and greeted him.

'Whatever have I done to deserve this?' he asked, amused.

'I've discovered a church.'

'A church?' A puzzled look appeared in his face.

'It has a Ladies Benevolent Society and they're holding a
bazaar.'

'That'll be the All Saints' Church in the bund.'

'You know it?'

'One of the chaps at the Kobe Club is friends with the
bishop.'

'You might have told me.'

'I had no idea you were hankering to attend church. I
thought you'd given all that up.'

Whatever had given him that idea? There were times she
thought he really didn't know her at all.

'Ernest, will you take me?'

'I'm meeting Frank Parker at the club, but the church is
nearby. I'll drop you there.'

That Saturday, Emma had butterflies in her tummy as she
stepped down from the pony cart and beheld the stout building
of the church with its arched narthex and square tower rising
up above the roofline. Without the pram for once, she gripped
Gladys's hand as she crossed the concourse. A door was wide
open in the porch, centred in a side wall.

Inside, behind the rows of pews facing the altar, an area
had been given over to trestle tables laden with an assortment
of wares. A table at one end was dedicated to refreshments.
The women behind the tables glanced over at her as she
approached. Eyes met eyes and smiles were met with smiles
and a warm glow grew inside her.

'Hello, dear,' said the woman behind the toys stall, her gaze darting down to Gladys, whose little hands reached up to pull at the leg of a knitted doll.

'Gladys,' Emma said. 'Don't touch.'

'What a pretty name!'

The woman picked up the doll and came around to the front of the stall. She knelt as she handed Gladys the doll.

'I have a niece just as pretty as you and I can't give her this doll. Will you have it instead?'

Gladys nodded shyly.

'And you'll promise to look after it for me?'

Gladys nodded again, backing away behind her mother's skirt.

'What do you say, Gladys?'

'Ta.'

Emma wished she would say the whole word, but Ernest was in the habit of encouraging the shorter version.

'I really must pay you,' she said to the woman.

'Beryl's the name and I won't hear of it. Are you from around these parts?'

'We live near Kitano.'

'Everyone seems to live in or near Kitano,' Beryl laughed. 'Your husband is a merchant?'

'Export manager for Guthries.'

'Then you must be at an absolute loose end. Why don't you join us? We women have to stick together in these parts. You're American, I take it?'

'My accent is rather a giveaway. I'm Emma.'

'I'm delighted to meet you. Come, let's have some tea.'

Within half an hour, Emma discovered the Kobe Ladies Benevolent Society was run by the bishop's wife and comprised a warm and enthusiastic group of middle-aged women whose husbands all worked in the British commercial community. It took another two hours of observing all who came to support the charity bazaar to realise the church itself played a prominent role in Kobe among the English. The men had their Kobe Club, which in the bund served as a replacement for the lack of a strong presence of Freemasons, and the church provided their wives with a focus of their own. One instant, Emma determined to fit in and the next, she found she did. She'd inherited a group of benevolent mother figures and planned on making the most of the opportunity.

Ernest, who was waiting outside the church when she stepped through the porch, encountered an entirely different Emma to the one he had known a few hours before. This Emma was buoyant, her heart fit to burst. Her new friend Beryl, with her frizz of hair and her freckles and green eyes, along with the other ladies, were sunbeams penetrating the thick cloud of her Kobe existence and she absorbed those sunbeams and radiated them at Ernest.

Taking in the sight of this happy version of his wife, his response was immediate.

'Let's take tea at the Oriental before heading home.'

More tea? Why not! Why not indeed! A celebration was surely in order.

She vowed from then on, she would attend every service held at the All Saints' Church.

Life, for Emma, improved enormously after the bazaar. In Yamamoto-dori, her daily walks took on a pleasant hue. She was no longer disturbed by the cool hostility she received from some of the local Japanese who seemed to regard her with resentment or sufferance or indifference but rarely with warmth and friendship. They were a closed community, she decided, and it was not surprising considering the bund had been dumped on their land and they were forced to observe foreigners getting rich while they didn't. She read in the *Japan Daily* cases of cruelty to servants, and she imagined how many of those arrogant, free-living men must treat their housemaids and cooks and rickshaw drivers. Perhaps the Japanese thought the same of her, those narrow eyes watching her wander up and down the streets; perhaps they thought she was cruel to Yu Yan. She almost burst out laughing at the thought.

Feeling more confident and adventuresome, one day she extended her daily walk and visited the Ikuta shrine. The walk was downhill from her home and the streets not as steep as those up to Kitano. She wandered around the grounds and admired the shrine with its upturned roof and its distinctive red paintwork, and she watched devotees and wondered about the Shinto faith. On the high side of the shrine, the mountains rose up just beyond the town. Roads heading off in all directions were flanked with shophouses, lanterns suspended from roof rafters swaying in the wind. She was, as ever, the only non-Japanese person to be seen, and although she attracted attention, she found when she made eye contact and smiled, she would receive a smile in reply.

Her weekly routine was broken up with church events, her new friend Beryl picking her and Gladys up on her way down from Kitano. Whether it be a service or Bible study or an afternoon tea, Beryl could always be relied on to take her.

Emma fitted right in, her experiences of expatriate wives in Singapore a distant cry from the mix of personalities among the Benevolent Ladies, which ranged from matronly to pious. When they discovered she was a nurse, her standing amongst them grew all the stronger and in her presence, conversations invariably dwelled on the ailments of all and the condition of expatriate health care in Kobe at the missionary hospitals. She forgot about Ernest at work or at the club... forgot that she played a bit part in his life, second or even third to his dogged pursuit of advancement. She forgot that despite all of her efforts to accentuate all the positives in his nature, she couldn't quite fully embrace the Ernest that he was. She forgot all that, in the face of her new female friends, who no doubt harboured similar views of their own husbands, although, unlike Dottie and Cynthia, she suspected they would never give voice to their complaints, even in confidence.

Spring had at last brought warmth and sunny days. Life was ticking along nicely until one morning Emma awoke with heartburn.

Over breakfast she felt nauseous and Ernest's slurping of a coddled egg made her rush to the bathroom.

There was only one diagnosis to be made. She was pregnant.

She stood in the bathroom, gripped the edge of the basin, dry-retched and retched again. Once the nausea had passed, she took in her reflection as she stared into the months ahead, picturing her belly getting bigger. It wasn't that she didn't want a second child, a playmate for Gladys. It was the thought of bringing another being into this hollow excuse of a marriage. Would that she could summon the same fortitude evident in her church friends, a fortitude able to bury or deny her discontents. Was she wrong to feel this listless, this unloved?

She re-entered the dining room to face a quizzical Yu Yan, who took one penetrating look at her before a grin spread across her face, and she left the room, nodding and muttering to herself.

Emma sat down to her half-eaten toast and emitted a loud sigh.

Ernest put down his spoon and took a few gulps of his tea.

'We're not in the doldrums again, are we?'

'I'm fine.'

'You don't look it.'

'I said, I'm fine.'

'Then can't you raise a smile.'

His words seemed borne of callous indifference, but he didn't know. She should tell him. Instead, as he sat there slurping his egg, she stared down the chasm of the year ahead.

HAWAII AND MONTRÉAL

The kitchen window rattled in its frame as a ferocious winter wind charged down the street, the sort of wind that blew umbrellas inside out. Emma glanced out on the off chance of spotting that happening, but the only person she could see was a woman hurrying along in a kimono and a hat.

Emma pulled away from the window and drew her cardigan about her chest. With nothing to do, she tiptoed upstairs to the second bedroom and gazed down with loving eyes at her sleeping baby Irene snug in her cot. Gladys, having tired herself out on the rampage all morning, was sleeping as well, lying flat on her belly on her bed. It was a moment of blessed peace. Then Emma heard singing, followed by a shout and footsteps shuffling along the hall downstairs. She thought Yu Yan would appear at any moment.

She didn't.

Silence, and then Emma heard the front door close. Yu Yan had gone to the shops.

She felt her whole body relax.

She decided she could endure the monotony of her daily

routine with Yu Yan bearing down on her every move no longer. She thought she'd go mad.

The instant she had seen Emma was pregnant, her benevolent tyrant of a servant insisted on some dietary changes, including various kinds of raw fish, none of which Emma was able to stomach the sight of, let alone eat. Yu Yan would snatch away the untouched bowl or plate, tut-tutting or yelling her disapproval. She was sure Yu Yan's constant mithering had made her morning sickness worse.

She confided in Beryl one time, but Beryl found Emma's domestic situation hilarious and advised she keep her sense of humour. 'Better a fussing housekeeper than a lazy one, believe me.' She was right, Emma knew, but it hadn't made things at home any easier. And, having gained no sympathy from her friend, she kept her own counsel when it came to her frustrations.

Then the birth came and winter came with it, and it was cold and wet and miserable, and she had to spend all her days indoors nursing her daughter and keeping Gladys entertained with whatever was to hand. Toys were hard to come by in Kobe, but she had had the foresight to purchase back in San Francisco a doll, a teddy bear and a ball. Beryl had gifted Gladys a wooden horse she could pull along with a string and a Zoetrope, which never failed to captivate the little mite's attention.

For now, Irene could make do with Gladys's old rattles, but with Gladys reaching two and a half, Emma thought a dolls house and a tea set in order, and more dolls and a teddy bear for Irene. The generosity of Beryl and the other ladies had been overwhelming and even a little humiliating. Emma liked to buy things for her children herself. It was just that there wasn't much to buy in Japan, or at least not that she could find.

Emma always made good use of her time while the children

napped. On this occasion, with Yu Yan at the shops, she enjoyed complete freedom from interruption and forewent her usual tatting to write to her parents. It was something she'd been putting off. A letter from her father had arrived last week with the news that her mother's health was deteriorating. Emma responded with words of concern then went on to describe anecdotes of Irene and Gladys. When she reached the end of the page, her last sentence trailed off and she put down her pen with an ache in her heart. She felt duty-bound to see her parents despite the cool reception she would receive. There was a sense of urgency, too, if her mother was ever to meet her latest granddaughter. She continued with her last sentence, informing her father she would visit with the children as soon as she could arrange the travel.

The tranquillity, broken when Yu Yan returned and began her soft humming in the kitchen, came to its natural end. Gladys woke first and whined for milk. Her clomping about stirred Irene who rubbed her little face, opened her eyes and began to cry. Emma lifted her out of the cot. The rest of the afternoon was taken up with mothering and by the time Ernest arrived home, dampened by the rain and worn out from work, she was exhausted. She waited until Yu Yan had left and Gladys and Irene were asleep in their beds before broaching the topic uppermost in her mind.

'I would like to take the children to America to see my parents.'

Ernest looked up from his newspaper.

'When were you thinking?'

'As soon as it can be arranged.'

A doubtful look appeared in his face. 'Irene is rather young, don't you think?'

'All the more reason to go now, while she's easy to carry. Ernest, my mother is ill.'

She waited. She was not about to plead or even explain further. The situation spoke for itself and silence worked better than words when it came to exerting her will.

Eventually, Ernest said with marked indifference, 'I'll make the arrangements tomorrow.'

She thanked him and went to check on the girls, before settling down to work on a lace doily.

The following afternoon, Ernest arrived home with her tickets. She was to travel on the Matson Line in four days' time.

'I thought you would need some time to pack,' Ernest said.

She found his casual, business-like manner disconcerting. It was almost as though he couldn't wait to see the back of her and the children, which could hardly be true, at least with regard to Irene and Gladys who he plainly adored. As for her, he had shown not one iota of interest in her in the intimate sense since Irene's birth.

They would be away for three months and much of that time would be spent travelling. She might have gone for longer, but she decided about a month was ample time to spend in Montréal. Too long, probably. Not that she was eager to return to Kobe.

It was a blustery mid-February day with Irene not yet three months old when they boarded the steamship bound for Hawaii, where they would need to change ships for San Francisco. Ernest helped her with the children and made sure the porter took her luggage to her cabin. He even heaved her trunk onto one of the beds and unstrapped the leather tie. She took in her new surroundings, reassuring herself she had everything she could possibly need. There was a small writing desk bolted to the wall below the porthole. A small wardrobe and a dressing table with a mirror above. Another door led to a bathroom. The fittings were highly polished, the décor pleasing if dark. Only the best for Mrs Taylor, it would seem, and she was grateful to her husband for securing her one of the ship's best cabins.

'Will you be alright?' he said with last minute concern.

'Don't worry, Ernest. We'll be fine.'

'Bye-bye, little darlings.'

He kissed both his daughters on their foreheads. She was about to gather the girls and follow him out of the cabin, thinking to wave to him once he was standing on the pier, but he insisted she stay put.

'I will be waiting for you when you return. Make sure to enjoy yourself.'

He squeezed her hand in an unusual show of affection.

'Don't work too hard, Ernest.'

'I shall be my diligent self, dear Emma.'

Their parting was warm, his best wishes heartfelt, and she wondered if she had slipped back into being unfair to Ernest these last months and failed to see him for all he was, good and bad. She vowed yet again to appreciate his attributes and not focus so much on his failings and, when she was back in Kobe, start afresh with some optimism for their marriage in her heart.

As it was, Emma was only able to appreciate his good points once she felt movement and the ship pulled away from the pier.

The voyage to Hawaii proved pleasant. Irene was a good baby and slept soundly. Gladys, well into the demanding two-year-old stage, was apt to stamp her foot and pout her lip, but aboard the ship she was lulled into silence by the motion and kept amused by the affection she received from the other passengers and the crew, who were all charmed by the little creature with the wide blue eyes and curls of chestnut-brown hair. Seeing how Gladys enjoyed the attention, Emma made a point of sitting in the lounge with her two infant girls, where Gladys could wander on her unsteady legs. The further away from Japan the ship travelled, the better Emma felt. She was lighter, less burdened, and she was filled with anticipation. She couldn't wait to set foot on American soil.

One afternoon early on in the voyage, the days were made all the more pleasant when a middle-aged woman approached Emma in the lounge. Emma had seen the woman in the dining room and in the corridors, but they had not had a proper encounter. The woman smiled and said, 'Mind if I join you?' sitting down in the seat opposite before Emma could answer.

Emma succumbed to a soft inner glow.

The woman introduced herself as Maud and proceeded to coo over Irene asleep on Emma's lap. Emma noticed tears welling in Maud's eyes.

'Silly me,' Maud said, a touch embarrassed. 'Take no notice.'

'You've lost someone,' Emma said, her voice soft as she was catapulted out of her motherhood bubble, with all of its preoccupations, into the sudden realisation of the war.

Maud exhaled heavily. 'My sons. Both.'

'I'm awfully sorry. The war has to end soon,' Emma said. 'Surely it must end.'

Gladys came up and pressed against her mother's leg. The two women were silent for a while.

Maud broke it with, 'Where are you from in Kobe?'

'Up near Kitano. Do you know it?'

'Never been but I have heard of Kitano. Very pretty, they say.'

'Very steep. And you?'

Emma discovered Maud was living in the Yokohama bund, and rather than dwell on the horrors of war, the two women shared stories of the waterfront lifestyle, where the men had all the fun and the women were bored out of their wits.

'The temptations are too great,' Maud said. 'I think that is what draws most men to these outposts. The licentiousness. They go there to dally.'

'Even the married men?' Emma said, a little shocked, even as she knew Maud spoke the truth.

'I would say especially the married men. Why else would they come?'

'Ambition?' Emma said, thinking of Ernest.

'Perhaps. But most would do better in their own countries. They go to these far-flung locations for the adventure.'

It was not a conversation Emma wanted to have. She told herself Ernest was different. He was not the dallying type. He was a company man, a social climber, and he was hell-bent on rising to the top, or at least as high as he was able to at Guthries. She asked Maud about the things she missed in England and they talked about needlework and shopping and the countryside.

'There's something soothing being in your own country, don't you think?'

Emma agreed, although inwardly she wasn't sure she had ever experienced the emotion.

When they put into port at Honolulu, Emma was one of the first on deck despite her two infant charges, all three of them uncomfortable in the sticky heat and the bright sunshine. All she could think about was getting off the ship and onto the next. Her new friend Maud came and stood beside her. Before long, the deck filled with other passengers, everyone eager to disembark.

The gangway was lowered and the ship's purser, distinctive

in his white uniform and hat, stood authoritatively by the railing as another uniformed man, big-bellied and with an ostentatious moustache, stood on the pier, oozing authority. Behind him stood some American navy officials. The moustached man put up his hand in a gesture. One by one, the passengers fell quiet and still. Then he walked up the gangway, where he beckoned to the purser. There was a long exchange of words, the purser's gaze drifting down to the navy officials. The officious man left the ship, chatter rose up among the passengers, and then the purser called everyone to attention with a shrill whistle.

The passengers fell into a disgruntled silence.

'Ladies and gentlemen,' the purser said, 'the US Navy has commissioned the SS *Maui* for military service. All those due to depart for San Francisco are to wait here on deck. Everyone else, please make your way off the ship.'

There were mutters of confusion that grew into loud voices and then shouts of indignation from some, while others tried to quell the irritation with comments about supporting the war effort. The purser ignored the milling passengers and saw to it that those bound for other destinations disembarked.

Emma stood back out of the way as those disembarking pushed past. After what felt like far too long, most of the passengers remained on board. Irene stirred and threatened to cry. Gladys was restless.

The purser again called everyone to attention, this time without a whistle. 'Arrangements are being made for you to remain in Honolulu until the next ship arrives from San Francisco.'

'How long will that be?'

'A week.'

'A whole week!'

Everyone spoke at once. Businessmen complained they

would miss important meetings. A mother would be missing her daughter's wedding. Someone else needed to be by the bedside of a dying relative. Before they left the ship, there was another long delay as each passenger was given the opportunity to send a telegram to notify their contacts. Emma told her parents she would be a week late. It was not a delay she was looking forward to one bit.

Maud remained by Emma's side. Once their feet were on the pier, she said, 'Don't worry, I'll stick by you so we don't get separated. Heaven only knows where they are taking us.'

They were bundled into awaiting liberty trucks and transported to a hostel. By now, everyone was complaining. The consensus was they should at least have been installed in a decent hotel, given the inconvenience, or even an acceptable hotel, but to have to suffer a basic hostel, comprising a series of huts with low ceilings and no fans, was beyond the pale. The navy, it seemed, did not deem the passengers worthy of much consideration. Making matters worse, the ship's staff, whom the passengers had grown accustomed to, had been replaced with indifferent naval personnel, who made no response to the carrying-on and focused instead on ensuring everyone's luggage was placed in the appropriate cabin.

One couple, who had travelled first class and were furious at the lack of regard, demanded to be taken to a hotel. They were successful, and that was the last Emma saw of them. The others were in varying degrees more accepting. As everyone chose where they wanted to be, Maud bundled her way into Emma's cabin.

'I'm hardly going to get one to myself and I would much rather be with you than that lot,' she laughed, claiming one of the top bunks with her handbag.

Emma would rather have been alone with her girls but, considering the crowded conditions, that was not an option and besides, she enjoyed Maud's company and some help with her daughters in the heat would not go amiss. Although she did wonder if Maud would find the constant presence of the girls wearing, especially as she so plainly missed her sons.

The hostel had communal kitchen facilities and the purser had assured the passengers they would also be fed by the navy. And fed they were, not by sailors in uniform but by friendly local women, who came and took over the kitchen and cooked up all kinds of exotic dishes no one had seen or heard of before. There was tropical fruit, which Gladys adored, and noodles and fish and coconut. For breakfast, there were spicy sausages and eggs. In Emma's view, no one had a thing to complain about except for the heat. Most of the others settled down, with the exception of a pair of stalwart complainers who everyone else ignored. Maud even managed to source fresh milk and chocolate for Gladys.

Their cabin enjoyed views of the forested mountains and Emma spent much of her spare time gazing out, wondering at the sorts of people who lived on the islands, the natives and then the Americans and the Chinese and the others making the location their home. The upshot of the requisition of the SS *Maui* for Emma was that she gained even more support than ever from the other passengers, and there was always someone to mind her babies if she needed to take a shower or rinse out some clothes or even go for a short walk.

Gladys formed an affectionate bond with Maud. She would follow the older woman around or fall asleep on her lap listening to Maud's tales of the adventures she had had as a child, and make-believe stories of fairies and angels and furry animals.

When the children slept, Maud spoke of other stories, ones suited to Emma's ears, of loves lost and found, of siblings and her favourite aunts. She asked Emma about her life, too, and at first Emma was cautious. She described her childhood in Philadelphia, but with little detail, quickly skipping forward in time to offer vignettes of nursing and then life in London. It was only when Maud revealed she had a deep interest in the spirit world that Emma, in a moment of weakness, let down her guard and told Maud of her Mennonite heritage.

'Then you are German,' Maud said, lowering her voice to a whisper.

'No, I am American. I was born in Philadelphia,' Emma lied, a dart of terror flying through her.

'And your parents are naturalised?'

'Yes.'

More lies and, feeling the colour rising in her cheeks, Emma knew Maud knew it, but she didn't seem to mind.

'I expect the Germans will be hated all the more now America has joined the war,' Maud said reflectively. Then, much to Emma's relief, she changed the subject, preferring to dwell on religious matters.

'I knew a Mennonite family once. They were neighbours. Kept themselves to themselves. Strange woman, the mother was, if you'll pardon me for saying.'

'There are all kinds of Mennonites,' Emma said, wondering where this new topic was leading. 'Some are intensely private. Fearful, maybe.'

'I don't suppose the Mennonites have any time for matters of the spirit world.'

'What do you mean?' Emma said, taken aback and thinking only of the Holy Ghost.

'Contacting the departed.'

Emma felt deflated. What was it with the world today and this peculiar interest?

Her mind darted back to that time when Ernest had dabbled with a Ouija board on the ship bound for Singapore.

She thought then as she thought now, that he had allowed evil to enter their lives and the consequences were playing out, the evidence his absence of moral fibre.

'Séances?' she inquired politely.

'I suppose.'

'I have always thought of them as dangerous.'

'You are talking of Ouija, no doubt. Most people think it is a silly parlour game and nothing more. I don't practice anything of the sort.'

'You're a Spiritualist?'

'You've heard of us?'

'Only vaguely.' Her mind drifted back to Singapore. To a remark Cynthia had made outside the Theosophical Lodge when they were out buying Emma jutties.

'I'm a Christian, Emma, like you.'

'But you do contact the dead.'

'The souls of the departed, yes.'

'How is that possible?'

'We believe evolution does not stop at death. We commune with the spirit world. It's all done in the name of Christ.'

'But not in a church.'

'Yes, a church. Not a grand cathedral, mind. More a chapel. But the weekly service is the same.'

Church or no church, Emma baulked at the very idea of contacting the dead, deciding then and there she would be too frightened to have anything to do with these Spiritualists. As though answering her thoughts, Maud said, 'It's the only connection I have with my sons.'

Emma could think of nothing to say. She could hardly refute a grieving woman, and on what basis? Maud was still a Christian. She still went to church and believed in God. Spiritualism was unconventional, but then so were the Anabaptists, including the Mennonites. She'd become a roving believer, content to attend any old church rather than none at all. Would she attend a Spiritualist church if there was no other alternative? Never.

She was saved from any further awkwardness when Irene woke up with a grizzle that turned into a disgruntled cry.

The week in the hostel soon passed. They boarded the ship bound for San Francisco amidst an uproar of cheers and, in what felt like no time, Emma was standing on deck at the ship's starboard, watching the approaching hills as they cruised into San Francisco harbour.

She let Maud help her disembark, but when it came to managing the rest of her transfer to the train station, she told her friend she was familiar with the city and would have no trouble finding her way. She felt a touch guilty, knowing she had maintained her friendship with Maud throughout the second part of the voyage with mixed feelings. She had been cordial, but not open and forthcoming. No matter how hard she tried to rationalise, deep down she found she had nothing in common with a woman who carried a passion for contacting the dead, even if they were her own sons. She knew it was prejudice but as far as she was concerned, Maud's interest in Spiritualism, in the final analysis, eclipsed all of her other qualities, good as they were. Some part of Emma recognised her reaction was unfounded, but this recognition gained no purchase in her defensive armoury. As they bid each other goodbye, Emma felt a twinge of guilt over her cool treatment of Maud, who clearly adored Gladys and had taken much solace in the child's company. To atone, Emma promised to write. They had exchanged addresses the night before.

Emma had spoken the truth when she claimed she knew her way around San Francisco. Besides, there would be many people ready to assist should she find herself stuck. The train journey was more challenging with two babies to care for, but yet again goodwill and human kindness prevailed, and she spent a very pleasant if exhausting five days making her way across America.

It was only when she arrived at her parents' home that her optimistic mood changed to one of profound solemnity. Her mother had just turned sixty-nine. Emma had missed her birthday by three weeks. Her father greeted her at the door, acknowledging his granddaughters in a perfunctory manner before taking her jacket and ushering her into the sitting room.

Her mother was seated by the fire, benefitting from the warmth of the flames dancing in the grate. An ageing woman, she gazed at her grandchildren with something like love in her eyes, but it was love coloured with sadness and regret. Emma knew her mother would take those emotions to her grave.

She unbuttoned her cardigan, hesitated, then took it off. Even after her week in Hawaii, Emma found the room hot and stuffy. The spring air outside was a little cool, but even so, she wanted to throw open a window to let in some fresh air. Instead, she settled her girls down and made small talk while they waited for the maid to bring tea.

It wasn't just the air that was stifling. Her mother's lack-lustre appearance, the uptight expression she wore on her face, her manner altogether spoke not just of illness or of sadness and regret, but of scarcely veiled blame and reproach. Why did she have to hold on so fiercely to her daughter's exodus from the confines of the faith? For that was what Emma saw in her mother's demeanour and it hurt and that hurt made her angry. Emma stared into the weeks ahead, wishing she could change her ticket and head back across America sooner.

The atmosphere in the house was subdued for other reasons, too. The war was taking its toll. Over dinner that evening, her father explained that the hatred against the Germans was just as strong in Canada, but at least Herman was left alone on the farm. It was in Montréal, in the shops and in the streets, that he had learned it was better not to open his mouth to speak unless he had to. Which explained to Emma in the ensuing days why he never offered to take his daughter and granddaughters out. Not even for a walk in the park. Emma was forced to go alone.

To make matters even worse, no one had heard news of George since before the start of the war. Almost four years had passed since then. Emma had to listen to her parents' speculations – perhaps he remained in prison as a conscientious objector, or his uncle was managing to keep in him in hiding at the back of his shop and didn't dare write and let them know – all the while knowing George had enlisted to fight. Only she suffered imaginary images of his suffering and death, while her parents held fast to the belief that their youngest child was a civilian, alive and in some degree safe and well. Their musings were hard to listen to. They'd created a fantastical portrait of her brother; George the hero, George the stalwart Mennonite standing up for his faith against the demands of his country, a true believer who would ultimately triumph and return to the fold. Several times during their consumption of the pot roast and then the apple pie and custard, in moments of weakness and frustration, she almost let slip the truth. But she stopped herself. It would have been churlish and counterproductive. Let them have their dream.

Herman seemed to carry the burden of the absent George the heaviest. He visited the following Sunday and, watching him interact with their parents as they sat down to another pot roast dinner and another fruit pie and custard, it was as though he had to be two sons to make up for his brother's absence.

No one had heard from Karin, either. But then, as Emma

kept telling her parents – to reassure herself as much as them – how was anyone to expect a letter from Germany when there was a war on. No doubt letters were surreptitiously ferried across enemy lines, but not many and the sender would need contacts, and a pressing need. Perhaps there was no pressing need. No news meant there had been no tragedy and all was well. That was all any of them could hold on to.

As the days dragged by, spending time in her parents' house became increasingly oppressive, and midway through her visit Emma was consumed with guilt. She felt guilty for being who she was. Guilty at having escaped the vicissitudes of war, first in a colonial outpost and then in a bund. Guilty for following her heart and leaving her faith. Guilty for marrying a man who had taken her far from her own roots in Philadelphia and allowed her to masquerade as a British-American wife. Guilty for having brought into the world, and to her parents' doorstep, the thief's offspring.

Her daughters would never be Mennonites; not unless she abandoned the marriage and returned to the fold. Even then, she would remain something of an outcast, having committed that singular betrayal. She felt an absence in her heart, as though the ties had already been broken and would never be repaired.

It seemed pointless being in Montréal. She had done her duty and was rewarded with anguish. Yet she was so desperately unhappy in her soul. Despite the Benevolent Ladies Society, which was her singular distraction, she detested Kobe and dreaded going back to an indifferent Ernest, and yet she could not bring herself to confide in her parents. She could not burden them with her woes and she could not face their reproach. There was every chance they would think even less of her for even considering breaking her marriage vows. Besides, she had no grounds. Ernest had never been cruel and he had not committed adultery. His perpetual long absences from the family home did not constitute grounds for divorce. Not that she would contemplate a divorce, not seriously, the shame that came with it would be intolerable.

On the penultimate day of her visit, she managed to persuade her father to take her into Montréal city so she could find some toys for the girls. Once they were out in the hustle and bustle of the city streets, there with the grand buildings and the array of fascinating shops, passing by the Seville Theatre and gazing up at this and that, her father seemed lighter and happier. It was another world they were sharing. They strolled in small parks filled with spring bulbs in bloom, took a tram to the Place d'Armes and admired the grand Notre Dame Basilica. They forgot about the war and all that came with it and took pleasure in each other's company. It was the closest she had felt to her father in many years. After a simple lunch in a crowded café, Emma took them back to Morgan's department store on St Catherine Street and bought a doll's house, two Raggedy Ann dolls and a tea set. It was a lot to carry, but she was not putting up with bored daughters back in Kobe. Boredom, she thought, was the curse of every woman rearing her children in isolation.

Back in her parents' mausoleum of a home, her father replaced his coat of good cheer with his normal sombre state of mind. Instead of relishing in the adventures of the day, over dinner that evening he insisted on discussing the anti-German sentiment in Canada and in Philadelphia. He said her uncle had written saying things were no better in Nebraska.

'It was not the people who chose this,' he said bitterly. 'It was those idiot politicians.'

Emma glanced at her mother, who just sighed. No doubt she had heard the same many times before. Emma sighed inwardly in unison.

He went on. 'Being German is one thing. Being a German pacifist is something the average American cannot comprehend.'

Hoping to deflect the rather tired topic, Emma asked after news of her uncle.

'He's fine. Last I heard, your cousin Hans had purchased land in Fort Morgan, Colorado.'

'Fort Morgan? The train goes right through there,' Emma said.

'You should write down his address, Emma,' her mother said. 'In case you feel like visiting on your journey back.'

She doubted she would, as it was much easier to remain on the train with her luggage, but she made a note of his address anyway, to be polite, and vowed to pay attention as the train made its way across the prairies and think of her cousin as they passed by.

The following morning, as she was due to depart for the station, she promised her father she would visit them again next year.

'Perhaps the war will be over by then and we can celebrate.'

'Will you move back to Philadelphia?'

'Will you?'

'I doubt it. Nothing for us there. And Herman seems settled.'

'He'll want to return to his training, surely?'

'There are hospitals in Montréal.'

There was no response she could give. For her father, the war had defeated the purpose of migrating from Germany. They had sought relief from persecution, only to be persecuted once more.

She kissed his cheek and said her goodbyes.

She left Montréal confused and sad – yet as first one train and then the next passed through state after state, she began to dismiss her unhappy frame of mind as unacceptable and unappreciative considering all the suffering going on in the world, and above all it was un-Christian of her to be so self-centred. She needed to shake off her own unhappiness, restore her faith that had taken a battering simply because she was dissatisfied. She had two beautiful little daughters to fill up her life, she had the Kobe Ladies Benevolent Society and the All Saints' Church to occupy her, and she was married to a man who held a very good position in a mercantile business, a position that would be the envy of many. She should, she must be grateful.

When the train passed through Fort Morgan, she thought of her cousin Hans and his wife Sophia and their young family. She doubted she would ever meet them, but it was comforting to know they were there.

A RIOT IN THE BUND

Summer brought fine and warm days to Kobe and made the daily walk along the streets of Yamamoto-dori pleasant. The community seemed to have accepted the presence of this foreign woman with her pram and her toddler, a woman they had been seeing every day for the last eighteen months, and sometimes the Japanese women would offer Gladys a shy smile. Language posed the greater barrier; Emma had little opportunity to learn Japanese and she lacked the confidence to speak the few words she did know. She had always been an intensely private woman, and she wasn't given to offering winning smiles and muddled hand gestures to accompany her attempts at communicating; not that she thought it would have made much difference and might even have proven counter-productive. Kobe locals remained uneasy and suspicious in the face of outsiders encroaching on their territory. And with good reason. Although she did wonder sometimes if perhaps she was too sensitive. She never felt unsafe, and she often reminded herself of that.

Emma found she had eased back into the rhythm of her life after her trip without difficulty. The tapestry was coming along nicely now she'd mastered some of the trickier techniques. Beryl collected her and the girls whenever there was something on at the church, and Ernest attended the Sunday service with remarkable regularity, after realising half the members of the Kobe club went as well. He was pleased as punch to show off his little family, bouncing Irene in his arms as he ingratiated himself with whomever he deemed important. Irene loved every minute of the attention, her silky auburn hair, nutty-brown eyes and pretty face drawing affectionate remarks from all.

In her dealings with the ladies' society, Emma was forced to maintain her guard, even with Beryl, lest her reactions to their talk of the war inadvertently revealed her origins. The effort of maintaining her British-American pretence was wearing, even as she developed a remarkable ability to hide behind the veneer. She was even able to complain about the Kaiser.

She almost came unstuck one day as they were having afternoon tea, when Maureen, a new and rather skittish member of the group, rather uncharitably said, 'I wish those bloody Germans would all just bugger off.' Emma had to hide her flushed face, lowering her gaze to straighten Irene's bib. Beryl quickly admonished Maureen, pointing out it was the countries who were at war, not the soldiers, and every death was somebody's son or brother or father.

There could be no greater truth in war. And since returning from Montréal, Emma had become more preoccupied than ever with the whereabouts and safety of George and her mother's failing health; preoccupations that encroached on her thoughts whenever she was alone.

When at home, she did her best to get through each day in

reasonable spirits for the sake of the children, who thankfully occupied most of her time, and at least when she focussed on them and them alone, she felt content. It wasn't hard to do, although it did come with weariness. Irene was now seven months old and her teething was in full swing, and Gladys was approaching three and as demanding as ever. Yu Yan would often keep Gladys entertained in the kitchen, chatting to her in her Chinese tongue, which Gladys found fascinating, and giving her tasty treats as she prepared the family meals. She offered some home remedies for Irene's gums as well, but Emma flatly refused to take them. Emma spent the afternoons while the girls were napping, pottering in the courtyard garden, dead-heading, tip-pruning, watering and pulling out any stray weeds, and admiring the flowers in full flush, dazzling whenever the summer sun shone down on them. When she tired of the tasks, she took up her tapestry. Or she would just sit and read the paper.

One Sunday afternoon towards the end of July, a shadow muted her enjoyment of the summer sun's bright rays. On page four of the *Japan Daily* there was a report on the social unrest in the Toyama province. The newspaper explained how rice, Japan's staple, had doubled in priced in a few months. Wages were low and people could no longer afford to eat. Emma had no idea where Toyama was. She asked Ernest, seated across the table.

'North,' he said without looking up.

'North?'

He graced her with his gaze. 'On the north coast. Why?'

Not wanting to enter into a discussion, she said, 'No reason. Just something I read.'

Satisfied, he returned to his book.

In the days that followed, what had begun as page four reportage became headline news as manufacturing workers organised sits-ins, marches and strikes. Sharecroppers were joining in. Women organised boycotts of ships exporting grain.

Then the *Japan Daily* announced that in Toyama, twenty-five thousand people had been arrested.

Twenty-five thousand!

She put the newspaper down on her lap. It was evening and the girls were asleep. She looked over at Ernest. He again had his head buried in that book. It wasn't a novel. It was *Morals and Dogma of the Ancient and Accepted Scottish Rite of Freemasonry* by Albert Pike. She didn't dare ask him about it and she had never seen inside; he took the leather-bound volume to Guthries and when home, he never let it out of his sight. What worried her, her with her traditional Christian faith, was the deepening of his interest in Freemasonry, which she had presumed he'd only become involved in again in Kobe – he'd joined a Lodge back in May – to further his career. Now, he was engrossed in something esoteric and she didn't like it, not one bit.

She didn't like the numbers of rioters, either.

When Ernest at last bookmarked his page, she asked him if he thought they should be concerned.

'Don't fret, Emma dear. Those rioters are far away from us and the authorities are stamping down hard. They'll have put it to rest in no time.'

'But what if they don't? What if they come to Kobe?'

'They won't come here,' he said with astonishing assurance.

She took no comfort in his assurances. She had no idea how he arrived at such a conclusion when it was obvious to her the people in the very streets where they lived were discontented.

She also had no idea what the Japanese shoppers and pedestrians and patrons of cafés were saying when she passed them by on her daily walk, but their looks at her were growing darker by the day and there was a definite mood in the air. She no longer felt comfortable pushing the pram up and down the streets with Gladys holding onto the handlebar.

In early August, the unrest escalated when fifty thousand protestors descended on Nagoya. Her mouth fell open as she read the article. Fifty thousand was an awful lot of people.

'Flies will get in if you leave it open,' Ernest said.

Emma closed her mouth. Then she said, 'Where's Nagoya? Do you know?'

'The other side of Osaka. Why?'

'Have you read this?' She pointed at the article.

'I told you not to worry, old duck.' Ernest laughed. It was a patronising laugh. 'Nagoya is a very long way from Kobe. Those protests won't come here.'

She wished she had his confidence. And she wished he wouldn't call her an old duck. She wasn't old, and she certainly was not about to start quacking.

The unrest in Nagoya continued and the *Japan Daily* devoted pages and pages to the unfolding events. There were attacks on the offices of rice merchants. Protestors were setting buildings on fire. The police tried to erect barricades, causing the numbers of protestors to swell to one-hundred and thirty thousand. A quarter of Nagoya's population, the journalist said. A quarter! Emma tried to picture that number of people out on the streets. The very idea terrified her.

She grew too apprehensive to go to church. Beryl had the same reaction. The Kobe Ladies Benevolent Society suspended activities until things settled down. Then the bishop suspended all services.

Emma took to praying with renewed conviction. She prayed for her family's safety. She prayed for the protests to die down. She prayed for the government to do something to lower the price of rice. She had no expectation that her prayers would be answered, but there was some solace in the act. At least she was doing something.

As the protests continued, Ernest maintained his belief that the government would soon gain control. He had no sympathy whatsoever for the protestors. They should all work harder if they wanted to put more food on the table, just like he did. Strikes, protests, riots – to him, they were tantamount to high treason and should be punished as brutally as any law enforcer saw fit. She was appalled. Despite her gnawing apprehension, she found herself firmly on the side of the protestors. She couldn't condone the violence, but it hardly seemed fair that the people should suffer because of all those merchants, Guthries included, who had driven up the price of rice locally by exporting the bulk of it. Through the lens of the reports she saw, as though for the first time, the injustices that arose from the exporting of goods. And it added a fresh dimension to what she had begun to recognise deep in her heart was a growing contempt for Ernest in every respect.

Although she had to admit that in one respect, so far, he was right. The riots had not reached Kobe and it didn't look like they would.

Relief came when the tense atmosphere lifted at the start of the Obon holiday. Workers were about to enjoy a whole week off for the festival. The *Japan Daily* devoted a double page to the Buddhist tradition, explaining Obon was the Japanese festival of the dead, when families came together and remembered and commemorated their ancestors. The feature article included a photograph of a previous festival, of some children all dressed up with painted faces. Emma had been looking forward to Obon week. She'd had to forego participating in the previous year's festivities as her ankles had started to swell due to her pregnancy, much to Ernest's consternation. He had felt duty-bound to keep her company on his week off and to his credit he had. Although she did allow him to take Gladys out for an afternoon.

This year, Ernest was keen they should all participate. He awoke on the first day of the festival in an exuberant mood. Emma had given Yu Yan the week off and was happy to attend to their domestic needs, with her husband at home being a parent. Ernest was always so marvellous with the girls. All morning he entertained them. Emma looked on, pleased he displayed such unstinting affection for his daughters.

He still hadn't the slightest interest in her; not since Irene's birth had he required her to fulfil her conjugal obligation and that was eight months ago. At first, she was relieved. Then, she hadn't minded, but now she began to wonder if he found her repulsive. Irene had left her a touch disfigured about the abdomen, something she knew to be a normal hazard of pregnancy. To be rejected by your own husband on the strength of that disfigurement was incomprehensible. Perhaps he was simply too busy and tired. Perhaps they had reached that stage in a marriage when the romance had naturally waned. Or perhaps he had difficulties of his own he wasn't divulging.

After the girls' afternoon nap, he suggested they walk down to the waterfront to participate in the merrymaking. Despite wanting to experience a little of Obon Week, Emma was not sure it was appropriate to take a baby out in all the crowds. Besides, the festival was for the Japanese, not for them.

When she voiced her view, he said, 'Nonsense.'

'It's too far.'

'A mile is not too far to walk. Irene will be in the pram and I will carry Gladys.'

With your bunions? She didn't say it. Instead, she folded her arms across her chest to convey her displeasure.

'Come on. We haven't had any fun for ages. It will be a treat.' He gave her one of his playful smiles.

She could hear the merrymaking through the open window. Perhaps he was right. The change would do them all good. Besides, she could see he was adamant.

Resigned to an evening of festive entertainment, she even allowed herself to look forward to it. While Ernest changed his attire, she tidied up and readied Irene and Gladys. Seeing him all dapper in a new suit, she put on the smartest of Dottie's summer dresses – layers of fine red muslin of varying lengths, scalloped at the hem – and a tailored jacket that sat snugly at the waist and straw hat to match. By five, they were ready to set off.

Stepping through the front door and out onto the street, they entered another world. Kobe was abuzz and it felt exciting to be amongst it all. Ernest was right. She was taken out of herself. Everywhere they walked, red and gold lanterns were hanging outside the doors of houses and shops. She heard flutes and Japanese drums coming from the direction of the Ikuta shrine. Ernest did a little dance on the pavement and Gladys giggled. The streets were filled with women and men garbed in brightly coloured yukatas with their wide belts and typically long, flowing sleeves. Children had painted faces similar to those she had seen in the newspaper. The celebrations were blessed with balmy evening air and there was not a breath of wind.

Emma could see many of the revellers were already drunk and everywhere she looked, men and women were slurping glasses of beer. Some had sake. Not given to drinking alcohol, she did her best not to judge, telling herself it was all part of the celebrations.

Down on the waterfront, Ernest insisted they dined at the Oriental Hotel. As they climbed the steps and passed between the stout pillars and entered the main foyer, Emma was reminded of the only other time she had been inside the opulent building, their first night in Kobe, the night she thought Irene was conceived. They made their way through a wide arch to the hotel restaurant.

The room was ample and high-ceilinged and lit by elegant chandeliers. Plants in large tubs decorated the space. Circular tables draped with white linen were arranged in low rows, many of them vacant. Emma spotted Maureen, one of the ladies from the church, and her husband seated at a table below one of the grand, multi-paned windows. She thought of taking a table nearby, but on seeing the children, a waiter rushed over and steered them to an out-of-the-way table near the kitchen. He brought a highchair for Irene and a cushion for Gladys to sit on. The moment the toddler sat down her hands reached for the potted plant perched on the table edge. Quick off the mark, the waiter took it away and returned with the menus.

'Beefsteak is in order, don't you think?' Ernest said, loud enough for the departing waiter to hear. 'We are in Kobe, after all.'

He was clearly in a lavish mood and he wanted the world to know it. A different waiter came to take their order, an exceedingly polite waiter – they were all exceedingly polite – only this waiter had a disconcertingly obsequious glint in his eye.

Ernest ordered turtle soup and steak and a carafe of sake, and French fries and lemonade for Gladys.

'No expense spared, dear heart,' he insisted when Emma chose duck pate followed by fried fish, a conservative option, she knew.

He managed to slosh half the sake before their entrées arrived and proceeded to dominate the conversation, teasing Gladys and making Irene giggle with his silly faces and little games. Emma gave him free rein.

Grabbing hands and messy faces aside, the meal was most pleasant. Emma thoroughly enjoyed the food and the setting. It was delightful to be out in Kobe on a festive night, to feel the cohesive intimacy of her family, to watch Ernest be a good if indulgent father to their children.

'Try some sake,' he said at the end of the meal, pouring a little into her glass before she had a chance to decline. She was still feeding Irene and it did not seem right to ply her body with alcohol.

'It's Obon week,' Ernest said. 'You have to try it. Just a sip.'

She obliged, only taking the smallest amount to satisfy his will. As she swallowed, the liquor burned her throat and she realised she had probably sipped too much. She set the glass down and refused to bring it to her lips after that, and she busied herself with Irene and Gladys as she watched Ernest slosh back the rest of the carafe. Thinking, hoping the enormous steak he had consumed would lessen the intoxication.

In her side vision, Emma saw Maureen and her husband leave the restaurant, dodging by a man in a white suit who'd paused to look around. Spotting Ernest, the man headed over.

'Ernest, old fellow. Enjoying the festivities?'

'I am indeed, Humphrey.' He proffered his hand. 'This is my wife, Emma.'

'Charmed.' Humphrey gave her a small bow. 'And what delightful little cherubs you have.'

He grinned and winked and ruffled Irene's hair. Then he poked out his tongue at her and Emma felt instinctively protective, as though in the face of a predator.

After a brief exchange with Ernest, Humphrey took his leave. Emma wiped sticky hands and faces while Ernest paid the bill. Sated, they left the restaurant and re-entered the festive atmosphere of the night. As they walked along the wide promenade between the trees and the long strip of fenced-off lawn, Ernest related all he knew about Humphrey. A Freemason – Emma had already guessed – with commercial interests in the bund, as had every other Englishman they encountered. 'He's never married, you know.'

Emma was not surprised. If anyone they knew partook in the loose women of Kobe, it was Humphrey.

They arrived at the end of the promenade and ambled back along the other side of the lawn, closer to the water's edge. The Oriental Hotel stood tall and proud in the row of other fine colonial buildings facing the harbour. Behind the rooftops, the mountains loomed. The locale was quieter and much less crowded than the backstreets, and they paused to watch the jumble of fishing boats sway gently and tug on their moorings. Ernest pointed out their features to a bemused Gladys.

'Can we go on one, Daddy?' she begged, and Ernest laughed.

Gladys started to whine and tug at her father's hand.

Behind them, Emma heard raucous shouts and cheers coming from a side street. She glanced around but couldn't see who was making the noise. Irene stirred and Emma rocked the pram to settle her. She caught Ernest's attention and said she thought the girls had had enough and they should perhaps head home.

Ernest was about to protest when Gladys yanked his arm and whined, 'Daddy, I want to go in a boat!' She was easily fixated and stubborn as a mule, qualities Ernest was for once having to contend with. His solution was to quickly hoist her onto his shoulders, much to the amusement of onlookers.

Leaving the harbour behind, they crossed the road and turned down a side street and made their way through the crowds and food stalls towards the sound of beating drums.

They were yet to arrive at the next cross street when there was a loud bang and then another. Fireworks, Emma thought, gazing up at what sky there was to be seen, anticipating sparkles. Instead, there were loud shouts and people running.

A horde of revellers came barrelling down a street to their left, from the direction of the Chinese quarter. Emma and Ernest hurried on, dodging past people heading every which way.

At the next intersection, they found the party atmosphere had transformed. No longer were there throngs of happy people drinking and dancing. Instead, they confronted an angry mob of rioters yelling and waving their fists.

Emma froze where she stood. Even if she had wanted to carry on through the bund and up to Kitano, she couldn't push the pram through such a dense tangle of people. The crowd thickened and thickened. People swarmed to join the protestors.

She looked around, stricken. Ernest was nowhere to be seen. She had no idea in which direction he had gone. She peered down at Irene, who was crying in distress. Emma dared not pick her up, yet she seemed vulnerable in the pram. What on earth was she to do? She tried to edge away but the people to the front of her would not budge. She couldn't manoeuvre the pram in any direction. She was stuck.

Panicked thoughts raced through her mind. She stood out like a beacon in her smart straw hat and fine red dress; a foreigner, the very reason the hungry, angry locals were rioting. It was fortunate the crowd was so dense or she would have been even more visible. After all, she could become a scape-goat. But no one took much notice of her. They were too busy yelling and raising their fists in the air.

She heard a roar and she followed the sound with her gaze. Further down the street, about one block away, she saw flames, red-hot tongues licking up the sides of a building. Then there was the shatter of glass, an explosion, followed by high-pitched screams.

The crowd started squeezing and heaving this way and

that, some wanting to get closer, others wanting to run away. People shoved past her, bumping into the pram. She still couldn't move. She watched as the flames took hold of the building, enveloping it, devouring it with a preternatural hunger. In too little time, the blaze had become an inferno. She could feel the heat from where she stood.

Minutes passed. Her heart was thumping in her chest. She kept looking around for Ernest but she'd lost him.

It was bedlam. As the crowd heaved, she noticed a policeman, and then another. Relief washed through her. Safety and sanity at last.

The officers, ten, twenty of them now, were trying to disperse the crowd. The protestors on the fringes, no doubt not wanting to be arrested, drifted away. Every gap she saw, she moved into it and gradually made her way to the other side of the street.

To her complete astonishment, there was Ernest, standing in a doorway, easy to spot with Gladys still on his shoulders. When she got near enough to be heard, she told him to carry Gladys on his hip. He hesitated, puzzled.

'This instant!'

She had never shouted at him in public before and his reaction was immediate. He obliged, offering an apology that came with a rush of sentences defending his decision.

'And you think our daughter needed to witness a riot?'

'To her it was just a lot of mayhem. She was in no danger.'

'You don't know that. How can you even think that?'

She carried on past him, pushing the pram through the crowd with him trailing behind, her anger causing anyone approaching to give the pram a wide berth. She thought she might escape the worst of the revellers and protestors if she kept heading in the direction of Kitano, but she seemed to be taking them deeper into the furore.

At the next intersection, she looked down the side street and not fifty yards from where she stood, another building was ablaze. Flames reached skyward in a terrifying roar. Above the yells and the screams and the chanting she heard crashes of falling timbers. The police presence had grown stronger. They were trying to calm and disperse the crowd, but the protestors were having none of it. Tensions were mounting. Violence was sure to break out.

There was nothing to be done but hurry on by in the hope that eventually the horde would thin, that some sense of normalcy would descend on Kobe.

The moment she saw they were through the worst of it, the streets no longer thick with drunken and irate Japanese, Emma quickened her pace, ignoring Ernest puffing and panting behind her until, at last, they arrived at their front door.

By then, Gladys was crying and Irene was screaming at the top of her lungs and rubbing her little face. Ernest soon started adding his voice to the upset, but Emma snapped at him to be quiet. She, meanwhile, was shaking. She could scarcely get her key in the door.

Ensconced in their living quarters, Emma went around securing windows and drawing blinds. She felt like sitting in the dark lest someone saw a light on and decided to break in and attack them. Paranoia, true, but her heart was racing and she struggled to breathe.

Irene's caterwauling prompted Emma's attention. Leaving Ernest to settle Gladys, she picked up her baby and took her into the bedroom and sat down in the chair beside the electric heater to feed her. Both mother and baby slowly regained their equanimity. A nappy change later and Emma wandered into the living room as Ernest emerged from the kitchen with a milk chocolate bar and a bottle of whisky. Gladys trailed behind him, sucking her thumb. Emma welcomed the chocolate and, for once, she welcomed the whisky as well.

The rioting lasted a whole week. For the duration, the Taylor family did not leave their house. Ernest, who up until the riots reached Kobe had maintained a casual calm, became protective and wary and conceded to Emma that she had been right all along about the threat. He said he had no idea if they would be targeted if they went out.

'I underestimated them, Emma, I really did. The people here, they seemed such a peaceful sort, obedient.'

'If people are oppressed enough, they will do anything. They are hungry, at risk of starving, Ernest. You do realise that?'

'I do now.'

Without Yu Yan, Emma faced a mountain of washing and cooking. They ate what there was in the house, which turned out to be plenty as Yu Yan liked a well-stocked pantry. From time to time, Ernest kept vigil, observing the street outside the kitchen window and assessing the situation.

By Friday, it was obvious the protests had calmed down and he ventured out to purchase some groceries and a newspaper. Emma refused to go with him.

The next Monday, Ernest returned to work. Emma spent a restless day of careful listening at home, her solitude broken when Yu Yan appeared unexpectedly, apologising for her lateness. It took some time before Emma ascertained how Yu Yan had been affected by the riots. She lived in the Chinese quarter and her son, who owned the shophouse where they all lived, had taken a beating when an angry mob looted the shop. He had a broken arm along with cuts to his face and two black eyes, and the shop was badly damaged. Yu Yan indicated she was not sure how the family would recover from the loss. Sympathising with Yu Yan's plight, Emma faced divided loyalties, to her family and Yu Yan's on the one hand, and to those poor, half-starved locals deprived of their staple, rice, on the other. There were no winners in the situation. Even the merchants had taken a bashing and everyone was doomed to live in tension and uncertainty and fear until the government acted. She wished they would hurry up about it.

That night, Ernest came home and said there was more trouble in Kobe, this time a violent strike by workers at the Mitsubishi shipyard.

'They want better wages, I expect,' he said.

'Yes, better wages. Why ever not?'

He didn't reply.

As usual, Ernest had brought home the *Japan Daily*. In the quiet of the evening, Emma read the headlines. To her horror, the unrest had swept through the whole of Japan's industrial heartland. Japan was suffering its own domestic war, the result of the war unfolding beyond its shores, a lack of government regulation and the profiteering of greedy individuals all serving to hike up the price of rice. It seemed to her insane that things had been allowed to deteriorate to such a degree. Every nurse knew you had to get to a wound fast or it would fester.

Emma decided she had had enough of Kobe and enough of Japan. She had sympathy for the locals and their plight, but this was no place for a British-American to bring up children. She wanted to leave Kobe for good. Although she knew she would never persuade Ernest to relinquish his posting, not when trade was booming. And she had nowhere to go other than to her parents, and she would not feel comfortable doing that, knowing she was not welcome. Impulse vied with practical common sense. She thought about it for the rest of August and the whole of September. Even when Prime Minister Terauchi and his cabinet resigned at the end of that month, Emma had no confidence Japanese society would remain in peace. All she could do was ride out the situation, praying the icy air of winter would drive people indoors in front of their fires; praying that Ernest would soon be posted elsewhere.

INFLUENZA

On a cold and miserable November evening, Ernest arrived home, slapped the newspaper down on the coffee table beside her and said, without much cheer, 'The war is over.'

His lack of enthusiasm was puzzling.

'Over?' she said. 'Really?' She glanced at the girls playing happily on the living room rug and drew the newspaper closer to read the headline.

'We won,' Ernest said. 'The Germans have surrendered.'

He left the room. With another glance at the girls, she gathered up her knitting, bundled it safely away from little hands and followed him into the kitchen.

He went to the window and stared out at the street. Emma watched him, her balding, portly husband in his fortieth year, hands thrust in his trouser pockets, reflecting on goodness only knew what, but no doubt it had to do with him and not the world at large.

Emma wasn't sure how to feel about the war's end. She felt relieved, absolutely she did, but the sense of victory did not embed itself in her. After all, she was German. She did not agree with the attitude of the Kaiser, but neither did she hold in her heart any strong loyalty towards America or Britain. How could she? A large portion of her extended family lived in Germany. Her sister and her family, and her brother, her dear, dear George, had moved back there. She was compromised. Not that she would have wanted Germany to win the war. Really, she had no idea what to think other than of all those wasted lives lost in the trenches.

Ernest pulled away from the window and looked at her strangely.

'You seem troubled,' she said, thinking he must be considering her awkward situation.

But no.

'Guthries has been trading in Japan on the back of this war. So yes, I'm troubled. Now demand for Japanese exports will decline.'

'Meaning?'

'This is my life, Emma... our lives I am talking about. Suddenly, my position here in Kobe might be compromised.'

She instantly saw red. The selfishness of the man was boundless.

'Is that all you can think about?' she snapped.

'I beg your pardon?'

'How many millions have died? And all you're concerned about is your job.'

Ernest reacted, but not with words. Instead, he walked over to the table, angrily thrusting in a chair, and then picking up a book and slamming it down. Pencils, cups, a small plate, everything rattled. Across the hall, through the open sliding doors, Irene looked up at him, shocked. She started to cry. Gladys, sitting on the floor with her Raggedy Ann, joined her. He took one look at his daughters, shot Emma a steely glare and announced he was taking a walk.

'Suit yourself,' she whispered to herself behind his back.

After the front door slammed, she went and distracted the girls with a picture book. Bedtime was approaching but they wouldn't sleep if they were upset. Once they had calmed down, she sat down on the floor and organised their toys, occupying Gladys with her doll's house and Irene with her stacking blocks, her thoughts returning to George. Surely she would hear news now the war was over? She imagined the chaos, the communication difficulties, and told herself in all likelihood she would not hear from him for months.

Since she couldn't write to him, she wrote to her parents instead, expressing her relief that the war was over and wishing them well. She told them she hoped to visit again once the winter was over. She didn't mention the rice riots. She wrote about Irene's teething and attempts at walking. The letter took over an hour to compose and as she put down her pen, Ernest arrived home with a bunch of flowers and an apology.

'You're overwrought,' he said. 'I should have been more considerate.'

She thanked him. There was no point holding a grudge. He had his own pressures, she knew that, and perhaps she had been too harsh, too quick to judge.

'Shouldn't you write to your sisters? Find out about Edwin?' she said as she folded her letter and slid it into the waiting envelope ready for Yu Yan to post.

'All in good time.'

He sat down on the floor with the girls and before long there were giggles and squeals of laughter. She was about to tell him not to excite them close to bedtime, but curbed the impulse.

Watching him dote on his daughters, she was puzzled, yet again, by Ernest's lack of affection for his own family. Or perhaps he wasn't given to writing letters of that sort. Perhaps she should write to Edwin, to Sarah, to Hannah. They were sure to have news of their own to impart. She considered it, but decided the task belonged to Ernest. After all, she had only visited Edwin once, Hannah that time at the party in New Jersey, and Sarah never. Emma never could ascertain why Ernest chose to keep his distance from his siblings. He'd created another family at Guthries, she supposed, and at the Kobe Club and the Lodge. Always the Lodge. Perhaps it didn't matter. Yet there were consequences. Her lack of bonds with the Taylors reinforced her own feelings of fragmentation. There were cousins for Irene and Gladys, a sense of belonging, all of it forfeited to Ernest's dogged independence.

Two weeks later, when optimism was seeping back into the soul of humanity, a double-page feature article on the alarming death toll from a lethal disease appeared in the *Japan Daily*. They were calling it Spanish influenza, many suspecting the disease had its origins in Spain as that was the location of an early outbreak. Emma was glad to be reading the piece after dinner when the girls were asleep. She refrained from remarking on the news to Ernest, who was sitting in the other chair, happily immersed in another Freemasonry book. He'd only accuse her of fearmongering.

Emma's eyes took in the words in the newspaper, reading over each sentence twice as the reality sunk in. The disease, which killed many of those infected in a matter of days, continued to sweep across the world. The journalist stated deaths had been widespread since September and the disease had spread throughout America like a wildfire. She had read snippets in earlier editions over the last weeks, brief mentions, the journalists focusing on overseas news. Now she was told there were already about nine thousand cases in Kobe alone.

That put the pandemic on her doorstep.

The article stated Japanese morgues were already overflowing. Schools were being closed by order of the government. Nearly a thousand people had died of the flu in Tokyo alone in just four days.

She paused. The hospitals wouldn't cope with that caseload. The wards would be overrun. Where would they put everyone? Field hospitals would be required. She'd nursed respiratory illnesses before, watching the gravely ill struggle for every breath as their airways narrowed and their lungs filled with fluid they were too weak to expel.

She pictured the nurses forced to cope with the suffering.

The last article she read sent a chill through her. Many millions of soldiers in poor condition after fighting in the trenches had succumbed to the disease. Many millions. Those poor young men. Did the number include George?

She put the paper down on her lap. Until now, she had resisted contemplating the full extent of the pandemic, the danger they were in. In her mind, she made plans. She knew what was needed. She would not allow any unnecessary risks.

She interrupted Ernest with, 'You must be vigilant. Tell me at the first sign of a sore throat.'

'I beg your pardon?'

'There's an influenza epidemic. Here, in Japan.'

'Oh, that. Worry not. I shan't put myself at risk. All I do is travel to work and sit in an office cut off from the rest of the staff.'

'What about the Lodge? The Kobe Club?'

'I very much doubt any of those men will contract this disease. Seems to be hitting the young.'

'You know all about it, then?'

'Only what I've heard.'

'It isn't only the young. It says here,' she said, stabbing the newspaper, 'that factories have been closed. People are being advised to stay out of public spaces.'

'A bit extreme, if you ask me.'

'Extreme? Have you any idea how many people stand to die from this? It's killing victims in a matter of days.'

Ernest peered over his glasses at her and gave her a patronising smile.

'Don't believe everything you read in the newspaper. They are probably exaggerating. And even if one of us did catch the bug, that doesn't mean we will die. Word at work has it most survive.'

'Oh, and you believe Guthries over governments and doctors?'

'I am only telling you what I've been told.'

Ernest was right, of course. There would be many more survivors than victims. Her work in infectious diseases had taught her that. Even so, with such a virulent disease on the loose, she decided she would remain indoors with the children as much as she could. She was not even sure she could trust to have Yu Yan around.

Ernest was furious when he came home the following day to discover Emma had let her go.

'You'll need to keep paying her. She has a family of her own.'

'Aren't you taking things a bit far?'

'I would rather this than lose a child.'

He huffed and he puffed like the big bad wolf in the nursery rhyme. Emma took no notice. In the days that followed, she adopted her own emergency measures. First, she cut up three of Irene's dresses that she'd outgrown and made triple-thickness masks for them all. Then she went to the local grocery store, the pastel pink mask covering her mouth and nose drawing the gazes of all, and handed the grocer the list she had asked Yu Yan to write in Japanese along with instructions, arranging for the basic food items to be delivered to her door every day. She refused to open the door until the deliveryman had gone away. With gloved hands, she collected the box and took it to the kitchen. She took out the items and then put the box outside the front door, away from grabbing hands. The groceries themselves might also carry the germs, so she wiped down the jars and cartons with hot, soapy water and disinfectant just in case.

She had no idea how long the germs could live outside the human body, but she thought twenty-four hours a reasonable guess. Whenever the girls were asleep or occupied in the kitchen, she would fully open the sliding doors in the living room to let in the fresh air, despite the wintry chill. Minimising the risk through these simple precautions seemed basic common sense. Knowing she was doing everything possible to protect her offspring, if either did contract the illness, her conscience would be clear.

Ernest, oblivious to most of her precautionary efforts, was another matter. Reining in his cavalier attitude was a daily chore. She forced him to scrub his hands upon entry to the house after work each day. He moaned and complained, but she insisted.

Her new regime was tedious and her domestic duties time-consuming. Yet they all remained healthy. Eventually, Ernest had to concede she was right in protecting the family after one of Guthries' staff came down with a terrible fever and died three days later. After that, Ernest assured Emma he would take no risks at work and stay away from the regular office staff as much as he could. He even dutifully wore the mask she had made him out of one of his old shirts.

The death toll rose. Schools remained shut and the atmosphere in the whole of Japan was grim. All anyone could do was ride out the ordeal and hope. It was a lonely time. She had scarcely begun attending church services again after the riots when the influenza struck and she was forced into self-imposed isolation. She missed the companionship of the ladies of the benevolent society enormously.

It seemed she was not the only one who felt lonely. Every few days, Beryl would call in bearing gifts of produce from her garden and treats for the children. Emma gave the treats the same treatment she did the groceries.

'You can't be too careful,' she said, the first time Beryl came by.

'You're an example to us all,' Beryl said, a bemused look in her eye.

Beryl's visits were always the same. Emma made tea and they would chat about the world, the suffering, the war and then the pandemic.

'Surely soon, God will decide humanity has had enough.'

'It'll be a relief to get back to normal.'

Then Beryl would help keep the girls amused and tidy up after them before she left. She played her self-appointed role of grandmother perfectly.

In December, a letter arrived postmarked Montréal. Emma tore open the envelope and extracted a single sheet of paper containing a few lines. She caught her breath as she read.

Her mother had passed away. She had died of a heart attack. It was quick, her father said. She didn't suffer.

Emma's eyes swam over his words. The letter was so very short, she wondered why he hadn't sent a telegram. There was no news of George or Karin and he didn't mention Herman. No news of the funeral or his future plans. Just the cold, hard truth that she no longer had a mother.

It was still early in the day and outside the sky was grey. Irene and Gladys had just eaten. There was the washing to do, the house to tidy. She could face none of it. She felt oppressed. The house was stifling, the walls crowding in. She needed fresh air, open space. She bundled Irene and Gladys in coats, hats, scarves and masks, put Irene in the pram, donned her own mask and went out. Blinded by tears that refused all her efforts to stem them, she pushed the pram down to the Ikuta shrine and back to the corner of her street. Then she turned around and headed back to the shrine again. If anyone approached, she held her breath as they passed, but mostly the streets were empty. She walked until her legs ached. She walked until Gladys moaned and she had to carry her. She walked until she was exhausted and still she walked. Only when the rain that had been threatening all morning finally came down in quick patters, did she hurry back to the house, cursing her lack of foresight at having failed to take an umbrella. She had half a mind to grab one and head out again. Instead, she heaved the pram indoors. It was only then she considered the risk she had taken with her family's health. She decided it was minimal.

She unbuttoned coats and removed shoes and gloves and hats and masks. Some food and milk and a nappy change for Irene and she settled the girls down in the living room. She sank into Ernest's favoured armchair and there she sat, keeping an eye on the girls with half-attention. She couldn't bring herself to even move, let alone attend to the daily chores. Her gaze fixed on her tapestry ensconced in its small wooden box. The one occupation that might potentially have brought solace required a level of serenity and focus she simply didn't have. How ironic, she thought with an inward scoff, and she vowed to find a different pastime, something easy like knitting scarves in garter stitch. Well, perhaps not quite that easy, but still...

For the rest of the day, she did nothing but stare vacantly at furniture, at walls, at floors, rousing herself to change nappies and feed hungry mouths. She couldn't eat. Her mind kept trotting off to fetch the ball of grief she did her best to toss away, bringing it back to drop at her feet like a well-trained dog. She would pick up the ball coated in the dog's slobber and hurl it away and the faithful dog would bring it back again. And she would stare into her mother's face, recall the hurt, the reproach, and descend into a pit of guilt. Now there would be no opportunity to heal the rift that had grown between them these last twelve years, ever since Ernest had arrived on the scene. She hadn't realised how much she had wanted her mother's forgiveness, her understanding and, above all, her affection. Too late. And she hadn't anticipated the grief she would feel at the loss.

Compounding her pain was the punishing knowledge that, in abandoning her family, she had missed being there for the crucial years of her mother's decline. Worse, she felt estranged from those who were left. Would she see Herman again? Her father? What if she lost all of them, too? And then there was George. When she thought of him, she couldn't bear it. If she lost him, she would be destitute in her heart for the rest of her life.

Hoping for solace, she waited for Ernest to come home. He had already lost both parents and she thought he would understand the shock, the grief. But when he arrived and found her all maudlin in the dim light of living room and she told him her news, he offered little sympathy and proved of small comfort. Instead, he looked around the room with a critical eye – there were toys scattered end to end, along with dirty plates and cups – and told her they must ask for Yu Yan to return as she clearly wasn't coping. Emma relented. She knew Ernest was right. Yu Yan did make things easier and she was company.

Within the first hour back on the job, as Emma entered the

kitchen, Yu Yan caught her despondent look and said, 'You no happy.'

As if on cue, tears trickled down Emma's cheeks.

Yu Yan stood before her and reached out to wipe her eyes. 'What happen?'

Realising Yu Yan was not going anywhere without an explanation, Emma told her she had lost her mother.

Yu Yan's face filled with sympathy. 'I lose mother and father very young,' she said. She went on to explain, using hand gestures and a lot of repetition, how they had both died. Emma still wasn't sure she had understood, but the effort of trying had released her from the burden of her grief.

'You need to let your mother go,' Yu Yan said softly. 'She happy now.'

From then on, Yu Yan told jokes no one understood and did funny walks and kept the children entertained. Emma grew ever fonder of her Chinese servant and when she taught Gladys to understand simple words, drawing pictures and writing down the letters, she also taught Yu Yan. Learning beside her, Gladys, at three and a half years old, was twice as engaged and learned twice as much in the process and even Irene, at not much over one year old, took an interest.

When Yu Yan went out, Emma taught Gladys the same words all over again, in German.

Christmas came and went without much festivity, the pandemic dampening the spirits of the expatriate community. Although Ernest managed to enjoy himself. The Kobe Club put on a party, for members only. And the Lodge held a dinner, again for their members. The Ladies Benevolent Society held a luncheon at the church the day before Christmas Eve, but no matter how hard Beryl tried to persuade her to attend, Emma wouldn't breach her own home-quarantine protocol.

She made an exception for the Christmas Carols service,

accepting Beryl's offer of a lift in her husband's new Mitsubishi motorcar, leaving the girls at home with Ernest. She wore her mask for the entire time, even in the motorcar, much to Beryl's amusement.

'It's rather annoying to have to take it off and put it on again,' Emma said, by way of an excuse.

The truth was, she couldn't be certain Beryl had not come into contact with an infected person and be infectious herself, even though she displayed no symptoms, and in the confined space of the motorcar, she was sure to breathe in Beryl's exhaled air in any case. Emma had no solid foundation for her belief and she wasn't about to express it for fear of being mocked and accused of over-reacting. Better to keep quiet. Better to be safe.

Dottie sent a Christmas card which arrived after Boxing Day with news that Lizbeth and Gustav had managed to leave Australia and were heading back to Singapore. Ian had succumbed to the dreaded influenza but was thankfully on the mend, largely as a result of Cynthia's devoted care. She and Edgar were well and just the same as ever, and Eve and her husband were returning to England. *They will be missed. Whatever will I do with my time now there's no need to raise funds for the war effort?* Dottie wrote, and signed off with love.

The days slid by. Winter in January had a nasty bite to it. The icy air blew down off the mountains, making even the shortest of walks an ordeal. Even with Yu Yan for company, Beryl's visits for entertainment, and the girls to occupy her days, life in lockdown was monotonous. Every day, Ernest brought home the *Japan Daily* which carried yet more bad news of the flu. Thousands were dying every week, with fresh outbreaks occurring all over Japan. Whole villages were wiped out. Along with wearing masks, the authorities advised gargling to flush away the germs before they took hold. Emma was kept busy cutting up more of Irene's dresses to make masks for Yu Yan's extended family.

Just when everyone thought the flu in Japan was on the wane, another wave hit and the death toll spiked. By mid-March, Emma was reaching the end of her tether. She'd been cooped up in the house for months without much respite. First the riots, then the flu. She would be forgiven for deciding her departure from Kobe was long overdue. She craved open spaces, not narrow streets on a strip of land hemmed in by the sea and overshadowed by the mountains. She craved to be somewhere familiar, somewhere she felt she belonged. Above all, she yearned to see her family, what was left of it.

With the warmer weather, it appeared cases of influenza were falling, the *Japan Daily* carrying an air of optimism in its reportage, although she wasn't sure she could trust that sentiment. Highly infectious diseases had a nasty habit of lurking in dark corners, reappearing just when everyone let down their guard. Even so, little by little, she braved the outdoors, taking the girls for longer walks each day. Beryl invited her to attend the Ladies Benevolent Society meetings, but still she declined, saying she would rather wait a little longer, to be safe. The truth was, Emma had become broody and withdrawn, the result of her self-imposed confinement. She would rather sit on a low chair and entertain the girls, and teach Gladys the alphabet and how to count to ten in both English and German, than sip tea with the ladies of Kobe expatriate society. In her quiet time, she forwent working on her tapestry and set to work instead tatting a lace tablecloth – a mammoth task she took on to keep busy.

As March shaded into April, every day she thought of her father and brother in Montréal a little more. In her mind, they served as a tempting lure. A third outbreak of influenza had peaked in America and the newspapers were reporting far fewer deaths. She weighed up her options. Stay in Kobe and ride out the epidemic that might or might not be abating. Or catch a steamship to San Francisco and weather the long journey to Montréal by train. She couldn't decide. What she did know was she had fallen into an attitude of marking time. As though some major change was imminent, and even essential. As though she needed to break out of her own skin, start afresh somehow. But she was married with two toddlers. How was breaking free even possible? The best she could hope for was another long holiday, which would mean the inevitable return to Kobe. Picturing that return, she could scarcely bring herself to leave in the first place, for surely she would feel even more listless faced with nothing significant to occupy her other than handicrafts. She knew the source of her frustration was her nurse's training, which fitted her for the workforce in an essential capacity and rendered her useful. Yet she couldn't work in Kobe. She wasn't registered. She wasn't Japanese. She would simply have to ride out Ernest's posting and hope it wouldn't be forever. And in the meantime, she supposed once she had finished the tablecloth, she might as well make lace doilies for the church fetes. It was time-consuming, satisfying and she was good at it.

Maundy Thursday arrived. She had agreed to meet Ernest at the Oriental Hotel for lunch. She rarely visited the waterfront and had made a vow to herself, now the girls were a little older and Gladys easier to manage, that she would spend more time in the bund, especially now the Japanese death toll from the pandemic was showing definite signs of decline. Lunch at the Oriental would be a celebration after many months of isolation. And besides, she couldn't have declined in the face of Ernest's enthusiasm.

Yu Yan was enthusiastic, too.

'I clean everywhere. You come back to sparkling house.'

Ernest had arranged for a car to collect Emma and the girls. The driver arrived an hour early. Fortunately, she had already dressed the girls for their outing. It never occurred to her to send the driver away and ask him to return at the correct time. Instead, she flew around the house gathering her things and hurried out the door. Irene had been in a fractious mood all morning after Gladys had whacked her over the head with her Raggedy Ann. Emma hoped a drive and then the stimulation of the waterfront and the Oriental Hotel would lift all their moods.

The moment the car arrived at the hotel, a doorman came forward to assist. She let him pick Gladys up and pop her down on the pavement and then she clambered out of the back seat holding a still disgruntled Irene.

With Irene propped on her hip and Gladys's hand firmly in her own, Emma stopped at the bottom of the steps, not knowing whether to head inside the hotel and wait or go and look at the ships. Irene was whining and arching her back and Emma thought a walk along the waterfront would be the best option.

She must have dithered too long, for a man approached her from behind and said, 'Waiting for someone?'

Embarrassed, Emma spoke quickly. 'My husband. But I'm awfully early.'

She glanced behind the man at the sea. Irene started to cry.

'Oh, don't cry, little one.' He smiled and pulled silly faces and played peek-a-boo with his newspaper until Irene's face broke into a cautious smile.

'What lovely auburn hair she has. Must take after her mother.' The man caught Emma's gaze. 'I'm Mr Smith.'

Emma dimly recalled Ernest mentioning a Mr Smith at Guthries and wondered if it might be him. She rearranged Irene, who had slipped down off her hip, straightening her jacket and skirt which had ridden up in the process. As though she had been cued, Irene restarted her grizzling. Emma ignored her.

'Are you a Guthries' man?' she said, seeing that Mr Smith had decided to keep her company.

'At your service.' He bowed and they both laughed.

'I'm waiting for Mr Taylor.'

'Ernest? He's back at the office.' He hesitated, looking from Emma to the girls. 'It's not far. May I?' He bent down and offered Gladys a broad smile. 'And who is this pretty young lady?'

Gladys turned to bury her face in her mother's skirt.

He laughed. 'I don't bite. Come on.' He reached out with his hand. She held out hers for him to take.

Emma followed him, hoping the motion would calm Irene. It didn't.

They only had to walk one block before they entered the foyer of the Guthries office.

The atmosphere of the dark, wood-panelled foyer was austere. Emma didn't feel she belonged there. Not with two toddlers in tow. Especially as Irene would not stop her grizzling.

Mr Smith let go of Gladys and went to fetch Ernest. Emma felt awkward as she watched him walk away down a short, dimly lit corridor. She didn't know whether to follow him or wait. Before she could make up her mind, Mr Smith hurried back and caught her free arm at the elbow and tried to whisk her away, saying perhaps they could take tea while they waited.

Instantly suspicious, Emma freed her elbow and pushed past him and headed down the corridor.

'You can't go in there,' Mr Smith implored.

She took no notice. Two seconds later, she wished she had heeded Mr Smith's plea. For there, right before her through a glass-panelled door, was Ernest and he was not alone. He stood leaning with his back against his desk, holding a woman in a passionate embrace. Emma stared for long enough to see the woman was Chinese. She was small and also very young. The translator. She pushed open the door. There was a long moment in which shocked gazes locked with one single horrified gaze. Before Irene could reach out for her father – something she was wont to do the moment she clapped eyes on him – Emma marched out of the office, past a stunned Mr Smith and out of Guthries. She took in a few deep breaths of the warm spring air and then headed back to the hotel, where she found a pony cart to take her and the girls back home.

Yu Yan was surprised to see her.

'You can go home now,' Emma said.

'I no finish.'

'Yu Yan,' she said, her tone commanding. 'Go home.'

Yu Yan hesitated, puzzled and hurt. Then she fetched her bag and headed out the front door.

Emma felt no remorse. As much as she had grown fond of her housekeeper, she was not about to confide and she knew Yu Yan would have quizzed her until she let something slip. Revealing the death of a parent was one thing; a husband's betrayal was quite another. The humiliation would have been overwhelming. It was bad enough that Mr Smith had borne witness to the tryst. Who else knew? Who, out of Ernest's cronies at the Kobe Club, the Lodge and even their church knew he was having an affair? She could never show her face in Kobe again. She wouldn't want to be seen even by Beryl. For all she knew, the entire Kobe Ladies Benevolent Society had heard the news. She would never know the truth, as she would never admit it to them and they would never admit it to her.

The girls grew restless. She had to fix them some lunch. As she cut and buttered bread, she mulled over the true reason

Ernest was concerned about having to leave Kobe if Japanese exports declined. His floozy. She might have been upset, and a part of her was deeply hurt, but most of all she was livid. How dare he carry on behind her back while she was stuck in this godforsaken place bringing up his daughters! She refrained from crashing about and slamming doors. Instead, she watched the girls eat their lunch and she brooded. Then, she crammed her trunk full with all of her things, along with another two cases of Irene and Gladys's clothes and toys.

When Ernest finally arrived home, all remorseful and apologetic, she had calmed down enough to say, rather quietly, that he was to buy her a ticket for America the very next day and she would be staying at the Oriental Hotel until her departure.

'One way will do,' she added.

He couldn't help but notice the packed luggage.

'You're leaving me?'

'What do you expect?'

'And the children?'

'Don't be ridiculous.'

He didn't contest her remark.

'When will you return.'

'Don't ask me that, Ernest Taylor. I do not know if I shall ever return.'

She was back at the Oriental Hotel with Gladys and Irene that very night.

1940

COTTENHAM HOUSE

Emma pulled her cardigan down to cover her hips, then adjusted the blanket draped over her knees and tightened her scarf around her neck. An icy wind entered Cottenham House through every cranny. Thick curtains over black-out drapes didn't prevent some of that air entering her bedroom. The pads of her fingers were sore from threading her shuttle through the warp, the cold having drained the buoyancy of her flesh. She was halfway along the roof section of her tapestry – depicted in dark mahogany and shades of beige – and she was determined to finish it. Before she inserted the shuttle, she sat back for a short rest, her gaze drifting around the room before settling on her dressing table, where a simple oval frame contained the first wool tapestry she ever made, the one Mrs Carver gave her, the one that helped distract her from her anguish as she waited for the ship to take her and the girls back to America.

She had met Mrs Carver at the Oriental Hotel on the first day of her stay. She was the wife of a British merchant based in Yokohama, there enjoying the sights of Kobe while her husband attended business meetings in the bund. Eager for company, she all but accosted Emma in the foyer as she exited the dining room and insisted on helping her with the children.

'How simply marvellous to encounter a young mother here in the bund,' she enthused, in a manner a touch gauche for Emma's sensibilities.

Emma allowed her unsolicited escort to walk her to her room, even as she knew from then on, she would be anticipating a knock on the door at any moment.

The knock came later that same day, Mrs Carver marching straight on in as Emma pulled open the door, her arms laden with treats for her daughters. Mrs Carver plonked herself down on the end of Emma's bed and proceeded to engage Gladys and Irene as she unfurled candy bars and cheap but pretty toys.

'You really shouldn't have.'

'Nonsense.'

It took more than an hour before Emma let down her guard. She didn't confide in Mrs Carver, the bund environment was much too tight-knit for that, but she did allow her to entertain the girls and, in the days that followed, to demonstrate the tricks of wool tapestry. Not that Emma needed much educating. But she humoured Mrs Carver, too polite to tell her the wool tapestry in her hand paled when compared to the complexities of working in the ancient Chinese methods of silk. As Mrs Carver issued her instructions, Emma recalled Chun back in Singapore; the patient way she'd demonstrated the finer points of the craft, the pleasure she took in teaching her Englishwoman employer.

A single black rose on a pale background. That image struck her now as symbolic, as though when Mrs Carver gave Emma the tapestry, she already knew of Ernest's treachery.

Facing the tapestry on the other side of the dressing table was a portrait of Ernest, all dapper in a 1920s suit. That photograph was taken in Wimbledon. Emma couldn't recall the year. Between the tapestry and the photograph was a crystal dish containing an assortment of clip-on earrings gifted her by Gladys and Irene, earrings she wore on special occasions.

Leaving Kobe the way she did was Emma's last impulsive act. She had regretted it ever since. Had she stayed, had she forgiven him, stood by him, perhaps then he might have stood by her. Instead, years later, when Irene was ten years old and Gladys a petulant twelve, Ernest embarked on a ship bound for Australia and never returned.

During those eight years when they were back in London, his business trips had taken him away from his family for many months at a time. Emma and the girls had grown accustomed to his long absences. But in 1928, after six months had passed and Emma had not received word, not one letter, she presumed the worst.

She wrote to his employers, at that time a metal colour-printing firm who specialised in brewery trays. Ernest was by then employed as general manager. She addressed the letter to his secretary. The reply informed Emma that he had failed to return from his trip and the firm had no idea of his where-abouts. The letter was signed by the new general manager.

There were no further inquiries to be made. Emma was left not knowing if he were dead or alive. Sometimes she thought he had got lost in an Australian desert. That he had met with foul play or had a fatal accident of some kind. Sometimes she suspected he'd run off with another woman, but she dismissed that idea. He would have had no qualms about abandoning her, of that she was sure, but his daughters were another matter. He doted on them. He would never have cut them off so brutally.

The income she relied on disappeared as well. The little Taylor family went from riches to rags within a month. A resourceful woman, she signed up at a local nursing agency. In a matter of days, she had her first clients, all of them wealthy enough to afford a private nursing fee despite the depression. She bathed and fed and administered medications and dressed wounds and none of it she minded. Above all, she sat by bedsides and offered words of comfort. She had to forego the more lucrative and secure live-in positions and at first, the work came intermittently and money was tight. There were weeks when she went hungry to feed her daughters. Weeks when she drank water instead of tea. It took a few years to establish a reputation. Only then did she enjoy the benefits of recommendations, many of them arising through the Spiritualist church. By the time Gladys and Irene were teenagers and needed her less, she was in high demand and took on longer hours. Then the girls complained they never saw her. She couldn't win. It had come as a considerable relief to her when they both left home and she was able to take on live-in positions.

In those years of hardship, Emma had met many interesting people, Wimbledon and the surrounding suburbs supporting a colourful demographic.

Now, more years of hardship were upon her. After a decade of making do and mending, she, like the rest of Britain, would have to make do with rations. The government had announced the new restrictions the previous week. Bacon, butter and sugar.

At dinner the previous night, Mrs Stoker complained there would be no more cake, no more apple pie. 'I have nine mouths to feed here. Nine. I've no idea how I'm to make two ounces of butter each last a whole week. Two ounces, I ask you. It'll be bread and scrape from now on. Mark my words.'

'There'll be plenty of sugar if we don't put it in our tea,' Emma suggested.

'I'm not drinking unsweetened tea,' boomed Frank, the chauffeur, plainly outraged by the idea.

Emma smiled inwardly. Frank was wont to shovel two heaped teaspoons into every cup.

'You could try halving the amount,' Mr Holt said.

Mrs Davies gave the men a censorious look.

'I'm sure you'll find a way to sate our appetites, Mrs Stoker,' Emma said.

Susan sat taller in her seat. 'I worked for an Italian family once and they used oil instead of butter in their cakes.'

Cradling a pile of dirty pudding bowls, Mrs Stoker looked shocked. 'Oil? What sort of oil?'

'Olive oil. The cakes turned out very nicely.'

'Well, I never.'

'Mrs Stoker can use margarine,' said Mrs Davies.

The entire table screwed up their faces in disgust. Margarine was clearly beneath the Cottenham household.

There was a long period of silence, broken by Mrs Stoker's movements and the clatter of crockery over by the sink as Miss Hint, who'd finished her meal long before the others, washed up.

When Mrs Stoker returned to the table, Frank caught her gaze, a shifty gleam appearing in his eyes. 'I know a man at the mechanics who knows the local grocer...'

'That's quite enough, Mr Weaver,' Mrs Davies cut in.

Mrs Stoker, who'd stopped in her tracks to listen, carried on taking away plates. Everyone knew she'd ask Frank later.

'We'd better get used to it,' said Mr Holt. 'Word is there'll be a lot more rationing to come. Mrs Davies, I suggest we expand our vegetable beds. Dig up a bit of lawn for potatoes, that sort of thing.'

Susan, who was too young to recall the way things used to be, fidgeted in her seat. 'Do you think the war will drag on that long?'

'If the last one is anything to go by, yes, it will. And we better be prepared to hunker down until it's over.'

Will Irene have enough to eat? That was all Emma could think about at dinner.

It was all she could think about now as she threaded her needle with more cobalt blue. A war was no time to have a baby. She knew that better than most. Irene had a month before she reached her term. Her ankles had swollen so much, she spent all day with her feet up.

Emma tried to visit her every week on her day off, taking the bus to Raynes Park, then crossing the railway line and walking the rest of the way along Kingston Road, veering off along a footpath that took her to the top of Richmond Avenue. Irene and George ran a little four-room hotel, although there was talk that George, a chef by trade, would need to enlist. Emma wasn't sure what her daughter would do should that happen. Run the hotel by herself with the baby? Gladys lodged in one of the rooms, but that wouldn't be for much longer, not with talk of the wedding.

Emma told herself she mustn't worry. She'd brought her daughters up to be hardy and resilient and they were.

The following morning, Emma was forced to run through the new rationing again with Adela.

'How much?' Adela asked as Emma removed the breakfast tray.

'Two ounces'

'That won't go far.' She shot Emma a desperate look. 'I do find it hard to swallow dry toast.'

'I'll make sure Mrs Stoker boils you a soft egg. Will that help?'

'Will we run out of jam?'

'Mrs Davies assures us the pantry is full to overflowing after last season's bumper fruit harvest.'

'Well, that's something.' She emitted a soft sigh. 'Mrs Davies is a marvel, don't you think?'

'Let me straighten your pillows.'

Adela raised her head a fraction. Emma, placed her hand under the back of her head as she shifted and plumped until satisfied that the pillow arrangement was to Adela's liking.

'There,' she said, easing Adela's head back down.

'You're a marvel, too, Emma, dear.' A thoughtful look appeared in her face. Emma was instantly expectant. More talk of rationing? Not likely, given Adela's short attention span. More Oscar?

'Mrs Taylor.'

'Yes?' she said, taken aback at being formally addressed.

'No, it isn't Taylor anymore. Didn't I decide I preferred your maiden name?'

That was months ago. Emma decided not to answer. She wondered where Adela was heading with her musing. She didn't enjoy being the object of the old lady's scrutiny.

'What is it again?'

'What is what?'

'Your maiden name.'

She turned her face to Emma. There was no avoiding the truth.

'Harms.'

'Ah, that's it. Harms. I knew a Harms once. A long time ago. It isn't an English surname. I suppose you know that.'

Emma did know that. She had always known that. It was why, growing up in Philadelphia, she could pretend to have been born in America once she acquired the accent, but she could not deny her German heritage. Stay out of Harms' way, that was one of the taunts. The children must have been coached by their parents. Harms was a rare surname, tightly linked to the Mennonite exodus to the United States of

America in the mid to late 1800s. Her father was proud of this fact. Adela, she thought, had no idea. But Emma anticipated where her patient was going with the conversation and again, she offered no reply.

Adela persisted. 'I've a challenge extracting the truth from you.'

'I am not sure I know what you mean.'

'Emma, you may have had an Englishman for a husband and you may have grown up in America – anyone with ears will confirm that as you have a peculiar way of saying "Tuesday" – but, you see, this Harms chap I knew, he was *German*.'

Her stress on the last word caused Emma to freeze inside.

'You're German, too, are you not?'

'Miss Schuster, please.'

'Thought so. But fear not. Your secret is safe with me. Are you a Hitler supporter?'

'Certainly not.'

'Glad to hear it. We're all human beings, Emma. What matters is how we treat each other. And you treat me very well. Makes no difference to me where you come from.'

But it did, it must, or why bring it up? Idle curiosity? Cantankerousness? Would Adela let the revelation slip to the other members of the household? Emma scrambled for precedents either way. She had never known Adela to gossip about her staff. She had only ever offered praise. It was the only reassurance Emma could hold on to. That, and the fact that she was forgetful.

And Emma could always deny the truth. There was no evidence; her papers were incinerated. A prudent move, as it turned out.

No matter how much she tried to tell herself she had nothing to fear, she knew she would spend the rest of her stay at Cottenham House with the horror of internment bubbling away in the depths of her mind. Perhaps she should resign. Find another posting. But there was a war on, which meant positions might be in short supply. And besides, Adela was fond of her.

The following morning, Emma woke up with cold feet. She hurried herself out of bed and washed and dressed and exited her frigid room for the warmth of the kitchen, vowing to mention to a recalcitrant Mrs Davies for the umpteenth time this winter that the radiator in her bedroom wasn't functioning correctly. It appeared her comfort was not a priority.

Miss Hint was laying a fire in the living-room grate as she passed by. Mrs Stoker had prepared bowls of steaming porridge for breakfast. Emma sat herself down in her usual place and accepted the cup of tea Mrs Stoker set down before her.

Emma didn't rush. She wanted her feet to warm up thoroughly before she went out to catch the bus to Raynes Park. She had risen early so she would be back by ten-thirty to relieve Susan.

At the hotel in Richmond Avenue, Irene was in one of her acerbic moods and the doilies Emma made to help decorate the hotel were not received with much grace. Emma sympathised. Her daughter had become something of a bloated heifer with tree trunks for legs, only able to waddle back and forth to the lavatory, something she complained she was cursed to do about twenty-four times a day. At least.

'Can't you hold on a little longer?'

'No, I can't. This monster of a baby is pressing down on my bladder.'

'I expect you're carrying a lot of water.'

'Were you like this with me?'

She eyed her daughter seated with her feet up in the only

armchair in the room, pictured her as a little tot, the same curly auburn hair, the same adventuresome spirit in the eyes, and she decided not every woman was cut out for motherhood. She was too wilful, too spirited, too hungry for living. A child forced a woman inwards, into her domestic sphere, and outwards only as far as the child beneath her gaze. Her will bent to her child's. Her needs took second place. That was how it must be, how it had always been, but perhaps not how it would be for Irene. She might fare better with a boy, with an active, energetic boy, Emma thought.

'Is there anything I can do?'

Not waiting for an answer, Emma filled the kettle and lit the gas cooker. She collected the used tea cups scattered on side tables and gave two a rinse. She found a packet of biscuits in the pantry, already open.

'Are you short of anything?'

Piles of second-hand baby clothes Emma had sourced at jumble sales were folded on top of the dresser alongside a similar sized pile of nappies, a small tin of nappy pins and a tin of baby powder. She went back to the pantry, scanned the contents, pressed her lips together.

'George is taking care of all that, Mum.'

Emma closed the door and dashed to the kettle as it began to hiss. As if on cue, George entered the room, a tall, dashing young man, keen to prove he was eminently capable as he took over making the tea, forcing Emma to take up a chair at the table. She suddenly felt superfluous, although George was no Yu Yan. Still, she felt pushed out, denied a role, and wondered what being a grandmother to Irene's child would be like.

Back at Cottenham House, Adela was in a jovial mood. The moment Emma appeared, she exclaimed, 'Thank goodness you're here. I've been trying to explain to Susan the virtues of our church, but she's not taking the least interest.'

'I'm sure that's not true.'

Emma winked at Susan, who rolled her eyes behind Adela's back, stifled a yawn and whispered, 'She's in a right chirpy mood this morning. No idea what's got into her.'

Susan removed Adela's morning tea tray as she left the room.

'Now, sit yourself down, Emma,' Adela said, patting the bed. 'Or should I call you Mrs Harms? He-he. Now, I've been thinking. Why don't we arrange for your lovely reverend to have a little service here?'

'I'm not sure we'll be able to get you down the stairs, Adela.'

'Why not have it right here?'

'In your bedroom?'

'It's certainly large enough.'

The thought of bringing the congregation of the Wimbledon Spiritualist Church into Adela's bedroom seemed to Emma ludicrous. As she pictured the scene, she stifled a laugh.

'What prompts you to want to host a service?'

She already knew the answer. Why not just hold a regular séance? It would be far simpler. Or perhaps Adela sought solace of a different kind. Emma didn't think she was close to her passing, not yet, she was much too chipper, but the elderly and the infirm were apt to take sudden turns.

'Do you remember that day we were squashed up together in the middle row one Sunday and you dropped...what was it you dropped?'

'My prayer book.'

'That's right. And I reached down to pick it up and stabbed your thigh with my hatpin. And you yelped. What a way to make someone's acquaintance!'

They both laughed.

It was only a shallow puncture wound, although it would have been much worse had it not been for the thickness of Emma's skirt.

'I'm not sure I ever saw you at church much after that.'

'I go every week.'

'I have never been one for regular attendance. I was only there on that occasion to witness Leslie Flint.'

'He was a remarkable medium.'

'So I discovered. He received a message from Oscar. Do you remember?'

'He told you Oscar wanted to thank you from the bottom of his heart for all you did for him.'

'That was such a comfort.'

Emma waited as Adela gathered her thoughts. Once Adela latched on to the topic of Oscar, there was nothing for it but to let her reflections run their course.

'I did do a lot for Oscar, you know.' She pushed a stray wisp of hair from her forehead. As she turned her face, the loose folds of flesh about her neck jiggled a little. She reached for Emma's hand and gave it a soft squeeze. 'I tried to help Constance and Oscar to reconcile. I wrote so many letters to all sorts of people. But the couple wouldn't be persuaded. I think Constance felt too betrayed.'

'Betrayal is difficult to forgive.'

Quick as a flash, she said, 'You found that, did you?' And Emma was left wondering if all her talk about Oscar was simply a ruse to probe her about Ernest. As if by his very name, Ernest, he had become a centrepiece of importance in Adela's thought garden.

'You were talking about Oscar,' she said softly, hoping to divert her thoughts.

'Yes, yes,' Adela obliged. 'Well, she wasn't the forgiving

type. But she was by no means the villain of the piece. She was, in truth, one of the victims. But she was... how can I put this?... a little too uncompromising for my liking.'

'Who was the villain?'

'The villain? Oh, Bosie's father, of course. The worst of the entire situation is, Oscar could have fled and avoided prosecution. He had the opportunity. A full hour and a half, in fact, to get himself to France. But he wouldn't. He didn't want to appear a deserter or a coward.'

'That's noble of him.'

'Oh, it is. It is. He was arrested in 1895. When were you born, my dear? Was it then?'

'1885.'

'I must write that down.' She cast around for an imaginary notebook and pen. Finding none, she said, 'Really, it was all Bosie's doing.'

'Bosie?'

'Fancy trying to get Oscar to sue his father! It was never going to end well. If you had only known that vile Marquess of Queensbury, you'd agree with me without hesitation.'

'Did you know him?'

'In a fashion. One moves in the same circles, so naturally, I came across him. But I didn't know him in the familiar sense of the word.'

Adela fell into a moment of private reflection as Emma imagined the lavish social gatherings, the garden parties, the balls. It was a world far removed from her own; a world of fame and notoriety, an exclusive world in which the extraordinarily wealthy and privileged mingled amongst themselves; a world, at times, that resulted in public scandal, and then the ordinary people watched on, in amazement and disgust.

She was jolted out of her reverie when Adela emitted a soft cough.

'The fact of the matter is, Oscar would never have been disgraced had that silly Bosie not persuaded him to sue for libel after the Marquess called him a sodomite.'

Emma caught her breath. Adela's face wore a rueful expression.

'Indeed. What a horrid word. Truly. But there are times one must rise above the slander. Claim the higher ground. And in a fashion, this is what Oscar was aiming to do. But he should have refrained from a lawsuit because it backfired horribly, because the allegation was true. He *was* a sodomite.'

Her head slumped back on her pillows. 'Oh, the injustice! My poor, poor, Oscar.'

'Try not to upset yourself, Adela. Think of your heart.'

'*My* heart? I can only think of *his* heart. The betrayal, yes, I can understand he broke his vow of fidelity, but surely a man is entitled to explore true love!'

Emma didn't know how to answer. She held no prejudice. It was just that she had no experience with men loving men. Fortunately, she wasn't required to offer an opinion.

Adela took a few breaths and went on. 'It was all downhill from there. Since his homosexuality had been publicly exposed, the next logical step for the authorities was to arrest him and have him charged. It was at that juncture, Emma, that he made the noble decision not to bolt for France. But, oh, such humiliation. They had chambermaids testifying against him. It was ghastly.'

Adela's breath quickened and she made a vague grab for her chest. Emma rushed forward and took her pulse. 'Please, Adela, you mustn't excite yourself.'

'I'm alright. I want you to hear the truth. Don't you see? I want you to know I am a true and loyal friend who can be trusted to stand up for those who have been put in the wrong. You must understand this, Emma. You must. I will go to any lengths, within my own limits. When I discovered Oscar was in financial distress after his bankruptcy, I sent him a cheque for a thousand pounds. That's the sort of woman who is employing you, my dear, dear Emma. And I will move heaven and earth for you as well, if it comes to it.'

Emma released Adela's wrist as she slowly absorbed that last remark. Her employer was not about to forget her true nationality. If anything, she was holding on to it, dramatizing the situation, the potential for internment. Emma wished she had the propensity to lie. For if she had, she would never have divulged her maiden name. She would have said Smith or Jones. But not Harms. Never Harms.

Adela wasn't finished. 'Prison. They sent him to prison. I wrote to him often in those years. My letters were of tremendous comfort to him, you know. He told me that. I was one of the few who did. His fellow artists, the entire society surrounding him, they all rejected him.'

'That's awful. I can't imagine why people would do that.'

'To save face. Oh, Emma, Pentonville prison is such a hellhole. That was where they sent him to start with. Pentonville. His beautiful hair was cropped short. He was forced to bathe in filthy water and the cell he was given was much too small, and all day and all night he had to listen to the other inmates and their caterwauling.'

'I've heard it is a harsh place.'

'Harsh is an understatement. He had a complete breakdown in there. He didn't eat or sleep. He was so weak he kept falling down. Damaged his inner ear. Ross and Harris eventually succeeded in having him moved to Reading Gaol, which was a little better. Two whole years of hard labour he served, the poor man. I kept trying to persuade him to keep writing. But he wouldn't. Or couldn't. I don't think at the time I truly grasped just how wretched he felt. I was much younger back then. And it isn't until one suffers that one can fully appreciate the suffering of others.'

She stopped, as though arrested by her own thinking. Emma seized the moment.

'I'll read some more *Dorian Gray* if you wish.'

'That will be splendid, just splendid. Now, where were we up to?'

1919

A CHANGE OF PLAN

Emma was due to board the ship for Honolulu at ten o'clock. She rose early and organised the children and the rest of the packing before heading down to the dining room for breakfast. She was buttering toast when the head waiter came over, proffering a small silver tray.

'A telegram, ma'am.'

She put down her knife, brushed some crumbs off her fingertips and took the small, thin envelope. It was addressed to Yamamoto-dori. She was grateful to Yu Yan – or possibly Ernest – for having it sent on.

She hesitated with the envelope in her hand, not sure whether to open it then and there in front of all the other diners, or retreat to her room. Her hands had a mind of their own, opening the flap and pulling out the small piece of folder paper. The message was brief. It was from her uncle in Montréal.

The words were few and as she read, her hands trembled and her breath caught in her throat.

Father and Herman dead. Stop. Influenza. Stop. Signed Uncle Wolfgang.

There was a moment of disbelief. Then the bottom fell out of her life. Thoughts jumbled as her heart formed a tight fist. She fought back the tears, trying desperately to hide her reaction from her children. Irene reached for the toast on Emma's plate and she hurriedly cut a soldier and handed it to her, thankful for the tiny distraction.

Incomprehension gave way to a slow realisation. Her father and brother had both succumbed to Spanish influenza. She pictured them in the Canadian house, feverish, delirious, gasping for breath, suffering. Would either of them have lived if she had been there to nurse them? But she would only have put herself and the children at risk of infection. And besides, how would she have known, how would she have got there in time if she had? It was hopeless to self-recriminate when there was nothing to be done. She could not possibly have reached Montréal from Kobe in time. She faced the cold, hard truth. She had no mother and now no father or brother. There were only Karin and George left, if they were still alive.

The shock of the news had left her stunned. She grew aware, dimly, that Gladys was tugging her arm.

'Mummy, more please.'

Emma looked down at her daughter's empty plate. Gladys suddenly had a voracious appetite after spending a whole week in the hotel picking at her food at mealtimes, the result of Mrs Carver's treats. Irene, too, was ravenous. Emma attended to their demands. She had no choice. She could not break down in tears in the dining room. She must perform her motherly duties, focus on her daughters and their needs.

She also needed to think. She could change her plans and go back to Ernest, to her humdrum life as his wife. His betrayed wife. That thought made her feel queasy. Since Montréal was out and she was no longer in contact with anyone back in Philadelphia, there was only one place she could think of to go.

As she brought her teacup to her lips, Mrs Carver appeared, pulling out the spare chair and sitting down, chatting gaily. Then she caught Emma's gaze and fell silent. Emma quickly looked down at her plate.

'Whatever's the matter?'

All Emma could do was pass across the telegram. Mrs Carver opened the thin paper with caution. It took her no time to take in the news.

'Emma, no. I'm so sorry.'

Gladys started rocking in her seat. Mrs Carver distracted her and kept both girls occupied as she spoke.

'You're due to board in an hour.'

'I should cancel.'

'And do what?'

She didn't answer.

'Emma, I wasn't born yesterday. Whatever has happened in your marriage is between you and your husband, but it seems plain to me you were not leaving to have a nice holiday. I suspected from the moment we first met that you were running back to your family.'

Emma inhaled to speak. Mrs Carver raised a censorious hand.

'Let me finish. There must be some other options for you. Other family members.'

'I can contact my cousin in Colorado.'

'Then you must send a telegram. '

'I hardly know him.'

'Doesn't matter. Times are desperate. Besides, Japan is no place for you to be right now, what with so much influenza around. You'll feel safer in your own country, believe me. Now, dry those eyes.'

Mrs Carver insisted she mind the children while Emma went to the reception desk to send a telegram to her cousin in Fort Morgan, letting him know of her arrival. They had never met. Her mother had given her Hans' address, but she had no idea if her cousin even knew of her, other than that she existed.

As she arranged to settle her bill, she felt the presence of Mrs Carver behind her. She turned and beheld the older woman's benevolent face.

'You've been so kind.'

'Nonsense. You've been marvellous company for this lonely old fool.'

It was then Emma realised she hadn't once seen the mysterious Mr Carver for the entire week.

'I'm a widow,' she said as though reading Emma's mind.

A widow with an ache in her heart and a hole in her life. No wonder she'd latched onto Emma like a clam.

They bade each other farewell, promising to write.

'I don't know your first name.'

'Norma.'

With that, Mrs Carver took off upstairs to her room. Emma watched her disappear from view, aware for the first time of her companion's own burden of grief.

Emma had decided to let Ernest help her with the children when it was time to embark. They had arranged to meet on the pier. She was typically early and stood with her luggage near the gangway, enjoying the morning sunshine on her face, grateful that both girls were being quiet. A vigorous wind rushed down from the mountains looming behind the town and she turned her back to it, preferring to observe the goings-on aboard the ship.

The sun slid behind a cloud and the air grew chilly. Ernest, she thought, was late. Some of the other passengers had already embarked. She turned around, thinking of seeking the assistance of a porter when Ernest appeared, emerging through a group of onlookers. He rushed over and her heart unexpectedly lurched. She was still furious with him and upset at his betrayal, but she also knew she was taking his children away and he had no idea when he would see them again. If the boot was on the other foot and that were her and not him, she would have been distraught. He retained his composure as he greeted her, but behind his smiling eyes she detected deep sadness and remorse. She could not bring herself to utter a single word lest she broke down and changed her mind.

There was no sign in his manner that he knew anything about the telegram. She voiced in her mind a short prayer of thanks to Yu Yan.

They stood in a sea of luggage. He gripped the handle of her trunk with a heave and a grunt. She caught the gaze of the porter walking down the gangway. Between them, the men managed the luggage and Emma took charge of the children. It felt good to be moving, good to be heading up the gangway, good to finally never have to tread on Japan's shores again. As they found her cabin, dodging by other passengers, she recalled last year when she had boarded a similar ship, and the mixed emotions she had felt leaving Kobe. It was the last time she had seen her parents. Her heart squeezed at the thought.

She went inside with Irene on her hip and Gladys clinging to her arm and pressed herself against the back wall between the two single beds as the porter and Ernest set down the luggage on the floor and on the beds. They were second-class passengers, Emma forfeiting the opportunity of a first-class passage to quicken her departure. When the porter left, Emma sat the girls down on the floor and took up the cabin's only chair. What with the addition of a cot for Irene, it was a cramped space, too confined for all of them. She steeled herself to wish Ernest goodbye, but before she could open her mouth to speak, he reached into his pocket and extracted two small presents: for Irene, a wooden horse on wheels, and for Gladys, a Japanese doll. The girls delighted in the novelty. Ernest looked on, then sat on the side of a bed and bent over, talking to them in soft tones. Time moved slowly. He lingered, dragging out his goodbyes to his daughters. The parting fast became unbearable and when she could tolerate his cuddles and chatter no longer, she announced it was time for Irene's nap and hadn't he better be getting on? As he stood, she hurried him to the door.

'I will let you know when we arrive in Montréal,' she said, maintaining her best poker face.

She couldn't tell him. He'd only beg her to stay.

They'd made it to the threshold, Emma standing squarely inside the cabin to block his re-entry.

Gazing past her to watch the girls seated on the floor, he said, 'It's not too late to change your mind.'

'Ernest, what you did was unforgivable.'

He said no more. Clearly, he was not about to beg. She watched him walk away before closing the cabin door.

She rummaged in her carpetbag and fished out some toys for Irene and Gladys. Keeping an eye on their antics, she began unpacking and arranging their things, listening to the sounds beyond the cabin door of passengers going by, the bustle of porters, then at last the deep, rumbling blast of the ship's horn and the drone of the engines as the ship pulled away.

Fascinated by the motion, the girls grew restless. She hefted Irene onto her hip and ushered Gladys to her side. It was a short stroll down a carpeted hall to the lounge, where Emma determined to spend most of her time.

She had become accustomed to long voyages and no longer felt sickened by the motion. The forced week in Hawaii aside, the previous passage across the Pacific had been pleasant, the ocean for the most part calm, the swells insignificant. She looked forward to a similar journey. Only this time, inside of her a void threatened, eager to swallow up all her attention, all her resolve. There would be no returning to Kobe. There would be no awkward weeks spent with her parents in Montréal. And there was nothing in her, not even in the most faithful corners of her being, to make her look forward to spending time in Fort Morgan with her cousin.

The ship ambled up the coast of Japan and that afternoon pulled into Yokohama. It was sunny and Emma took the girls out on deck to watch the activity on the pier. As passengers crowded up the gangway, she headed to the ship's bow to take in Yokohama and point out to the girls the junks and the fishing boats. Like Kobe, the mountains rose up behind the town. On the waterfront, the Grand Hotel, distinctive with its long rows of Georgian-style windows, stared back at her. Mrs Carver had mentioned the Grand Hotel. It was famous, she'd said, for its exceptional cuisine and for attracting the likes of Rudyard Kipling whom Mrs Carver, Norma, claimed she had met. The Oriental Hotel was perhaps a small step down from that high calibre, and as Emma pictured Mrs Carver boarding the ship for Kobe, she wondered what had propelled her to make the trip. Who was she, really, other than a widow? Emma realised she knew nothing about her strange companion. Theirs had been an encounter that revolved around the welfare and amusement of the children, adult conversations amounting to little more than light-hearted chitchat about the climate, the customs, the tribulations and the excitement of living in Japan.

The bunds were small enclaves. Perhaps Mrs Carver knew her travelling companion, Maud, who'd been so kind to her in Hawaii. Maud with the repellent, if curious, spiritual beliefs. Emma half-expected to see her again as she wandered back along the deck, but the woman who'd lost her sons in the war did not appear among the embarking passengers and she was nowhere to be seen in the lounge when Emma returned to claim her favourite seat by the window.

It occurred to Emma as she sat down that Maud must have drawn enormous comfort from the Spiritualist church. Perhaps she shouldn't have dismissed her faith so readily. Now, as she was poised to traverse the Pacific Ocean to a hollow existence bereft of any sense of familiarity or belonging, she could well understand reaching out, to God, to Christ, to angels, to the spirit world, for solace.

All Emma could do was settle into the rhythm of the journey, spending as much time in the lounge as she had done before, where the girls had more space and she could pass the time of day in conversation with her fellow female travellers. In the quiet of her cabin when her daughters napped, she worked on the wool tapestry. A welcome distraction. All she could do otherwise was wait and let time heal her aching heart.

In the lounge, Irene stole the attention this time, with her bright brown eyes and striking auburn hair. At eighteen months, she was a touch precocious, and she enjoyed the attention of onlookers as she toddled up and down the aisles with Gladys, her mother observing all the open arms ready to catch her should she threaten to lose her balance.

Three days out to sea, and Irene had to forgo her little ritual as the ship started to pitch and roll heavily. The captain had warned of a storm. By mid-morning, the swell had increased to a treacherous height and within the hour, just before the passengers were due to move to the dining room for lunch, the pitching and rolling grew too much. The horizon rose and fell alarmingly. A woman covered her face with her hand and rushed off as waves crashed against the ship, sending spray up on deck and dousing the windows of the lounge. Someone let out a scream. Many passengers started retreating to their cabins. Others, the stalwarts, remained where they were, one or two continuing to read their newspaper or book. By now, Irene was huddled in her mother's lap and Gladys's face wore a worried expression.

'We're alright,' Emma said reassuringly. 'It'll soon pass.'

As if in response, the ship lurched forwards and then rolled to the starboard before regaining its poise for a brief moment, then listing heavily to port. A chair slid and then toppled over. A woman cried out. Emma looked over, hoping to convey with a stern gaze that she didn't want anyone to frighten the children more than they already were. Then the heavens opened and rain obscured any sign of the ocean.

Almost no one made it to the dining room that day. Emma made the effort, thinking her children might be hungry. She had the good sense to treat the stairs down like a stepladder, taking the treads backwards.

The waiters had put side walls on the tables and dampened the table cloths. The salt and pepper jars were lying on their sides. Cutlery and plates still managed to slide about with the pitching and rolling of the ship and it was as much as Emma could do to eat the meatloaf before her. Irene, seated proudly and securely in her high chair, ate the most out of the three of them. Emma had to steady Gladys's hands as she tried to drink from her beaker.

That afternoon, Gladys was first to fall ill from the motion. She was sick in the bowl Emma had pre-emptively placed between the beds, and she looked dreadfully ill. Emma didn't feel much better. Her head ached and she had to use all her will not to vomit. Irene fared the best, but she had little appetite after that hearty lunch. For the rest of the day, Emma and Gladys lay down on their bunks and waited for the storm to pass, Irene crawling and flopping down around them.

They had a long wait.

Few were present at breakfast, lunch or dinner the next day, other than the same stalwarts who devoured their meals with gusto, as though defiant or perhaps determined to show off their resilience. Emma dragged herself to each meal with two very weary girls, dehydration her biggest concern.

The crew appeared indifferent to the storm and Emma took much comfort in that. If there had been anything to be concerned about, their faces would have conveyed it, and they did not. Yet the heavy seas did not abate for a whole week and throughout the ordeal the lounge was for the most part empty. On one occasion, a passenger attempted to venture out on deck, but he had only managed to open the door when he was hurried back inside by a concerned crewman.

Eight days into the terrible weather, the ship's captain graced the dining room with his presence at dinner and explained to a few bemused and listless diners that the ship had caught up with a storm and had been forced to travel along with it until the storm veered north.

As they neared Hawaii, the seas grew calm again, the lounge room filled and everyone appeared much relieved. Emma resumed her favourite seat at the end of the room with a view out of one of the windows. From there, she could keep a watchful eye on her daughters. She realised as she sat that she had not thought of Ernest at all during the last week. She never once wished he was there to support and comfort the children in their sickness and distress. Quite the opposite. If she had thought of him, and perhaps on reflection she might have had one or two fleeting thoughts, it was only to affirm his absence. He would have been a bother, not a help; an irritation, not a salve. Besides, she had never been more resolute about anything before in her life. The man was a cad, an abomination, a womanising, deceiving hound entirely unworthy of her favours. Nothing, not even wild horses, would make her go back to him.

Changing ships proved smooth and hassle-free and they were soon on their way to San Francisco. She had no idea what to expect in America after the war and the influenza had taken their toll, or what she was going to do in Fort Morgan with her two small children to take care of, but Ernest had provided her with a small allowance and she would have to make do with that until she found a way to move on with her life.

The sum he had offered sounded ample at the time, when she envisaged staying with her father. Now, the amount seemed barely sufficient to cover rent or board, and she would only make it do as long as she was frugal. Placing her faith in her telegram, that it had arrived and had been received with an open heart, when the ship put in to port after days of smooth sailing, she summoned her wits, ferried her daughters down the gangway and organised her luggage between the ship's porters and a cab driver and the porters at the railway station. She bought herself a first-class ticket to Fort Morgan, her last lavish expense – Gladys travelled half-price and Irene free – and boarded the afternoon train, justifying this one extravagance as she was not prepared to rough the hard seats and the lack of privacy in an open carriage.

Throughout the journey, she couldn't stop thinking she ought to have bought a regular fare, but last year she saw how non-first-class passengers were forced to travel and couldn't countenance the ordeal. She had a small cabin to herself and she whiled away the hours keeping her children fed and clean and amused, continuing with her wool tapestry and gazing through the window at the mountains and the desert that seemed to go on forever.

And at night, when there was nothing to look at and the motion of the train put her daughters into deep slumber, Emma wrote letters. She wrote to Dottie in Singapore, struggling to find words to convey the truth and deciding instead on a made-up version, with the exception of the passing of her father and brother. She wrote to Ernest, informing him of the deaths as well. She kept her words to him to a minimum. She wrote to Uncle Wolfgang to let him know she'd received the news and that she and the girls were well. Then she wrote to Karin, the hardest letter of all.

Karin had never been large in Emma's life. She was already married with a family by the time Emma was five and left with her parents and brothers for Philadelphia. It didn't seem likely Uncle Wolfgang had sent a telegram to Germany, although he might have sent a letter. Assuming Karin had survived the war, Emma felt duty-bound to relate the news, using the opportunity to ask after George. Perhaps there'd been word? Emma spoke of Gladys and Irene. She said Ernest was well. As the words dawdled from her pen, her heart ached in her chest. Before she signed her name, she mentioned visiting Germany one day, now the war was over.

She left a space at the top of all the letters for her new address, whatever that might be. Satisfied, she folded each letter in its allotted envelope, addressed each one and slid them into her handbag.

The following day was bright and the scenery pleasant as they passed through the Rocky Mountains. Not long after lunch they reached Denver, and soon the train traversed the pancake-flat plains of eastern Colorado.

When the train pulled into Fort Morgan station, her eyes were everywhere. She looked for a man she could recognise as her own blood, but the few who were on the platform all looked more or less the same and nothing like her. She propped Irene on her hip, hefted her bulging holdall onto her shoulder as she reached for Gladys's hand and went to open the carriage door.

Seeing her struggle, the station master rushed over and helped her down and then led her to the guard's van, where the rest of her luggage was being deposited on the platform.

Only two other people had alighted at the stop and they were greeted by awaiting men. She began to feel desperate, panic rising as she contemplated finding herself stranded in Fort Morgan, in the unfamiliar state of Colorado. It was only as the train was pulling out of the station that she saw a thin man with dark-brown hair standing by the station fence, and the relief reduced her voice to a sigh.

'I'll be alright from here,' Emma said to the kindly station-master, who left her with her trunk and suitcases beside her and disappeared.

The thin man came forward and took off his cap. 'You must be Emma.'

He didn't smile or hold out his hand in greeting.

She gazed into his face. He had light-blue eyes and one of them was lazy, as though it couldn't be bothered following the other one around.

'Hans, thank goodness you're here.'

He glanced at her luggage and then back at her.

'You planning on staying a while, then?'

'I was planning on staying in Montréal. Then I received news that my father and brother had died. I was due to embark.'

'You didn't think to stay in Kobe?'

It sounded like a reproach. She glanced down at the children. Tears welled. Seeing her distress, he said, 'Tell me later. Come on.'

He heaved the luggage onto his pony cart, and Emma helped Gladys mount the steps up to the single bench seat. With Irene held tightly in her arms, Emma sat at the end. Hans mounted the cart in two large steps and took the reins and they proceeded at a slow walk, away from the station and down a wide, tree-lined street. Everywhere was green and orderly. Houses stood proudly in their own blocks. At the edge of the town, no more than ten minutes from the station, Hans pulled on the reins and the pony came to a halt.

They all decanted and Emma stood waiting for Hans to unload her luggage as well, when he said, 'What, out of all this, do you need for tonight?'

The question took her aback. She realised with a sickening thud that they were not going to be staying with Hans. She indicated the smallest bag.

'I'll leave the rest on the cart, Emma. Don't worry, I'll cover it up and the cart will be in a shed in any case. But we've no room here for you and the girls, as you're about to see. I'm sorry.'

Emma was crestfallen and she had to force herself to hide it. The realisation that she had made a terrible mistake curdled her insides.

Hans led Emma and the girls through to the kitchen – large, square and basic – where his wife stood with her back to the stove, a welcoming smile breaking out on her face.

'I'm Sophia,' she said, rounding the table and reaching out to hug her.

Feeling the warmth of the other woman's embrace softened Han's blunt announcement, but not enough to bring Emma equanimity.

Small voices behind her caused Emma to glance around to find a huddle of children of various ages standing in the hall-way. She counted six: two boys who were almost men, two girls and two younger boys. Sophia introduced them as Emil who was fifteen, Ernest a proud thirteen, Hilda a shy eleven, Alvin a lively nine, Louisa a shy six, and Arthur a cheeky four.

'Hilda,' Sophia said to the eldest girl. 'Take your sister and

Arthur and go keep this little one amused. Her name is...?'

'Gladys.'

'Gladys. Off you go.'

Hilda reached for Gladys's hand. Gladys looked up at her mother, who gave her an encouraging nod.

'Sit yourself down,' Sophia told Emma as the children took themselves off up the hall. 'I'll make coffee. You must be exhausted.'

Emma pulled out a chair and sat down, perching Irene on her lap. Hans took up the chair opposite.

'I'm sorry to descend on you like this.'

'It's no problem,' Sophia said, her voice firm.

Hans and Sophia exchanged glances.

'We're sorry for your loss, Emma,' Sophia went on, speaking for the both of them. 'To lose your father and brother to the influenza like that. So bad.'

'How long were you planning on staying with your father?'

'Hans,' Sophia said abruptly.

'She has so much luggage.'

'It's alright,' Emma said. 'Indefinitely, I suppose.'

They both looked shocked.

'What about your husband?' Sophia said.

'Ernest is still in Kobe.'

'He'll be joining you?' said Hans.

'I've no idea. I had to get away. I needed time to think.'

'You don't need to say it,' Sophia said, and after a quick glance at her husband she winked at Emma and added, 'Men.'

Emma took small comfort from Sophia's remark and welcoming gestures, not in the face of Hans' sullen attitude.

'You have a very nice place here,' Emma said, hoping that would be enough to steer the conversation away from the awkwardness. It was.

The kitchen soon filled with the smell of percolating coffee.

When Sophia at last joined Emma and Hans at the table, they chatted about the weather, the war, the influenza, Woodrow Wilson. Hans disappeared outside, and Sophia and Emma moved on to discuss the children.

'You're a nurse,' Sophia said. 'That must be hard work.'

'I enjoy it. Or I did. I worked in Singapore before Gladys was born.'

'I wish I was good at something. Outside the home, I mean.'

'You have your hands full here, I imagine.'

She laughed. 'True.'

Irene started reaching for things on the table. Sophia left the room and returned with a play pen and an armful of toys.

With so many mouths to feed, preparing dinner took a while. Emma helped, offering to peel a small pail of potatoes, while keeping an eye on an increasingly restless Irene. Hilda appeared and asked Sophia if she could play with the baby, and Emma went and knelt down and introduced her to her little cousin. Hilda led Irene away and for the next couple of hours Emma kept an ear cocked for any sounds of distress. None came.

Dinner was wholesome and simple. Braised beef and boiled potato dumplings and steamed pickled cabbage. The gravy was rich with mustard, the German way. The family ate with little talk, the children clearly schooled in table manners.

After dinner, Sophia shooed the children out of the kitchen. Then she joined Hans, sitting across from Emma. An expectant atmosphere filled the room. Hans was the first to speak. He looked grave and his eyes held Emma's when he said, 'Where else can you go?'

Anxiety gripped her. Tears threatened.

'Nowhere. I don't know anyone else. I don't have anyone.'

'You should...'

'Hans, you're doing it again,' Sophia cut in. 'She's family

and she must stay near us. As close as possible.'

'There's nowhere in Fort Morgan.'

'I know someone,' Sophia said. 'You'll like her, Emma. She's Danish. Her name is Mrs Jensen and she runs a boarding house in Brush.'

'Brush?'

'Brush! I told you, she's not staying in Brush!'

'There's nothing wrong with Mrs Jensen's boarding house. I've been there. The rooms are very nice.'

'That's as maybe. But there's something very wrong with Brush.'

'Take no notice, Emma. Don't let your cousin alarm you. Hans is being a snob. Brush is more rugged than here. The people there are a bit rough around the edges, that's all. But Mrs Jensen runs a good boarding house at a very reasonable rate and I would rather you were there than in Denver. What do you think?'

'I suppose I could try it.'

'There you are, you see?' She poked her tongue out playfully at Hans and then grinned at Emma. 'I'll call her tomorrow.'

By the time the dishes were washed and put away, night was closing in. Sophia put the second eldest boy Ernest in with his brother, giving Emma a single bed for herself. Gladys could sleep top-to-toe with Louisa, and Irene had Arthur's old cot.

'I can't thank you enough,' Emma said, when she was alone with Sophia in the kitchen.

'Hans is a good man, you know that, Emma. I also know some men who are not so good. I know nothing of your Ernest, but I know you are not going back to Japan for a good reason. You don't need to tell me what he has done.'

She reached and took Emma in her arms and once again, Emma sank into the embrace.

BRUSH

Despite her troubles, Emma slept soundly that night and awoke to the smell of fried bacon. Her room was bright and sunny and brought her some cheer. She thought that perhaps, after all, Brush could well turn out to suit her fine.

Emma had overslept. When she entered the kitchen, the breakfast table was crowded with plates and bowls, cups of coffee and glasses of milk. She sat down in the only vacant chair at one corner, sandwiched between her girls who had already been organised by their cousins, and watched as the Harms family dove into eggs, bacon, muffins and hunks of dark bread, along with hominy grits and bottled fruit in bowls. Finding herself hungry again after the long journey, she joined in the feast. The coffee was good and strong. There was much chatter and clatter, unlike the night before, with neither Sophia nor Hans troubling much over table manners. Emma supposed with six children, they were a long way past the strictness she had had at first with Gladys. Last night's sombre and orderly behaviour must have been for show.

Sophia was about to re-fill Emma's cup when the phone

rang. 'That'll be Anna.' She set down the pot and left the room. Emma could only just make out her voice through the wall. When she came back, she wore a broad smile and said Mrs Jensen had a vacant room and was expecting them.

The Harms children had soon finished eating, and each took their cup to the sink, leaving their plate behind. Emma began tidying up her corner of the table.

'Leave all that,' Sophia said.

Emma ignored her. Between them, the table was soon cleared and cleaned. Sophia washed and Emma dried, and as she passed the tea towel over the wet plates, nostalgia washed through her. These people were her family, what was left of it. She wanted to know about Hans' brothers and sisters, his father and mother, but his manner, brooding and distant as he sat at the head of the table finishing his coffee, led her not to ask. The losses from the war and the influenza had hit every family hard. When Hans left to see to the pony and cart, she asked Sophia if he was all right.

A shadow crossed her face. 'Like you, he's burdened with much loss.'

She wondered if they had lost a child. But then it would have been Sophia, not Hans, who would have been grieving the most. Emma struggled to calculate the age of her cousin. She knew Hans was one of seven, but that was all she could recall.

'Did his brothers fight?' she asked tentatively.

'They were too old. We lost his younger sister Bertie at the end of winter.'

'To the influenza?'

Sophia nodded. 'In the same month, his eldest sister died suddenly. Her heart, the doctor said.'

'I'm sorry.'

She finished drying the last of the plates and looked around for somewhere to put them.

'In there.'

Emma opened a cupboard.

'What about his brothers? Are they close?'

'His three brothers have farms. Albert has a property in Fleming, which is on the train line. You'd have gone past it on the way to Montréal. Dierdrich took over the family farm in Nebraska when their father passed away. And Lawrence set himself up in Idaho. The youngest, Renate, married a farmer and they live in Nebraska on the Kansas border. They all have families.' She paused and, with her hands submerged in the soapy water, she turned her face to Emma's and smiled. 'Gladys and Irene have many cousins.'

It felt odd to think she had so many family members scattered through the region. Why had her father singled out Hans? Because he lived on the train line, she supposed, but so did Albert. Probably Hans was closer to her age.

He came in and announced the cart was ready. Emma put down the tea towel. Sophia reached out and embraced her for the last time and whispered in her ear not to be a stranger.

'Mrs Jensen has a telephone. Call me.'

'I will.'

The journey to Brush in the pony cart took over an hour, the road cutting through fields so flat they looked ironed. The impression she got was markedly different to the one through the train window with the fields whizzing by. Now she took in the crops, the narrow rivers, the few trees. She could not call the area pretty, but it had its own charm and felt remarkably safe. After the mutiny in Singapore and the rice riots in Japan, she looked forward to the tranquillity of this rural backwater, the perfect location to pause within while she determined what to do with her life, her future, the future of her girls. Her only concern was the distance from Fort Morgan, which seemed inordinately far, the further they went.

It was only when Brush appeared on the horizon that Hans, a man of few words, said, 'The car is having repairs.'

Emma could scarcely contain her relief. A car brought Brush much closer to Fort Morgan. Even so, with six children to manage, she doubted Sophia and Hans would make the trip to Brush to see her. At least, not often. She could only hope Hans would drive to Brush and collect her and the girls from time to time, to spend an afternoon in Fort Morgan.

Emma repressed her disappointment as farmland gave way to the town and she saw it was more or less as Hans had described it; a sprawling assortment of dwellings, some of them run down. They passed a Lutheran church on the right, a red-brick building and, shortly after, the railway sidings came into view. Brush seemed much smaller than Fort Morgan and nowhere near as pretty, although she could make no full assessment as Hans turned left up the first cross street before they reached the town centre and stopped outside a large, two-storey house on the next corner. Emma recognised the northern European, perhaps Danish style in the high, sloping roof line and dormer windows.

The front door opened and a woman appeared and came outside to stand on the path, watching. To either side of her were areas of lawn, unfenced, but Emma noticed a fence at the side that seemed to indicate the back garden was contained. Somewhere for the girls to play, and she knew they would be thrilled after spending weeks cooped up first on the ship and then the train. Even back in Yamamoto-dori, open space was limited.

Hans lifted Gladys out of the cart and Emma stepped down with Irene. A soft breeze blew. Emma looked over at the woman she presumed to be Mrs Jensen, still standing in anticipation. She was about Emma's age, tall, with blonde hair and a pale complexion.

As Emma approached, the woman said, 'Hello and welcome,' in a pure American accent that took Emma by surprise. 'I'm Anna.'

They exchanged a few words of introduction as Hans heaved the luggage off the cart.

'Will you be staying long?' Anna said.

'I've no idea.'

'It doesn't matter. Come inside and I'll show you to your room. It's upstairs.' She paused in the hall and giggled. 'Hans won't be pleased.' She leaned towards Emma and whispered, 'Make the men work, isn't that right, Emma?' She didn't wait for a reply as she mounted the stairs. 'Here we are, right in here. What do you think? It's my biggest guest room and you have a nice window with a view of the street.'

Emma drank in her new surroundings. 'It's lovely, thank you.'

'Have you eaten? I'll make coffee and we can have apple cake.' She backed out of the room. 'I'll let you settle in. Come downstairs when you smell the coffee.' Anna closed the door behind her.

The room contained a double bed centred in the longest wall, a single bed hard up against the wall behind the door, and a cot. A wardrobe and a large dressing table were positioned along the far wall, and a writing table sat below the window. There were two comfortable chairs facing into the room and positioned in front of a small wash basin in the corner next to the wardrobe. A chest of drawers filled the only remaining space on the far side of the double bed, with some shelves secured to the wall above. The furniture was dark, polished and well cared for. A large rug covered much of the floorboards. Pretty floral-print curtains framed the windows. The air smelled of fresh flowers and she saw there were roses in a vase on the bedside table. In all, it was a busy room, something of a jumble, but it was somewhere to be, somewhere to live.

Emma put Irene down on the bed as Hans came in, breathless, with the trunk. He deposited it just inside the door before heading downstairs to fetch the rest. On his final trip to Emma's new room, he said a brief goodbye.

'Sophia's right. You should be okay here.'

Emma watched him descend the stairs and slip from view before she closed the door. She felt suddenly, dramatically alone. But there was no time to indulge the feeling. Besides, she wouldn't give in to it. She fished out some of Irene's toys from her carpetbag and asked Gladys to mind her sister. Then she unpacked as fast as she could, first one case and then the other, placing clothes in the drawers and the wardrobe until everywhere had something in it. She put one case inside another and slid them under the bed. The trunk she tackled next, popping the knick-knacks on all the high surfaces and shelves, away from Irene's grabbing hands. She managed to deal with most of their possessions before Gladys lost interest in Irene. Emma thought she could smell of the aroma coffee wafting upstairs.

With Irene propped on her hip and Gladys trailing down the stairs behind, Emma followed the aroma and found Mrs Jensen in the dining room, along with an older couple. They were seated at a large, polished-oak table before a tray with cups, a large coffee jug, and plates waiting to be filled with a delicious-looking cake, all proud on its glass stand.

Seeing Emma enter the room, Anna stood.

'Emma, meet my mother and father-in-law. This is Carrie and Ben.'

Emma went over and shook both their hands where they sat. Anna invited her to take up the chair opposite. Emma arranged Irene on her lap and told Gladys to sit by her side. Facing the three family members seated in a row Emma suddenly felt under interrogation. She noticed toys on a shelf near the window. Anna followed her gaze.

'I have two sons. Harold is six. He's at school. And, ah, here's little Edwin,' she said as a skinny fair-haired boy with doleful eyes entered the room. 'He's four.'

The two mothers watched as Edwin approached Gladys and they sized each other up. With words of encouragement from both mothers, the pair went off to explore Edwin's toys. Irene eased herself off her mother's lap and toddled over to join them.

'My husband Jens is at work,' Anna said, pouring the coffee. 'He's a teller at the bank.' She raised herself up a fraction as she said it.

'And your husband?' Ben said, gazing at Emma over the cake, 'What does he do?'

'Father,' Anna hissed.

'It's all right.' Emma smiled to show she was untroubled, which was not exactly true, but she knew she needed to get used to explaining her circumstances to strangers. She drew her cup closer and said, 'He's an export manager.'

'That sounds very important,' Carrie said. 'What is an export manager?'

'You don't have to answer,' Anna said, cutting the cake.

Emma ignored her and went on, hoping a brief explanation would be all that was needed. 'He works for a large merchant company. They export all kinds of things. Rubber, tin, rice.'

'To where?'

Emma was beginning to feel embarrassed by the scrutiny. She told herself the old woman was taking an idle interest, nothing more, and she scrambled for the easiest way to explain the work of a merchant to Carrie, who did not appear to be all that worldly.

'They export goods all over the world. Ernest is in charge of the export side of things, but there are others who work in imports.'

'Imports, exports.'

'Just think of all those cargo ships going back and forth across the ocean,' Ben said, accepting the plate Anna set before him with a brief gesture of thanks.

'I cannot imagine it.'

'You have lived for too long in Colorado, my dear. I can picture it very well. Where is he from, this husband of yours? Is he American?'

'British.'

'British,' Ben repeated.

'Will he be joining you soon?' For all her apparent ignorance of the wider world, Carrie was sharp.

It was the obvious question, too, and one of them might as well have asked her to begin with, for it was no doubt the only information they were all waiting for.

'I expect so,' she said, fudging. 'I don't know. It's hard to say. He's in Japan.'

'Japan? My goodness, that sounds a very long way away,' Carrie said.

The two older Jensens were visibly shocked. Now it was Anna's turn to look awkward. Emma wished someone would change the subject before anyone could add, So you've left him.

She felt grateful to Anna when she said, 'You will meet Mr Callier and Mr Parsons at dinner. They both have work in Brush. Mr Parsons is Canadian. He has dealings with the hardware store. Mr Callier is here on agricultural business.'

The tension eased and Emma sipped her coffee and ate the cake, which proved as delicious as it looked and to some degree made up for the little inquisition she had just endured.

That afternoon, Emma took the girls out for a short walk, pushing Irene in a pram Anna had provided her with. It was almost summer and the day had grown hot and the westerly sun stung her skin. There was little shade beyond Custer Street. She went as far as the next corner and when she saw a shop nearby, she crossed the road to take a closer look, wondering what one might find in a small grocery shop in Brush, Colorado, in 1919. She was about to go inside when she noticed a sign plastered on the door's window: Germans must speak English. The words leaped out at her as though each letter was hitting her in the face. She stood there in the baking heat of that hot and still afternoon in Brush as though she were standing behind enemy lines. The war had ended months ago. Why were people leaving signs up? To taunt the Germans who lived in the town? Was there some problem here that Hans and Sophia had failed to tell her about? After all, Hans was as German as she. How many Germans were there in Brush and why were they so despised? More's the point, why was this shopkeeper allowed to leave that sign up now the war was over?

She was more indignant than uneasy. She had nothing to fear. There was not a trace of a German accent in her voice and she was a British national by marriage. Her indignation gave way to echoes of Kobe and the silent antipathy she had endured there from the locals in the streets, antipathy that culminated in the riots. She shooed the memories away. She didn't want them drowning out what little cheer had kindled in her heart.

The heat suddenly felt too much. She decided there was nothing in the window display to entice her into the shop and she walked away. She would save her explorations for the cool of the following morning – find a store without an inflammatory sign, she hoped.

That evening at dinner, everyone was present. Seven adults and four children made for quite a gathering. Anna served meatballs and caramelised potatoes and pickled cabbage to hungry and enthusiastic diners. The conversation was light and relaxed. Emma learned that Mr Parsons was single and a merchant, and Mr Callier was married and had an interest in photography. Both men were pleasant and well-mannered. Anna's husband Jens, small and neatly presented, was a man of few words, but he appeared nice enough.

After dinner, the male guests retired to their rooms and Jens withdrew to the living room with his parents, leaving the children with their mothers. Harold was busy inventing a game and trying to engage Edwin and Gladys. Irene was engrossed in some of Edwin's old toys. Seeing them all happily occupied, Emma asked Anna the question that had been nagging her all afternoon. She blurted it out without realising she might be giving away something of her own identity. Then again, surely Anna Jensen knew Sophia and Hans were of German heritage. Of course she did. With a name like Hans Harms, how could he be anything else?

'Why does the corner store have a sign telling Germans to speak English?'

Anna was quick with her reply. 'Oh, that. Ignore it. Some of the community here despise the Germans, just like the rest of America. It's a legacy of the war. Silly, really. The Germans living in Brush are no trouble and never have been. A lot are pacifists, mind. You know, conscientious objectors. That goes down none too well around these parts.'

She looked at Emma apologetically and added, 'Forgive me. I was forgetting. You are Hans' cousin, so you must be of German background too, originally. How foolish of me not to have thought. I do apologise.'

'No need,' she said quickly. Just as she was about to add, 'I'm American. I was born in Philadelphia,' to reinforce the point, they were interrupted by a screaming child. It was Gladys, who had fallen over and grazed her knee.

'I'll take them upstairs to bed, I think.'

'Come down once they're settled.' Anna drew close and said with a wry laugh, 'I could do with the company. We don't get many female guests.'

'If I don't, it is only because I have fallen asleep.'

Emma couldn't help taking to Anna. There was something about her that invoked trust and female companionship was always welcome, especially when starting afresh in a new location. Chun, Yu Yan, and now Anna, although she was not a servant, but rather the provider of a service. Nonetheless, Emma had always got along with those co-existing under the one roof.

Despite feeling a definite pull, she didn't go downstairs that first night, preferring to watch over her sleeping daughters, comfortable in an armchair with her tatting.

The following morning, straight after breakfast, Emma took the girls out for a walk. She was on a mission. She had a bundle of letters to post now she had a return address. The air felt warm on her skin and there was not a cloud in the sky. She headed down to the highway that bisected the town and then turned left. With the low sun beaming straight at her, she was forced to squint.

Hearing her coming, a dog started barking and as she approached the next house, she saw the large black beast in the front garden, her eyes tracing the fence to ensure it was enclosed. It was, but even so, Emma's heart beat faster. She urged Gladys to swap sides as she passed, the dog growling and snarling, rearing its front paws against the railing, its upper lip curled back revealing menacing teeth. Emma hoped the dog wouldn't leap the fence and attack. She couldn't get beyond that house fast enough and wondered if the owner was home.

Once she was safely past the dog, she relaxed, making a mental note to take a detour down a different street in future.

She had to wonder why such an obviously dangerous dog was allowed to terrorise passers-by in the neighbourhood.

When she crossed the next side street, she had a good look in each direction. All the streets were much the same as Custer Street. A most uniform small town, this was.

There was no one about. Six streets on and she arrived at the main shopping area of Brush. There was not much to it, just a long parade of small shops. To her disgust and dismay, Emma saw many more signs demanding Germans spoke English. Maybe those shop owners had forgotten to remove their signs, but even so, they should not have been put up in the first place. As it was, she could scarcely believe her eyes. Something wasn't right here in this small town. She never saw a single sign like this in San Francisco.

She knew that hatred could linger. Her father had spoken of the diaspora of Mennonite Germans into Canada who were fleeing violence and persecution, but she thought he was talking only of Philadelphia. She had no idea how widespread the feeling was. Although she might have guessed after her father's experiences of cool hostility in Montréal. Now she faced, right here in this town, what she could only regard as pure hatred. Not only against Germans, but, she decided, Mennonite Germans. The irony did not escape her, either, for if those Mennonites had been living in their homeland, they would have held fast to their pacifism and refused to fight just the same.

In the next instant, she thought of George. George who went against his faith to fight for his country. Oh, George.

It was with a mix of trepidation and defiance that Emma entered the post office, even though it was one of the few businesses not sporting one of those discriminatory signs. She presented her letters to the staunch postmaster, who eyed her suspiciously before lowering his gaze to take in the two children.

'Not seen you around these parts.'

'I've just arrived.' She pushed the letters across the counter. 'I'd like some stamps, please.'

The postmaster flicked through the letters as a short queue formed behind her.

'Japan, Singapore, Canada,' the man announced, in a voice loud enough for the entire building to hear. 'And Germany,' he added, raising his gaze to her face, his filled with truculent curiosity.

Emma froze. She wasn't about to tell him who she had written to.

'It probably won't get there,' he said as he turned the letter over and noticed the return address. 'Although I see you are anticipating a reply.'

There was a shuffle and a loud sigh behind her.

'You just wait, Mrs Pedersen. This lady is making her mail travel the whole world.'

There was a titter of laughter which ceased immediately when the postmaster added, 'For what reason that might be, we can only hazard a guess.'

His eyes had narrowed, his face filled with suspicion. Emma was incredulous. There she stood with two toddlers – one in a pram – and the postmaster thought she was a spy. She couldn't help blushing. Eager to mask her reaction, she reached into her purse and extracted a dollar bill. In her mind, she couldn't get out of the post office fast enough. Yet it took the postmaster a goodly while to give her the required change and find the appropriate stamps. When at last he had and they were affixed to their envelopes, she swung round, passed the two women queuing, their eyes boring into her, and stepped out onto the pavement consumed with indignation. She shoved the envelopes in the mailbox and marched back to the boarding house with Gladys almost running to keep up.

Once in her room, she came to the slow realisation that the town contained a prominent Danish community, including the Jensens, since Pedersen was surely a Danish surname. Surely it wasn't the Danish who were filled with animosity? It had to be the others, the local Americans. She was keen for clarification but she had no idea who to ask, for it seemed rude to inquire of Anna if her own people despised the Germans.

That evening after dinner, as she prepared her daughters for bed, she spoke to them softly in her native tongue. She had been teaching them the rudiments of the language back in Kobe, and on the way across America she had toyed with the idea of desisting as she could see no real benefit, yet now her heart filled with rebellion and she told them a German fairy tale before they slept.

The next morning, she left Gladys in the garden with Edwin under Anna's watchful eye and popped Irene in the pram for a walk. She decided to avoid the town centre and headed down the back streets instead. Perhaps there was a park, or, better still, a church. She had no mind to visit the Lutheran church she had seen that day when Hans brought her to Brush. Instead, she headed north.

It wasn't long before she saw one. It was a Presbyterian church. A grand building, too, most grand for this shabby old town, and she thought to enter before changing her mind at the base of the stone steps. The Presbyterians were no more her people than the Lutherans, although, with the mood she was in, she probably would have walked into any church in town. Except she thought she should explore all the churches before she made up her mind, so she kept walking. Three blocks on and she thought she glimpsed a church down a side street. She followed her instincts and in under a minute she was standing before a Congregational church. This time, she decided to go inside.

The minister was walking down the aisle towards the entrance as she entered the nave with her pram. He welcomed her, and she introduced herself. To her surprise and delight he was German. She recognised the accent straight away. There was an air of familiarity in the minister's manner and she wondered if this was where the old Mennonite families had established their faith. Her curiosity was aroused, but she had a more pressing question on her lips and here was the ideal person to educate her on the demographics of Brush. She explained she had just arrived and had seen the hateful signs in the shop windows.

The minister invited her to sit down at the end of a pew. He sat at the end of the pew in front and as he turned to face her, he said, 'This has been cattle country for generations. Then some farmers discovered how well sugar beet grows around here and German migrants were brought in from Lincoln, Nebraska, to work in the beet fields. The crop was so successful, the Great Western Sugar Company opened up a factory here and one in Fort Morgan. The locals resented the newcomers. It is often the way.'

'But many of them are Danish.'

'The Danish have no problem with us. It is more the cowboys and roughnecks. Like I said, this is cattle country. But many decades ago, some Danish families came here to grow crops. The Germans here are working for the Danes.'

She saw it then, the social divisions that provided fertile soil for the growth of animosity. At least she could take comfort knowing the Jensens had no problem with her heritage. Sophia had no doubt chosen her recommendation wisely. She would not have knowingly placed Emma and her girls in harm's way.

Perhaps this also explained why Hans disliked Brush, although there must be similar hatred in Fort Morgan.

'You have a lovely church,' Emma said, changing the subject.

The minister laughed.

'We took over this church after the Presbyterians built themselves a bigger church closer to town.'

An image of the church she had almost entered flashed into her mind. She thanked the minister for his time, took a note of the service schedule and left.

Walking back through the residential streets of Brush, Emma shrugged off those anti-German signs as the silly prejudices of the narrow-minded. Even the cool reception in the post office mustn't trouble her. It would pass; it was sure to pass a little more each day, now the war was over. People just needed time to move on. Meanwhile, she had nothing to worry about. If anyone asked, she would say she was born in Philadelphia and was married to an Englishman.

AN ILLNESS

The summer heat intensified. June gave way to July and the humidity rose. Thunderstorms were a frequent occurrence. At night, when all in the boarding house retired for bed, the various noises of the day were replaced with a near-deafening chorus of crickets and frogs. Emma made hats for the girls and only went out in the cool of the morning when there were few others about. When the days were at their hottest, she would sit with her daughters in their room and read to them in English and in German, and she would continue the German lessons she had started back in Kobe, introducing vocabulary and teaching them short phrases.

In the hour or two when the girls were napping, Emma would take out the wooden box containing her silk tapestry, having decided if she could shuttle silk through the warp in Singapore where the days were never cool, then she could manage here in Brush. It had been many months since she had had the frame of mind for the intricacies of the craft. Back in Kobe during the riots and the influenza, she had been too distressed to even try. Now, she forced herself, keen to enter that serene space within that only focussed attention on an absorbing task could provide. She was finishing one of the birds, its feathers of deep blue and fawn depicted in thin lines of silk, and progress was painstakingly slow. Time passed quickly and the girls soon stirred and Emma put away her tapestry in its special wooden box, ready for the next day and the next nap.

In the afternoons, she would take the girls downstairs to play with Edwin in the kitchen or the garden, and while away the hours chatting to Anna whenever she wasn't busy and there was no one else around. Emma found Anna to be an amiable soul and good company. Anna delighted in her stories of Singapore and Kobe. When Harold was not at school, he joined in with the other children from time to time, although he was a moody and reclusive child who preferred to be alone in his room with his trains. Anna said he was obsessed with trains.

Carrie and Ben tended to spend most of their time in the sitting room, reading the newspaper or a book, or playing cards together. Their daily habit changed when one day Jens brought home two new and comfortable outdoor chairs to replace the rickety old pair no one seemed game to sit on. Jens positioned the chairs on a small concreted area beneath the kitchen window that enjoyed the shade of the oak tree. From there, the couple could observe the children playing on the grass. Ben sanded back and repainted an old circular table to complete the outdoor setting. After that, the old couple relocated their activities outdoors whenever the weather was favourable.

One day in mid-July, Emma and Anna were chatting in the kitchen when a sudden shout followed by a succession of thumps brought their conversation to a halt. Ben came rushing in shortly after.

'Carrie's been stung.'

'A bee?'

'Wasp.'

Carrie entered the room clutching her leg.

'Darn thing tried to crawl up my skirt.'

She sat down at the table and peered down at her leg. A small red swelling was visible on her shin. Cassie deposited some spit on her fingers and dabbed it on the area.

'You need to wash it,' Emma said.

'Spit is good. We always use spit.'

'Coffee?' Anna said.

The back door flew open and Gladys ran in.

'Mummy, Edwin won't let me have my doll.'

Emma went and brought all the children inside, the outdoors suddenly seeming threatening, as irrational as she knew that was. Cassie and Ben retreated to the sitting room. Thinking it wise to leave the family in peace, Emma hurried the girls upstairs.

The following morning, when the three women were alone in the kitchen, Anna asked her mother-in-law if the sting was any better and Cassie raised her skirt. Emma leaned forward, seizing the chance to view Cassie's leg. She saw straight away that the sting site was inflamed and her calf had swollen. Ignoring her resistance, Emma went and put the back of her hand on Cassie's forehead. As suspected, she had a fever.

'You need to do something about that sting,' she said, sitting back down.

'It's just a flare-up. I'll be fine.'

'It's probably best to leave her to it, Emma. She doesn't like being fussed over.'

Clearly not, but Emma had dealt with plenty of belligerent patients. Still, she decided a watch and wait approach was wise.

By that evening, the leg and the fever were worse. Ben, Jens and Anna took Emma's view that something needed to be done.

'I'll see the doctor.'

'That won't be until Monday at the earliest. And it's Saturday.'

'That's only a day away.'

'Two days away.'

'One and a half.'

Losing patience, Emma cut in with, 'Either you call a doctor here right now, or you let me do something about that sting.'

'And what will you do?'

'I am a nurse, Cassie. I know exactly what to do.'

'That's as maybe, but you are not coming anywhere near my leg.'

'Then, to put it bluntly, you may well die.' She turned to the others for support. 'See that streak?' They all looked to where Emma was pointing. A small red mark had appeared on her skin above the sting site. 'That's the poison entering her blood stream.'

'Cassie,' Ben said with alarm, 'you must let Emma treat you.'

Cassie looked up and saw the resolute faces of her husband, son and daughter-in-law standing over her. She shrugged.

'Guess I'm well and truly ganged up on, here.'

Ben patted her shoulder. Cassie turned to Emma.

'You're not going to lance it?'

'I am going to use a poultice,' Emma said reassuringly. 'Anna, I need bread, linseed and mustard. Plenty of salt and a bandage.'

Throughout the rest of the weekend, every three hours, Emma changed Cassie's poultice. By the time Monday came around, the infection site showed a marked improvement and Cassie had changed from her initial resistance into the most placid of patients. She seemed to revel in the attention. It felt good to be useful and Emma was pleased with her progress. No doctor would be required.

Emma found it ironic that she could heal a patient but she couldn't heal herself, although her weekly attendance at the Congregationalist church services proved spiritually soothing. Emma had reconnected with her faith, at least a version of it. Church was the only place outside the boarding house where she received a warm welcome, the congregation eager to make her acquaintance. Although she was reserved when it came to making friends. She didn't want to form friendships in a place she was destined to leave and she didn't want the rest of Brush labelling her German by association. The faithful comprised a mix of young and old, many of them farm labourers and their families and despite her reticence, she gained a lot from their kind words and warm hospitality. But it wasn't enough. She didn't belong in Brush. She wasn't sure where she belonged. What she did know was she needed to receive replies to her letters. It would only be through communications from those who mattered the most to her that she would be able to make sense of her future.

It wasn't until the end of August that she began to receive those replies. The first to arrive was from Ernest. Anna passed the envelope to her across the breakfast table one morning and all eyes were on Emma as she tucked it away, embarrassed. She waited until she was upstairs in the quiet of her room before levering open the envelope. As she did so, she pictured the look on his face when he opened the letter she had sent. When he discovered she was living in a boarding house in Brush.

The letter was brief. He said exports were slowing and Guthries were deciding whether to wind up operations in Japan. He was worried he'd be out of a job before too long. No mention of the floozy. He hoped she could find it in her heart to forgive him. He missed the girls dearly. When the time came, should he come for her in Brush?

She replied straight away, wishing him well. She wrote of the boarding house, the Jensens and Gladys's new playmate, Edwin. She wrote of the infernal heat and the blandness of the town. No mention of the anti-German sentiment. She told him she'd found a church and was feeling quite settled. She didn't answer his question. She hadn't forgiven him. She didn't know if she ever wanted him back, although she didn't relish the alternative.

Instead of facing another silent interrogation at the post office, Emma thought to use the opportunity of a visit from Hans and Sophia to post the letter, as Hans was driving her and girls to Sterling for an outing. Surely in Sterling she wouldn't be treated with suspicion. Sophia's sister had a farm on the other side of the town, from where it was only a small detour to the post office.

At first sight, Sterling had a more open, pleasant feel, yet the same anti-German signs were propped in some of the shop windows she passed as she made her way from the motorcar to the post office. The reception she received from the postmaster was cordial if reserved, the overweight man in his too-tight uniform eyeing her as an intruder. But she didn't have the word *German* plastered across her forehead, or any other defining mark and her accent carried her through the ordeal of buying a stamp for a letter to Japan without fuss. With the letter posted, she was able to enjoy the day on the farm, watching the girls running free in the wide, open space of the farmyard with Sophia's youngest, Arthur, and her sister's twins, Caleb and Edgar. And then they feasted on an array of sandwiches, cold meats and pickled vegetables, and cake. The day out was the highlight of that summer.

In September, Emma received a letter from Dottie. Cynthia and Ian had moved back to England and Dottie missed her friend terribly. New neighbours had moved into Emma's former bungalow on Orchard Road and Dottie had encountered the wife in precisely the manner she'd first met Emma. The description brought back vivid memories and a touch of nostalgia. There she was, back at Dottie's, having tiffin, wearing her friend's old clothes. In the last paragraph, Dottie said she'd had word from Lizbeth, who was back in Germany with Gustav so that he could do his bit to help restore the economy. They were both fine and living life to the full, by the sound of it. Dottie admitted she felt bereft now she was the only one left and she hankered for the good old days. Emma wasn't sure they'd been anything of the sort, but then she'd never really been one for tiffin on the veranda.

It was such a depressing letter, it took Emma a couple of weeks to summon the enthusiasm to write back. There seemed little point in maintaining the friendship, but she had always been a loyal sort and Dottie sounded awfully adrift.

Having had letters from Ernest and Dottie, Emma anticipated a letter from Karin or even from Uncle Wolfgang, but none came.

By October, the heat had broken and autumn brought fine, sunny days and cool nights. Emma shifted her daily walk to late-morning. By four in the afternoon, the air grew chilly and Anna set about lighting fires. The highlight of the month was a little birthday party Emma and Anna organised for Gladys, who turned four. Not wanting to impose on her host's hospitality, Emma didn't invite her Harms cousins; there were simply too many of them.

Irene turned two in November. She, too, had a little party, Emma braving the stores in Brush to purchase a small gift. For both her girls' birthdays, the Jensens were generous,

Anna baking a cake and her and her mother-in-law buying gifts.

Life couldn't have been smoother in that large boarding house in Brush. Emma paid her board each month and she always maintained a certain distance out of respect for the Jensen's privacy, yet more and more she felt she was an integral part of the household, always chatting with Anna, with Cassie, always there at mealtimes. And of course there were the children, a powerful binding force, especially as Gladys and Edwin got along so well aside from the occasional scrap. Irene toddled about around them, mostly staying out of mischief. She was a less wilful child than her sister, her temper tantrums few, although she displayed a curiosity with her surroundings, an eagerness to explore and run off if she could.

Winter folded Colorado in snow and the nights were well below freezing. Despite wondering for how long she would remain in Brush, life at the Jensens grew increasingly pleasant and it became impossible to consider going anywhere else, especially as Christmas was approaching and everyone was filled with festive cheer.

The day before Christmas Eve, a large parcel arrived from Japan. Emma resisted opening it, placing it with the other gifts that were making quite a pile under the Christmas tree. That parcel jarred. Every time she looked at it, she was transported out of the little bubble she found herself in, and catapulted into the harsh reality of her situation. She was a woman separated from her husband, a husband who had betrayed her. She had two small children to care for and nowhere to go beyond Brush. All of her own immediate family were gone other than Karin, who was too far away, and George, her missing brother. If it hadn't been for that present, Emma might have fooled herself that all was well in her heart. As it was, for the next few days Emma participated in all the Jensens had planned, putting on a smile for the sake of the children, but the loss of her parents and her brother and the demise of her marriage, along with no word from Karin and the lack of knowledge about George, left the larger part of her hollow and bereft. Throughout the festivities, Anna, who sensed Emma's mood, made a point of jollying her along, plying her with wine and rich food. And when the presents were opened, the girls were thrilled to receive a large doll each from their father. He'd sent Emma some fine Japanese cloth, which she took to be a peace offering and, when she next went upstairs, promptly packed away in her trunk. In all, Emma was grateful to Anna, to the whole Jensen family, and even, to a degree, Ernest. All through Christmas she let herself be mollycoddled, only shedding a tear in the quiet of her room in the dark.

THE CENSUS

January, and it was the dead of night when Emma woke up cold in her bed to the sound of a freight train rumbling through the town. She pulled the covers up around her shoulders and turned onto her other side. The rumble went on and on until the last of the carriages passed the end of Custer Street and the sound slowly faded away, leaving silence in its wake. On the bed against the wall, Gladys slept soundly. Not a murmur from Irene.

Emma pulled the covers up to her chin and tuned into the soft breaths of her daughters, her thoughts straying all the way to Kobe, to Ernest, asleep in another bed, with his interpreter, no doubt.

To rid herself of the image, Emma pictured the others in the house, deep in slumber, especially Anna in the room across the landing. Emma liked to think of Anna. Whenever she did, she felt better about her circumstances. Their friendship had blossomed over Christmas and Emma thought of her new friend with much fondness. She found in Anna someone she could trust and had no qualms about divulging her background, her heritage, her stories of Philadelphia and London and what she recalled of Germany. It was a relief to share the truth and made the burden of being German in Colorado that much easier.

Anna was sympathetic, she knew, and approved of Emma teaching German to her children. 'How else are they to know who they really are?' she would say. Her mother-in-law Carrie was supportive too. Anna said Carrie had tried to teach the boys some Danish, but they had taken little interest. 'They are proper little Americans, those two,' Anna was fond of saying. Emma had no intention of rearing her daughters as 'proper little Americans'; not if it meant they would grow up hating their own heritage.

Sleep came eventually and when she woke up again it was daybreak. Irene was sitting up in her cot and Gladys turned over and rubbed her eyes. 'Come on, you two,' Emma said, throwing off the covers and reaching for her bathrobe. She could hear Anna downstairs in the kitchen, low voices, the sound of water gurgling through pipes.

She dressed the girls for the day and took them with her to the basin to watch over them while she washed. Then she slipped on the clothes she was wearing the day before. It was the same routine every day, the only change was the season. It was January, and as she drew the curtains, she saw more snow had fallen overnight.

When she exited the room for breakfast, she encountered Mr Parson making his way downstairs with a suitcase. Following him, with her girls trailing behind her like a pair of ducklings, she saw another suitcase by the front door. She had no idea he was leaving. A merchant, he came and went, staying at the Jensens whenever he was in the area. This time, Anna had not mentioned his departure and Emma was surprised, for Anna often discussed with Emma who was coming and who leaving, who she liked and who she didn't, and who she was suspicious of. She especially liked Mr Parson. As Emma ushered her daughters into the dining room, Mr Parson was right behind her and she greeted him with a warm, 'Good morning'.

'Good morning to you, Emma. And a frosty one it is.'

They sat down before the usual fare and as they tucked into their grits and eggs, muffins and coffee, Anna announced that the house would be receiving a new boarder that very afternoon. 'Mr Short is his name.' Anna shot a look at Carrie. 'Before you ask, Mother, I know nothing about him, other than that he's from Georgia. He sounded very nice on the telephone.'

Mr Short arrived at sunset. He brought a blast of icy air in with him when he walked into the hall. Emma was on the landing, about to descend the stairs and she felt that cold air swirl about her legs. She shivered involuntarily and walked softly to close the door to her room before returning to the landing like a spy.

Mr Short was, in fact, very tall and sported a beard that hid much of his face. His eyebrows were thick, his brow heavy. His eyes – small and dark – were acutely observant and he shot a quick look up at Emma, who froze. He was of an indeterminate age, but if Emma had to guess, she would have placed him in his forties. She found herself recoiling in his presence, but Anna seemed untroubled by his rough and ready manner. As she escorted him upstairs to Mr Parson's former room, Emma retreated to hers, her mind prickling with misgivings.

Dinner that night was a sombre affair. The family were seated together around one side of table as was their custom. Mr Callier, the photographer, a shy and sensitive man who had returned to capture the winter snow in Colorado – he was heading to the Rockies but had become captivated by the snow drifts on the plains and prolonged his stay – sat in his usual place, which meant he was next to Mr Short. Mr Callier did not appear comfortable being so close, although Emma might have been imagining his reaction. Emma sat opposite the family, with Gladys to one side and Irene the other. Not a happy arrangement. Poor Irene was situated between Emma and the new guest. Emma did not like the proximity of Mr Short one bit and had to quell an urge to draw Irene's chair closer to her own.

Ben attempted to strike up a conversation with the new guest.

'Anna tells me you're from Georgia. What line of work are you in?'

'Sales, since you ask. Truly it is nobody's business but my own.'

Ben raised his eyebrows. Carrie let out a soft gasp. Jens had just opened his mouth to speak when Anna placed a censorious hand on his arm and he shrank back in his seat. No one seemed to know what to say after that. The rest of the meal was consumed in silence.

The following morning, Hans came to collect Emma and the girls to spend the day in Fort Morgan. It was an infrequent occurrence and Emma was looking forward to it. Deep snow had prevented her spending Christmas or New Year with her cousins and this was the first opportunity since. It was Louisa's seventh birthday and Emma had purchased a small doll as a gift, forcing herself to ignore the offensive sign propped in the window of the toy store. All of the shopkeepers had chosen to leave those anti-German signs in their windows despite it being 1920. Forgiveness didn't seem to manifest in Brush, not when it came to the war. Emma did her best to ignore it.

The Harms' house had a festive air, with balloons tied to the front door and coloured streamers on the letterbox. Along with Sophia and Hans's six children, another four friends hovered around a prettily-turned-out Louisa. They made five giggling little girls.

There was jelly and biscuits and gingerbread and all manner of treats laid out on the dining room table. With the guests all present, Sophia went about telling the children to sit down. Hans and Sophia had organised some games between the party food and the birthday cake. The adults stood back and let the children enjoy themselves, intervening only when trouble brewed or a mishap seemed likely. Sophia introduced Emma to some of them, but Emma struggled to retain the names. When the feasting was over and Hans had marched the children into the living room for a game of blind man's bluff, Emma found herself listening midstream to a conversation nearby. One of the couples was discussing where to book their wedding anniversary dinner. Others were making recommendations.

'Have you tried Glenda's?' someone said.

'We can't go there. Remember?'

There were murmurs of discontent.

Sophia, who came up beside Emma, turned to her and whispered, 'Germans are not allowed in that restaurant.'

The anti-German attitude was prevalent in Fort Morgan as well? The war was over. Why, oh why wouldn't the locals let it go?

'I thought things were settling down,' a stout and kindly woman said.

'I wish that were true,' said the tall woman beside her. 'My boys were thrown out of class just last week for saying, "Guten Tag".'

A gasp of disbelief rippled around the group.

'That's outrageous,' the stout woman said.

The men in the group chimed in all at once.

'Something has to be done.'

'We must stand our ground.'

'And do what? Fight?'

Sophia interrupted with an offer of more fruit punch and cake. The mood lightened instantly, everyone realising they were getting carried away and a birthday party was hardly the place for such a topic. After the games came the cake, and then it was time for Emma to leave, as Hans wanted to be home before dark.

Emma carried an insistent unease away from the party. Trouble was brewing, she could sense it in her neighbourhood. The locals were spoiling for a fight.

Lunch the following day was a small affair. Jens was at work, Mr Callier and Mr Short were out, and Ben was spending the day helping an old school friend clear out his shed. Halfway through her sandwich, Anna murmured an apology and left the room. When she returned, she handed Emma a letter. Seeing the Montréal postmark, Emma opened the envelope straight away. She found her hands were trembling. It was from Uncle Wolfgang. She thought it a belated reply to hers, but it wasn't. Folded inside the envelope was another and it had a German postmark. She turned over the envelope and saw it was from Karin. The address was different from the one she had used when she wrote to her sister last June. She must have moved. She was desperate to open the letter but beneath the curious gazes of Anna and Carrie, she desisted.

Anna, ever discreet, went to fetch more coffee.

'Mummy,' Gladys said, 'I want to leave the table.'

'That is not how you ask permission.'

'May I leave the table, please?'

'Go into the living room with Edwin. And take Irene with you.'

Pleased not to have her tension observed by her inquisitive daughter, Emma sank back in her seat. She rode out the rest of the meal making small talk with Carrie and Anna. When at last it was possible to leave the table, she checked on the children, who were playing happily, and then raced upstairs and opened the letter.

Karin's writing was small and bunched-up. Emma was not used to reading German. She concentrated on the words, realising as she read that the letter was in response to one her father had written in the weeks before he died. Karin had no idea of his passing. She also had no news of George. Disappointed, Emma wrote back. Karin deserved to know the news as fast as possible and Emma couldn't assume Uncle Wolfgang had bothered to tell her. As she wrote, she tried to imagine her sister, but she had no idea what she would look like now, after all these years. A new idea formed in her mind as she wrote and when she drew the letter to a close, she promised to visit Hamburg the moment she was able, adding that now they had no parents and no Herman, they should pull together as sisters, if only for the sake of the children. She hoped that by now, Karin had received word of George. She must have done. The war ended over a year ago. She slid the letter into the envelope, sealed the flap and wrote Karin's correct address on the front and her own, in Brush, on the back.

She raced downstairs and asked Anna if she would mind keeping an eye on the girls while she went out.

'It's freezing out there.'

'It's only an errand.'

Emma raced back upstairs, donned her coat, hat, scarf and gloves and was through the door and hurrying up the street before she gave the postmaster a thought. Needs must, she told herself.

Snow was banked up to either side of the footpath. The

frigid air stung her lungs. She pulled her scarf up over her face, covering her mouth and nose. Not wanting to be out longer than she had to, she took the shortest route past the house with the vicious dog, quickening her pace even more as she went by, cautious not to slip on icy parts of the pavement, grateful the animal was nowhere to be seen.

When she arrived at the post office, she paused to catch her breath, pulling the scarf from her face as she entered the warm, stale air, and breaking out in a sweat. The post office was empty of customers and the postmaster stood behind the counter, looking as officious as ever.

'Good afternoon, Mrs Taylor.'

She was shocked he knew her name and she didn't bother to disguise it. He seemed pleased she was shocked. Then she realised he probably knew the names of everyone in Brush.

'I want to post this, please.'

She passed the letter across the counter. The postmaster eyed the envelope suspiciously.

'To Germany? Again?'

'Why ever not?'

'We have plenty of German folks in this town, Mrs Taylor. And you know what? Not one writes home to Germany. Not one. Now, why do you think that is?'

Because they'd get the reception I'm getting now, she thought but didn't say. They no doubt posted their letters in Fort Morgan or Denver... anywhere but here.

The suspicion in his eyes morphed into open hostility.

'Who are you, Mrs Taylor? Or, to put it another way, *what* are you?'

She was instantly indignant.

'I'm a wife and a mother, waiting for my British husband to wind up operations in Japan and collect me and his children. We'll be heading back to England, where we're from.' It was all a lie. She had no intention of taking Ernest back, but as she spoke, she saw it might be her only means of escape out of Brush. And then she could visit Karin as she'd promised in her letter.

The postmaster gave her a sceptical look. 'Is that right?'

'Why on earth would you doubt me?'

'You've heard of Mata Hari.'

Outrage tore through her. 'I'm no Mata Hari!' she snapped. 'Will you post this letter or not?'

He weighed the envelope to calculate the postage. She passed the coins across the counter. He pushed the letter and the stamp towards her as though they were toxic.

She snatched them both and turned around and stormed out of the building, vowing never to post a letter there again.

A week later, she received another letter from Ernest. She was surprised to receive it as she hadn't replied to his last. There were no sweet phrases of endearment and she was glad of it, for they would have been out of character and therefore false. No desperate plea to have her return to Kobe, either. Not that she expected it. Reading over his words, the situation in Japan did not sound good. He said exports had plummeted and Guthries were continuing to wind back operations. Many staff had been posted elsewhere. As the export manager, he was unable to leave his post, but he did not think it would be long before the company pulled out for good. He missed her, he said, he missed his daughters and wanted nothing more than to see them all again. Then came the apology, the reassurance that it was over with his translator, and that he would never be so foolish again. Please, wouldn't she consider taking him back?

She folded the letter and returned it to the envelope and tucked it away in her cardigan pocket. She hadn't forgiven him and she didn't miss him and she certainly didn't love him. She also knew she couldn't stay in Brush forever. Yet she had nowhere else to go. The world was still picking up the pieces after the war. She had received no word from George and had no means of communicating with him. If she were to refuse Ernest, the only place she could go was back to Germany. Throw herself at the mercy of her sister. At least she was blood. She hoped Karin replied to her letter the moment she received it.

On her way to the Congregational church that evening, as she walked down the dimly lit residential streets, she passed by two men who were loud and drunk, despite the prohibition. They took no notice of her and once she had passed them by, she hurried on her way. When she reached the next corner, she heard shouts and looked back. The two men – thugs – were attacking another man and calling him names, German names, insults.

She rushed around the corner, terrified of repercussions should she draw attention to herself. When she got to the church, she was shaking.

She managed to regain her composure as she entered the building, taking a seat in a pew towards the rear, much to the surprise of the minister who caught her gaze with a brief smile. Others filed in, each letting in a rush of cold air. Before long, the congregation stood and sang a hymn. Then the minister spoke of loving thy neighbour and turning the other cheek and holding fast in an attitude of forgiveness. It was an unusual service. There was a cautionary tone to the ministrations. Another hymn, a Bible reading, prayers, and the service came to an end.

As the others filed out the door into the cold black night, she approached the minister and told him what had happened.

He looked at her gravely and said, 'You would be advised not to come to evening service again, Mrs Taylor. Not on foot.'

'Are things that bad?'

The mood in Brush had darkened since Christmas and the arrival of Mr Short, although she decided that was coincidental.

His face shadowed. 'Tensions are rising. There is some talk of a new group moving into the area. You may have heard of them. The Ku Klux Klan.'

She had. They were the scourge of the southern states.

'I thought they only targeted black people.'

'They now have a broader campaign in mind.'

'Germans,' she said flatly as a gear shifted in her mind. Mr Short was from Georgia.

'I'm afraid so.'

'But the German people are not to blame for the war.'

'You cannot argue with the forces of hate. They're taking advantage of the situation here. This has been a divided town for too long.'

'What can we do?'

'We must pray and be steadfast in our beliefs.'

She hurried through the back streets to the boarding house. On her way, she didn't think prayers and strong beliefs would be of any help if those attackers were to turn on her. When she saw the two thugs loitering on a side street corner, she all but ran back to the boarding house, repeating to herself that no one other than the Jensens knew she was German, not even the postmaster, and while that was the case, she was safe.

During the last week of January, a blizzard kept tensions in the streets at bay. In the confines of the boarding house, Emma felt relatively safe, although the presence of the dour and menacing Mr Short meant she could not relax completely. On the

Tuesday of that week, Jens announced after dinner when they were all gathered in the room that it was time to tackle the Census form. He had the form right there before him, pen in hand. Emma was ready with her answers. She hoped to go last, but Gladys snatched Irene's Raggedy Ann and Irene started whining and demanding it back. Emma took the doll from Gladys and scooped up Irene and held her firmly. Gladys started crying loudly and tugging at her mother's dress. Exasperated, Emma growled at her daughter. Jens looked up and, assessing the situation, he asked Emma for her details.

Emma tried to tell him the answers to his questions over Irene's loud complaining. Then Edwin started hitting Gladys and all hell broke loose among the children. Above the commotion, Emma quickly told Jens her and her daughters' ages. When it got to where they were born and their nationalities, Irene yanked her mother's hair and punched her neck. Embarrassed, Emma gave her daughter a soft slap. Irene used that as an excuse to cry at the top of her lungs.

'Be quiet, Irene,' Emma hissed. Irene took no notice.

Anna stepped in and said above the ruckus, 'Emma's German.'

The adults froze. Emma was dumbstruck. She had trusted Anna with that information, never anticipating the woman had a loose tongue. Although she was only being honest. Emma should never have confided in her. She should have maintained the story she always told, that she was born in Philadelphia to German parents. She was about to contradict the statement, but what was the point when it was true and Anna, at least, knew it.

The situation went from bad to worse when, looking down at the form, Anna added, 'Germany is her country of origin. And both parents are German.'

'What about the children?' Jens said, without lifting his gaze.

'Father England and English. Mother German and Germany.'

'I've got that. What language do they speak?'

Gladys, at that very moment, chose to yell out, '*Hör auf damit.*'

Emma shot her a censorious look and Gladys was instantly meek. Irene continued her bawling. Emma wished to God she'd never taught the girls German.

'So, they all speak German?' Jens said.

'That's correct,' said Anna.

'But I'm also a British subject,' Emma said defensively. 'Married to a British citizen.'

'Doesn't count.'

Mr Short, who had been sitting at the other end of the table during the entire fracas with his head bowed as though examining his fingernails, lifted his gaze and shot Emma a look brimming with menace and hate.

Emma shunted her daughters out of the room, offering a quick apology for their behaviour as she closed the door. The shaking didn't start until she was alone in her room with her two belligerent children. She could have throttled them, but they were only little and had no idea of the trouble they had caused. She locked the door. She would have barricaded them in if she could.

From then on, she would have to sleep under the same roof as a member of the Ku Klux Klan, knowing she was a target of his wrath. She wanted to flee and had to steel herself not to starting packing.

ALL UNDER ONE ROOF

For the better part of a year, Emma had resided in Brush with resignation and at times with grim determination, her humdrum existence tempered by the conviviality of her friendship with Anna and the comfort of knowing her cousin and his family were just a train stop away in Fort Morgan. On census night, that had changed. Before census night, Emma could walk the streets with her head held high as an American, pushing from her the anti-German feeling in the town. No longer. In the weeks that followed, thanks to Anna's inadvertent betrayal, eyes followed her, blank expressions became scowls, and neighbours crossed the street rather than walk past her. Word of her true nationality had quickly spread, and she suspected Mr Short was behind it. She had no proof, as if there would ever be proof, but her instincts were strong. Being under the same roof as that man was a trial. After that fateful disclosure, at the dinner table he had not uttered one word to her. If he wanted the salt and she had it, he would ask Anna for it instead.

The local newspaper had started reporting on the growing

presence of the Klan in Brush and Fort Morgan. Mr Short's name was never mentioned. But Emma surmised he had much to do with fomenting all the malice in the community.

By spring, Emma's acute awareness of Mr Short proved a psychological strain. Ever since he arrived at the Jensens, the atmosphere in the boarding house had felt tense, but with his blatant animosity towards her, she could only relax in the house when he was out, and she took to spending most of her time when he was there hiding in her room, trying to blot him out of her mind by entertaining the girls, or, when they were napping, working on her tapestry.

What had begun as a challenging activity back in Singapore, became more than a pastime and more than a distraction. Now, weaving those thin silk threads grew into little acts of defiance, an assertion of who she was, a well-travelled woman with many skills, a trained nurse, a caring mother and a good Christian.

But she often failed to hold her mind steady on her task. Her thoughts were too intrusive. Emma could not understand why Anna had chosen to reveal where she really came from. How could it have escaped her notice that the town was filled with animosity towards the Germans and Mr Short was a troublemaker? It hadn't. So why did she divulge Emma's secret? Why sacrifice their friendship, which until then had bloomed petal by petal like a pretty rose, providing the only salve Emma had in this most difficult period of her life. It was too cruel to imagine.

Emma had no proof that Mr Short was a Klansman but her suspicions never went away. And she was hamstrung. She had not and would not divulge her suspicions to Anna. She did not want to create conflict. Things were awkward enough at mealtimes when she was forced into his presence. And besides, Anna, much to Emma's chagrin, had succumbed to the syrupy charm Mr Short lavished on her and Carrie. Emma knew if she did speak up about her misgivings, it would be she who would be put in the wrong, not Mr Short.

He gave her the silent treatment at mealtimes, but if they passed each other on the landing and he saw that no one was about, he made snide jibes and exaggerated gestures of avoidance. With nowhere else to go, all she could do was put up with it and bide her time, hoping that, sooner rather than later, Mr Short would leave.

It was Mr Callier who left, vacating his room in early March. He was replaced by Mr Vickers, a labourer from Louisiana who had a thick accent and a burly physique. His manner was sullen and he rarely spoke.

Emma could have had no idea that the two men were acquainted. They avoided interacting with each other at the dinner table, yet their twin presence at meal times lent a dour mood to the household. There was no more of Mr Short's attempts at being charming. Ben and Carrie had taken to eating with their heads bowed. Even the children were subdued. Many times, Emma caught Anna catching Jen's eye and quickly looked down at her plate.

The tense situation came to a head one evening in late March, as the lodgers consumed Anna's roast chicken. Mr Short, having devoured half the food on his plate, turned his face to Emma, waited until he caught her eye and said, 'Benjamin Franklin was a good man, don't you think, Mrs Taylor?'

She was shocked he had chosen to speak to her. 'I couldn't say,' she said, her heart beginning to race.

'He knew what was right for America.' He paused for effect, then he said, 'More's the point, *who*.'

Anna opened her mouth to speak. Jens put a hand on her arm and she slumped back in her seat. Gazes flitted nervously between Emma and Mr Short. Emma wasn't clear what he meant, but she suspected it had something to do with Germans.

He went on. 'Don't you agree, Mrs Taylor? Benjamin Franklin is what this country needs. Surely you can answer me, Mrs Taylor? If that is your name.' He paused again, looking around at the others as though to gain an audience. Mr Vickers set down his fork and looked fixedly in Emma's direction. Mr Short went on, 'Tell me what your real name is, Mrs Emma Taylor. The name you were born with.'

She looked down at her plate, refusing to meet those hostile gazes, reluctant to tell the room her maiden name.

'Why doesn't the woman answer!' He brought a hand down on the table. The crockery bounced and clinked. Carrie gasped. Gladys whimpered and Irene started to cry.

'Mr Short, I think that's enough,' Jens said. 'You're upsetting the table. Let us enjoy the food Mrs Jensen has prepared for us.'

Emma glanced up. For a brief moment, Mr Short looked fit to explode. Then he relaxed back in his seat, evidently changing his mind, satisfied he had caused enough of a stir for one day. 'As you wish,' he said to Jens. 'My apologies. I just thought the household would want to know who they have sleeping under their roof.'

'We already know, Mr Short.'

'I doubt it,' Mr Vickers said with a snort.

Emma had to curb an impulse to get up and leave the room. Her appetite gone, she focused on ensuring her daughters finished the food on their plates. As soon as she was able, she went upstairs, ushered the girls into her room and bolted the door behind her.

She was consumed with the urge to flee again, just as she had in Kobe, but she had nowhere to run to. There was no one in America, no one in Britain and nothing would propel her back to Kobe. Her only hope was a letter from Karin, a letter she hoped to receive, a letter with a welcome, an invitation. How much for the tickets? Emma checked her bank balance. She even counted the coins in her purse. She needed to prepare.

After the children were asleep, she prayed. She prayed for guidance, prayed for protection, prayed for release. She prayed and she prayed until all her prayers were spent.

That night, she awoke with a start. She heard the rumble of the freight train and thought perhaps that had woken her since all was still in the house. She thought she could detect the snores of Mr Vickers through the adjoining wall, a wall that felt to her much too thin for comfort.

She turned and lay on her side gazing into the dark. The train's whistle blew. In the wake of the shrill noise, over by the door, she made out a shape bounded in wisps of faint grey light. At first, she thought her eyes were playing tricks on her, until the shape grew more distinct and she found herself staring at the figure of a man, a young man. She held her breath, transfixed. A second later, and the visage slowly merged into the black of the door and was gone.

She exhaled long and slow, conscious of the heavy beat of her heart. To begin with, she was frightened. But that feeling soon gave way to an overwhelming mix of love and compassion.

Her mind mulled over the experience. She had never seen a ghost before, but she didn't believe what she had seen was in fact a ghost. More a vision of some kind, a presence. A benevolent soul? An angel? George? No, it couldn't have been him, surely. If George had come to her preternaturally, she would have felt sadness, grief. As she lay in the dark silence, she drew strange comfort from the supernatural event, in the final analysis believing her prayers had been answered; that she was being protected and that whatever happened, she and her children would be safe. So momentary was the experience that after a while, she even began to doubt it had occurred.

She rolled over onto her back and her bedsprings creaked. Irene stirred and turned over. Gladys didn't move. Emma closed her eyes and willed herself back to sleep.

The days dragged by. Gladys caught a cold off Edwin and gave it to Irene. The girls were all sniffles and coughs and whines and fractious moods. Emma kept them both warm and fed and corralled in their room. Now and then, she would dash down to the kitchen to fetch one of them a drink. There, she would find Anna and the two would exchange a few hesitant words before Emma rushed back upstairs, not keen to leave the girls alone a second more than she had to.

The moment they were well, she telephoned her cousin. She was desperate to get out of Brush, even for half a day. Sophia answered, sounding a touch breathless. Emma tuned into the background noise, more a commotion of thuds and high-pitched squeals.

'Hold on a second,' Sophia said and all went suddenly quiet.

There was a long pause.

Then Emma heard Sophia's voice again. After an exchange of pleasantries Emma said, 'I was hoping to come visit.'

'We'd love to have you. Hans has to go to Brush tomorrow morning. How about I get him to pick you up?'

For the first time in weeks, Emma felt a ripple of excitement in her belly. It was quickly dashed by the unexpected appearance of Mr Short.

The following morning, Emma and the girls were up and dressed and ready for their outing long before breakfast. Emma sat on the end of her bed with Irene on her lap and Gladys beside her as she listened for movement downstairs. She had taken to avoiding Mr Vickers and Mr Short by delaying breakfast until she heard the front door close. Then she would peer out her window for confirmation they had left the house. As soon as the coast was clear, she would bundle the girls out the bedroom door and head downstairs before Anna cleared away the breakfast things. It was a fine line between a cold and meagre breakfast and none at all, should the men leave late. This time, they left early and when Emma entered the dining room, she found Anna still eating toast and her mother-in-law sipping tea. Her appearance prompted movement and Anna stood and started tidying up and ferrying plates to the kitchen. The greeting, as usual, was subdued.

Emma was saved from having to make small talk by the early arrival of her cousin. She hurried Gladys and Irene through the remains of their toast as Hans chatted with Anna.

The drive to Fort Morgan across the flat Colorado plains was liberating. The ploughed fields, the emerging heads of sugar beet interspersed with grazing land, it all seemed bucolic and harmless. Evil hid in caves, in swamps, in the murk. No one could imagine such darkness could lurk in a wide, open space like this.

The welcoming smell of percolated coffee greeted her at the door and, to her delight, she found a second breakfast waiting for them at the kitchen table. Sophia rushed over and gave Emma a warm hug. Emma was pleased to find her in good spirits.

'Sit, sit. Tell me your news.'

Emma hesitated. Where to start? Should she outline her domestic troubles? There seemed little point in withholding the truth.

'That's dreadful,' Sophia said, stirring sugar into her coffee. Her sleeves were rolled up to her elbows. A lock of hair had come loose and fell across her face. She was untroubled by it.

'You'll leave?' Hans said, holding her gaze.

There was a roar followed by a cry and he stood up to go and deal with the children in the other room.

'I dearly want to,' Emma said in his absence. 'And I think I will.' There was that hesitation in her mind again. She overrode it and added, 'I can't stay at the boarding house much longer. We're not welcome.'

'I know. But Anna would never throw you out.'

'She wants to. I can see it in her eyes.'

'She's in an impossible situation.'

So am I, Emma thought but didn't say. There was no point. She had reached an impasse. Life seemed to offer no exit.

The rest of the morning was taken up in the garden, helping Sophia prepare for spring planting and supervising the children. Hans came over to take her and the girls back to Brush all too soon.

Emma watched the birds in the branches of the trees outside her window, while Irene was having an afternoon nap and Gladys played quietly with the toys on her bed. A squirrel scampered down the trunk. Now it was mid-April, the trees had begun to burst into blossom and leaf. Warmer days had brought optimism to the town, but there was to be no relief from the social tensions in Brush. Germans were as unwelcome as ever and low-level prejudice and the occasional skirmish were turning into overt hatred and violence.

Emma found herself spending even less time in Anna's company. Anna had grown cold, almost hostile around her. Yet Emma saw the fear in Anna's eyes and she recalled what Sophia had said, and she knew anyone running a boarding house could not afford to have trouble among the guests. It was a pity that it was she, and not Mr Vickers or Mr Short, who received the unwelcome attitude, but Anna was hardly going to confront those men. Emma knew her days at the boarding house were numbered, and all she could do was rely on Anna's good nature not to go through with the act so clearly playing on her mind.

The mood in the town was now so strongly anti-German, Emma rarely went out. The hostile looks she had gotten used to from shopkeepers and patrons alike had turned into aggressive scowls and taunts, and she did not want the girls to hear the name-calling. More people would cross the street rather than pass her by. She no longer visited the church. She missed the congregation but the minister was right – the walk there and back put her at risk. Her life had shrunk to the four walls of her room, while there, under that boarding-house roof, an even larger threat lurked right along the landing in the rooms of Mr Vickers and Mr Short.

One morning, while she was seated at breakfast with her daughters to either side, Mr Short and Mr Vickers both entered the room uncharacteristically late and sat down in their usual places, ignoring the surprised looks from Ben and Carrie, Anna, who seemed determined to ignore the tense atmosphere, presented Emma with two letters that had just arrived. She took the letters from Anna's hand with the weakest of smiles, not wanting the scrutiny of those vile men, especially when she saw that the first letter carried a German postmark. It was from her sister. Then, in a singular act of defiance and without looking up, she calmly levered open the envelope, unfolded the thin pages and proceeded to read, in German, what Karin had to say. She decided those men would need exceptional eyesight to know what language the letter had been written in and they could assume all they liked. For once, she was not going to be a coward.

Karin apologised for the late reply. She said she had had to wait for someone to translate what Emma had written.

And she had never been much of a letter writer. Could Emma read German? She hoped that was the case. She said she was well and the whole family had survived the flu. Her son Gunter, a conscientious objector who had chosen prison over war, had recovered his health and now had a job in the family business. He was twenty-two. Karin invited Emma and the girls to visit any time they wished. She went on to describe the sadness that still hung over the town – she lived near Hamburg – after so many young soldiers had lost their lives. And for what? She described the poverty, the difficulties after the treaty, and she questioned what all that fighting had really achieved. *Please come*, she said at the letter's end, and Emma knew she would. In her mind, she was already packing.

Seated at that table of hostility and fear, her mind flooded with memories of her parents and her brothers. She pushed them away. She could scarcely recall Germany. All she knew was that her extended family of origin hailed from Aurich, a town west of Hamburg, but that her mother's parents were both Norwegian and her father's German and Dutch. Some might say they were scarcely German at all and certainly not by heritage. Not that any of that would matter to Mr Short. She imagined with a small thrill disembarking at Hamburg and coming face to face with her sister, a sister she would not even recognise.

Emma folded the letter and returned it to the envelope. She looked around at the others with fresh confidence, enjoying a new resilience arising out of close family ties that bound her to her country of birth. Here, in America, and especially in Brush, she saw little but contempt for the German people and she wished with her whole being to be as far from this place as she was from Kobe.

The other letter, from Ernest, she pocketed. She did not

want to read his news in front of the others. She did not want to read his news at all.

To her surprise, Mr Short did not remark on her correspondence. He seemed in no mood to goad her. If anything, he appeared preoccupied. Even so, in the presence of those men, eating became intolerable and the moment she deemed her daughters had had their fill, she withdrew from the breakfast table without a word, taking them with her up to their room.

She had hoped to have an opportunity to collect her thoughts and make a decision about leaving Brush then and there, heading across America to New York and booking a passage to Germany, but she needed to think it all through and decide if she could afford all the expense. She didn't feel ready to embark on such an adventure when there was no future in it. What would she and the girls do after they had outstayed their welcome at Karin's? What if it turned out there wasn't even any room for her there? An invitation to visit was one thing. Accommodation another.

Her thoughts were interrupted by moans and whines and she saw she could snatch no time for herself with Irene in a fractious mood and Gladys deciding to antagonise her sister by snatching her toys. After enduring their squabbles for an hour or more, Emma thought a walk would do them all good despite the horrid atmosphere on the streets. She weighed up the pros and cons. Just when she thought she could not keep them a cooped up like chickens a moment longer, it started to rain. It seemed not even the elements were on her side.

With no sign of either daughter leaving her be, the morning looked set to drag on. She had no choice but to ignore the letter in her pocket, something she found easy enough to do. Whatever Ernest had to say could wait. She pushed aside all thoughts of a sudden flit and read the girls a story, and another. Then she found some paper and crayons and encouraged them to draw a picture of a house and watched over them, helping Irene, praising Gladys. When they tired of the activity, she spoke to them in her own tongue and taught them some more German words so that they would impress their Aunty Karin.

The minutes turned into hours and soon enough, it was lunchtime. She heard the familiar hoot of the midday train in the distance and steeled herself as she went downstairs with the girls, hoping Mr Vickers and Mr Short were dining elsewhere, as was their wont.

To her relief they were, and the Jensens and the Taylors sat around the dining table in a reasonably relaxed atmosphere. Carrie asked Emma how she was enjoying the spring warmth and flowers, and Ben wanted to know if Gladys had seen a squirrel in the tree. They were seated before a delicious-looking dish of potatoes and cheese. Anna, who seemed to carry the burden of Emma's presence, remained silent as she scooped portions onto plates and passed them around.

That silence had seeped into everyone else by the time the last plate was set down. Gone forever the cordial friendliness of the pre-Mr Short days, no matter what anyone did to ease the tension. Emma wondered yet again for how much longer she could endure the situation. She desperately wanted to break the silence, but there was nothing to say that would restore good cheer other than an announcement that she was leaving. Resigned to the atmosphere, she finished her portion of the creamy cheesy bake and helped Gladys and Irene with theirs. She was about to tap Irene on the hand for sliding her food off her plate and onto the table when there was an urgent-sounding rap on the front door.

Carrie stiffened. Ben placed a reassuring hand on her arm. There was a brief pause, leaving Emma wondering who was going to answer the door. Anna frowned, got up and left the room.

She re-entered the dining room and looked at Emma strangely. 'There's someone here to see you.'

Confused, Emma stood and prepared to go out into the hall. Who could be calling on her here at the boarding house? The minister? He was the only real friend she had in Brush, not that she had seen him in months. Perhaps he was paying her a courtesy call. Or could the caller be from some authority, evicting her and the children from an unsafe Brush before any real trouble started?

She braced herself as she went out into the hall. There, she came face to face with her husband.

She quickly closed the dining room door behind her and stood in front of it like a guard.

'Hello, Emma.' He reached for her but she took a small step back.

'Ernest,' she hissed. 'Whatever's going on?'

He appeared puzzled.

'Didn't you get my letter?'

She felt her cardigan pocket. 'No, I mean, yes, but it only arrived this morning and I haven't had a chance to open it.'

'Oh.'

He stood before her, a touch dishevelled, his hat askew, his paunch straining the buttons of his tailored suit. He'd gained weight in the last year and, she thought, perhaps a few wrinkles about the face. He was definitely careworn, she decided; more careworn than could be accounted for by a long train journey, especially as he had no doubt travelled first class.

'You'd better explain yourself.'

'Standing here in the hall?'

'I can't think of a better place.'

A deflated look appeared in his face.

'Very well. I had to leave Kobe. Japan's economy has

collapsed. The stock market took a plunge and now there's a run on the banks.'

Emma absorbed the information.

'Why didn't you send a telegram?'

'I thought my letter would arrive before I did.'

For an export manager, he appeared unable to have made a very basic calculation. Even she knew when a letter was likely to arrive, since the post cannot travel any quicker than a person.

'Where are the children?' he said, making to walk past her and enter the dining room.

'Wait. You can't just march on into our lives like this after a year of separation. It's too upsetting.'

'I have nowhere else to go.'

He did. Unlike her, he darn well did.

'You have your sister in New Jersey. Hannah would be thrilled to see you, I'm sure.'

'Gladys and Irene are my daughters. Surely you can understand me wanting to be with them.'

'Two letters in a whole year?'

'And a Christmas present.'

'For goodness' sake!'

'You know I am no good at writing letters.'

'Not even to your wife?'

'You walked out on me, remember?'

'With good cause.'

He gave her an imploring look.

'Come with me, Emma, please. Come to England. I'm a changed man, I promise you. My time with Guthries is over. I have been offered a new job. We can live in London. You love London. You can take on some nursing. You'd like that, wouldn't you? We'll be happy again. We can make things work.'

Before she had a chance to respond, Emma caught the

sound of footsteps on the path. There was a murmur of male voices. The door handle turned and she watched over Ernest's left shoulder as Mr Short and Mr Vickers entered the hall and came to a sudden and menacing halt.

Ernest turned and took a few backwards steps and stood with his back to the wall.

Mr Short glared down at him from his own formidable height.

'And you are?'

'I beg your pardon,' Ernest said, his voice filled with indignation.

The men exchanged glances. Mr Vickers let out a scornful laugh.

'An Englishman, by the sound of it,' he said.

'So I hear.' Mr Short paused, his top lip curling, his gaze flitting back and forth between Emma and Ernest, before at last resting on Ernest. Then he said in a low voice, more a growl, 'What are you doing married to a Kraut?'

Instantly indignant, Ernest puffed himself up.

'That's none of your business.'

Emma reached out a hand. 'Ernest, don't...'

Mr Short took a step forward and pointed his finger into Ernest's chest.

'It is so my business.'

He took another step forward and Ernest tried to step back. He would have stepped sideways but he was cornered. Mr Short seized his opportunity and rammed Ernest hard up against the wall.

Ernest emitted a yelp. Mr Short raised his fist, pulling back his elbow ready to strike. Then he snickered, unclenching his fist. Seeing an opportunity, Ernest took a sideways step, making to ease himself away. Wasting no time, Mr Short scruffed

Ernest by his shirt collar – forcing Ernest to tilt back his head – and hissed in his ear.

'Now you listen to me, you worthless piece of trash. I don't give a damn who you think you are. No law-abiding, god-fearing white man in this here town has any business wedding a German. You better get your ass out of this respectable boarding house and take that stinking vermin with you. Am I making myself clear?'

He gave Ernest a hard shake as he let him go.

'Well, I never!' Ernest blustered, shocked, outraged and terrified all at once.

'You better do as you're told, if you know what's good for you,' growled Mr Vickers.

Emma wanted to hurry Ernest up the stairs and out of harm's way. Before she could act, there was movement in the dining room. The door opened and Anna came out, her face flushed.

She took in the faces, the heaving chests.

'Whatever's going on?'

'I beg your pardon, ma'am,' said Mr Short, removing his hat. 'This man here calls himself her husband.'

'Emma, is this true?'

'Ernest has just arrived from Japan.'

'Then I think it is time you left my boarding house.'

'Yes,' Ernest said, finding his courage and turning to the men. 'Time you left.'

'Not him,' Anna said with quick anger. 'You. You must leave here, Mr Taylor. You too, Mrs Taylor. Take your children, pack up your things and leave. Right now. There is no place for you here in Brush.'

Emma was aghast at the suddenness of the command. She rushed into the dining room and gathered up her daughters.

Fighting back the tears, she hurried through the hall and up the stairs, urging Ernest to follow her. As the order of the eviction sank in, she knew Anna had had no choice. If she had tried to evict Mr Short and Mr Vickers, there would have been cause for retaliation. The Jensens could not risk the Ku Klux Klan burning down their house. But those thoughts did nothing to ease the humiliation. Still, it seemed life had made up her mind for her. She was leaving, this very afternoon. That thought alone was liberating.

Within an hour, they'd packed.

Emma was puzzling where to go when Ernest said, 'Is there a telephone in the house?'

'I'm not sure I want to ask Anna if I can use it.'

'You must. Call your cousin. Tell him I'll pay him handsomely if he would kindly come and collect us and drive us to Denver.'

'Denver?'

'At least it's civilised there.'

'But it's too far.'

'Nonsense!'

She ventured downstairs and found Anna in the kitchen, putting away the dishes. Carrie was seated at the table. An ally. At least, Emma hoped so. The two women stared at her, their expressions blank.

'May I use the telephone?'

Carrie shot Anna a glance, then let her gaze slide down to the floor.

'Go right ahead,' Anna said and turned to close a cupboard door.

Emma went back out into the hall. The telephone sat on a console table. It was impossible to hold a private conversation with the two women right there in the next room. She wanted to close the door but lacked the courage to do anything as assertive as that, given the circumstances.

She dialled the number and Sophia answered. Emma asked to speak to her cousin. 'He's busy, Emma.'

'But is he there?'

'He's here.'

'Then, please. I must speak to him. It's important.'

There was a long pause. Then she heard his voice. In a rush of hurried sentences, she managed to explain the need and the urgency.

'I'll be right over.'

'Are you sure?'

Half an hour later, she was seated in the back seat of her cousin's car with her daughters to either side of her. Never had she been more relieved to see the back of anywhere, even though she was leaving with her husband, which she supposed meant that they had reunited.

She told herself she would have gone with Ernest regardless, for Germany was that much closer to England and, after all she'd been through, she felt an urgent need to be on her own soil and near her own blood, and, if at all possible, find out what happened to her brother.

1940

A DAY OUT IN WIMBLEDON

One more thread of her needle across the warp of her tapestry and Emma drew her shawl more tightly around her shoulders and readjusted the woollen rug draped over her knees. Her fingers were cold, as was the tip of her nose. The winter freeze showed no sign of abating and big old Cottenham House had too many crannies allowing in the icy night air. The best place to be on a night like this was down in the kitchen or in bed, but with only a small corner of green to complete the cottage garden, she persevered.

It was when she stabbed the tip of her finger with the end of her shuttle that she paused to look past the loom, her gaze falling briefly on her one masterpiece hanging on the opposite wall, its soft colours highlighted by the lamplight below. She allowed her gaze to lower, to drift to other objects in the room. She was in the habit of avoiding looking that way. The tapestry hung there and was ignored, the memories still too strong. How long had it taken her to finish it? She cast her mind back. What began as a pastime in Singapore in 1914 occupied her loneliest hours in Kobe and Brush. Yet it was in Wimbledon that she finally completed the work, once her daughters grew older and entertained themselves and started school and she had much more free time. The techniques were fiddly and she recalled that moment when she threaded the little canoe shuttle through the warp for the final time and vowed never to tackle another silk tapestry again. Besides, wool was easily sourced, unlike the silk.

She told herself she ought to appreciate her work, considering how much effort went into it. Surely by now, she could admire all those fine silk threads without thinking of Ernest. She forced her gaze back, took in the gnarly cherry tree trunk, its thin branches bending, supporting a spray of pale-pink blossom. Two blue birds, one sitting on a branch, the other hovering in flight, looked at each other, their beaks open in chatter. The background of pale, peachy pink set off the arrangement beautifully. It suggested springtime and lovemaking and new life, and she supposed that was what she had lived through with the birth of both her daughters. But, unlike the tapestry, her life had not been lived against a backdrop of peachy pink.

The work, from this distance, appeared flawless. Even up close, it was fine and delicate and there were no evident mistakes. What there was instead, locked inside every silk strand, she didn't care to acknowledge, even now. So much discontent, so much anguish and heartache and confusion, always coming to terms with something or other, with a new situation, new people, Ernest. How did anyone come to terms with anything? By going over and over and over the same spot, weaving little threads of story, squashing them down one upon the other, building a picture, attending first here, then there, interlocking, dovetailing, making everything tie together to form a pleasing whole. Of all the tapestries she'd created over the years, the one she could scarcely look at and pointedly ignored, the one she had struggled to make, was the one that brought her the greatest satisfaction and pride: her masterpiece.

The almost finished work on her loom was evidence of decades of practice. It was a perfect work and it reminded her more of the tapestry hanging in Karin's house in Aurich. The one hanging above the fireplace in an ornate frame. The first time she visited, Karin told her their Norwegian grandmother had made it. Emma recalled standing enjoying the warmth from the fire in the grate and gazing in awe at the intricacies of the weaving. It was the first time Emma had seen Karin in over thirty years and she was meeting her nephew Gunter for the first time. He took to little Gladys and Irene the moment they walked in the door. It was the summer of 1921 and in Aurich, the mood was optimistic. Emma's German made a rapid come-back as she chatted with her sister.

After laying to rest the news of their parents' deaths and their brother Hermann, the conversation drifted to George. Karin said he was missing in action. Emma took in the news with a heavy heart. For seven years she had carried a sliver of hope that he would turn up one day. She would often picture him making watches and repairing clocks in Hannover. Then she recalled the apparition she had seen in the Brush boarding house. The war had been over for a long time before Emma saw that benevolent ghost, but she wondered if it might have been George, letting her know he was watching over her.

As she drew the shuttle through the warp for the last time, Emma confronted anew the realisation that she was the only remaining relative of her immediate family of origin other than Gunther, and her daughters had no contact at all with any aunts, uncles or cousins on the Taylor side of the family. And no father. There was no one to delight in the birth of Irene's child, other than her.

Although Emma missed her sister, she was glad Karin had

passed away before this new war began. It would have been a burden having her in Germany. And at forty-three years of age, Gunther was too old to serve and was saved the consequences of conscientiously objecting a second time, which was some comfort. Even so, he remained on the other side of the war, a ring-pass-not standing between them.

It had been easier not to take sides in the First World War. This time, Emma couldn't find any sympathy in her heart for Hitler. She was so far now from her German heritage that she felt no strong loyalty to her people. She prayed for peace, prayed for a quick resolution, yet she felt heavy, as though under a great weight, and she saw darkness descending on Europe as the Nazis pursued their agenda. Besides, Miss Schuster was a Jewish heiress and through her, Emma had come to learn of the persecution of the Jewish people, of all those fleeing Germany just as her own religious group had fled almost a century before. Now Britain was housing Jewish children fleeing concentration camps. Emma wished the government would do more, much more for all those parentless children.

A final tug of thread secured in a knot and her tapestry was complete. She left it there on the frame and got ready for bed. The following day was Sunday and she needed to rise early for church.

The pavement was icy. Standing at the bus stop, she lost feeling in her toes. She stamped her feet. Her gaze was pinned to the corner of the street as she waited, willing the bus to hurry up.

At last, there was the hiss of brakes and she greeted the conductor as she mounted the platform and headed on through, passing the side-on seats in favour of an empty seat at the front. It was her Sunday ritual and the conductor was a familiar face.

She paid her fare and wriggled her toes in her shoes, hoping to get some warmth into them before she alighted and made the brisk walk down Hartfield Road.

It wasn't far and the pavement was salted and reasonably free of snow and ice. Still, she took care, avoiding treading on any ice, stepping over patches of snow and avoiding slush. She listened to her footsteps, the only sound in the street. Up ahead, a tabby cat slunk by. Someone exited their front door as she passed and soon she heard the tinny clunk of a dustbin lid.

When at last she turned in at the low gate and pushed open the door, she found the reverend had turned up the heating for the congregation. Many had braved the cold like she had, but she noticed one or two were absent. She took her place in the front row, whispering hellos to her friends as she sat down. A few stragglers entered, each bringing with them a rush of cold air.

The reverend kept the service short, dwelling lightly on world troubles and praying for peace. There was the usual smattering of hymns. He kept his medium session brief as well, and it wasn't long before Emma was enjoying tea and sponge cake in the side room, which the reverend insisted at the start of his sermon everyone stayed for, if only for his wife's delicious raspberry jam.

It had always been this way at the Wimbledon Spiritualist Church. A devoted and close-knit congregation centred around a warm and giving reverend and his charming wife. Then there were the various guest mediums – they were on a circuit and the church was always packed on those occasions – and the faith healing, which she and another nurse provided as required in a small room at designated times.

It was the kind of conviviality and communion that had been missing from Emma's life until that day back in 1926, when the daughter of one of her patients – she'd registered at a nursing agency once Irene had started school – befriended her and asked her about her family and, despite her usual reticence, she had confided her story of loss. 'I just wish I could find out what really happened to my brother George. I know it's impossible, but without it, there's no sense of finality, just this nagging doubt. This "what if?"'

The woman had gazed at her sympathetically. 'What if I told you there was a way?'

'How? I mean, he's missing.'

'Would you like to come to church with me one day and find out?'

It was to prove a defining moment of her life.

Emma recalled the day she first entered the church, took in the splendid stained-glass window over the altar table, sat down amongst a small sea of open faces, and paid attention to the sermon delivered by a reverend with a benevolent air about him, who then, much to her surprise on that first occasion, acted as medium. She pictured that moment when the reverend said he had a message for someone special in the room, a new attendee, and his eyes bored into hers. Someone she was very fond of, he said. She sat frozen in her seat. Someone who loved her very much. She had no sense of what was coming. A watchmaker, the reverend said. And Emma caught her breath. When he said George wanted her to know he was happy and watching over her and the girls, tears welled and she could scarcely contain herself. Seeing her distress, her friend had rallied, as had all the others around her.

The comfort she'd felt then, she still felt now, the church becoming her new family almost overnight. Ernest had been away, as he so often was, on some overseas trip. Back then, he was working for Corfields who had a factory in Merton colour printing beer trays. South Africa, Australia and New Zealand had become his business destinations and she was never invited. Besides, the trips were lengthy, many months at a time, and they would have disrupted the girls' schooling. Ever since they had returned to London from Brush, Emma had spent long stretches of each year alone with the girls. The welcoming congregation of the Wimbledon Spiritualist Church had replaced all that was missing in her life.

Even when he was home, Ernest was not around much. He had never enjoyed church and he only went to the occasional Sunday service, something he did begrudgingly. By then, Emma had all but given up on the marriage except in name. After that year of separation in Brush, the relationship was never the same. The physical distance had left an emotional one in its wake and Emma could never trust Ernest again, even as she found it in her heart to forgive his betrayal. Of course, the girls adored him, especially Irene, the apple of his eye. And when he was home, he lavished them with presents and outings, anything they wanted. Which was why, when he left Southampton that day bound for Australia and never returned, Irene took it so badly. She was devastated. She wept. She sulked. She got herself into a tizzy over the slightest thing. Emma would never forget it. She was the one saddled with fake explanations and reassurances. Irene, by then nearing her teens, also resented the sudden tightening of the family finances. There was no more money for frivolities, no more expensive presents. As Britain sank into the depression years, Emma's household suffered this double loss.

But time healed as it passed and at least now, Irene was married, seemingly happily, and about to give birth. As Emma sipped her tea and bit into the last of the sponge cake on her plate, she decided, All's well that ends well, and so it had.

The air outside the church was no warmer when she left. There was to be no thaw that day. Emma hurried back to the bus stop, arriving just in time to catch the bus back to

Cottenham House. She was there within ten minutes. Miss Hint must have seen her from a window, for the front door opened the moment she entered the porch and she enjoyed the warmth of many fires. Poor Miss Hint was rushed off her feet delivering coal to so many grates. The house enjoyed central heating, too, but Miss Schuster demanded the fires be lit and Mr Holt made sure they were, despite the fact that Adela was bedridden and would never know if they weren't.

As Adela's heart condition slowly worsened, her demands on Emma's time grew and she could not recall the last time she had had a whole day to herself. Sunday was no exception. The moment she removed her outdoor apparel, she rushed upstairs to be by Adela's bedside, relieving Susan, who kindly covered her Sunday morning in exchange for a later start on Friday, which she used to visit her family and friends. When Emma opened the door, she was hit by a sudden rush of even warmer air and felt her own body heat rising in response.

Several large logs blazed in the fireplace. Mr Weaver had collected them especially for Adela. Emma unbuttoned her cardigan as she took up the bedside chair.

'There you are. Wherever have you been?' Adela said, smiling yet reproachful.

'Church, Adela.'

'Was it good?'

'The reverend's wife made a nice sponge cake with raspberry jam.'

'That does sound nice. Do we not have any raspberry jam?'

'Mrs Stoker hasn't said.'

'Never mind. It is not important. And, dear Emma,' she said, giving her a cheeky grin, 'I've been craving a little something of importance.'

Emma laughed as she reached for the book, her mirth

shading into apprehension. She wished Adela would stick with
Dorian Gray and not force her to read the plays.

'Now before you begin, remind me of where we're up to.'

'Lady Bracknell is quizzing Miss Prism about the mix-up
with the manuscript and the handbag.'

'Oh yes, my favourite part. Off you go then.'

Emma had not read two sentences when Adela interrupted
with, 'Stop, stop! You need more intonation, dear. "A handbag."
You say it blandly, if you don't mind my saying. You need to say
it with gravitas. Lady Bracknell is a formidable woman,
shocked and outraged at the thought of a baby in a handbag. A
handbag? Hear the difference? Do have another try.'

'A *handbag?*'

'Better, better. Again.'

Emma was about to give the phrase another try, when
Adela said, 'He gifted me that copy, you know, dear Oscar, after
he was released from prison.'

Emma knew better than to say, You told me already. The
truth would be a hundred times, no doubt. Instead, she said,
'Did he? How generous of him.'

'He was in a frightful state, I am told. After his release, I
mean. You know he worked hard for prison reform and for a
repeal of the act rendering homosexuality a crime. Wanting to
help other people. All those prisoners. Most good of him. Self-
less. Godly, almost, wouldn't you say?'

Adela scrutinised Emma's face.

'Charitable, yes.'

Satisfied with her response, Adela said, 'But then he took
off, you know, after his release, with that young Bosie.' She
shook her head. 'They went to Naples, of all places.'

'Naples.'

'It's very nice there. Have you been?'

'I've never had the pleasure.'

'The thing is, his wife Constance...' she paused as though for breath, but it was more of a sigh that she uttered, 'Constance denied Oscar access to his sons. Oh, how that must have hurt him. How could a mother do such a thing? It truly does beggar belief.'

Emma's mind darted back to that year in Brush. To that moment when she might have absconded had Ernest not turned up, and how she went back with him, put up with him and, above all, put up with his lack of presence, and then his sudden disappearance from their lives. She wondered if he had really cared about his daughters at all, for all his fawning and merriment in their company, and the indulgence he apportioned them.

She steered her mind back to the topic in hand and said, 'Constance must have had good reason, surely.'

'She suffered from a closed mind, Emma. Yes, Oscar and Bosie were quite shameless in their antics in Naples, but it had no bearing on his capacity to be a father to his sons. Oscar died not long after, never once seeing his boys again. What on earth was Constance thinking?'

Emma could think of nothing to say in response. This saintly Oscar that lived in Adela's mind had rejected Constance in favour of men. He broke his marriage vows, committed adultery and then tried to explain it all away with reference to the condition of his wife's post-childbirth stomach. Emma was aware that there was bound to be much more to the story, but that was the version that stuck fast in her mind and, in Constance's shoes, she would no doubt have reacted the same way. Perhaps Constance would have softened had Oscar lived long enough to see his boys grow older.

Adela was on her own thought tracks. 'She sent him photographs, apparently. Photographs!' she scoffed. 'Hardly a replacement for the real thing.'

Emma had to agree.

'He took it badly, but he did seem to forgive her. I admit I struggled with that. Children need a father, don't you agree, Emma? Of course you do. Here you are, without a husband for your girls, and me rattling on about Oscar. It is remiss of me.'

There was a long pause. Emma hoped Adela was finished with her topic, but she wasn't, not quite.

'He died, you know, of some horrible brain inflammation.'

'Encephalitis.'

'That's it. Sounds ghastly. The day before Christmas Eve, it was, and the news made for a wretched Christmas, let me tell you. I sent a wreath, naturally. And then that kind gentleman Robbie Ross sent me an account of those final months of Oscar's life. What an enormous comfort to me that was. To be regarded by Oscar as one of his special friends, too. Do you have anyone special, Emma? Someone you feel close to above everyone else?'

'It's my daughters I treasure most, Adela.'

'Of course you do. And why wouldn't you? It is as it should be. Well, I suppose in a fashion Oscar replaces children in my life. A woman must have an interest of some sort, mustn't she? Even at my age.'

The remark embedded itself into Emma's mind as she returned to her reading and Adela sank back into her pillows, content.

The following morning, as Emma was finishing her bowl of porridge and Mrs Stoker was busy frying everyone an egg, the telephone rang in the hall. Mrs Davies got up to answer it. She returned moments later, her face wearing an inquisitive look.

'Mrs Taylor, it's for you.'

Emma rushed from the room and picked up the receiver. It was her son-in-law, George.

'You have a granddaughter,' he said without preface, a little breathlessly. 'We're calling her Margaret.'

'Is Irene alright?'

'Mother and baby are fine.'

'I'll be over as soon as I can.'

George hung up. She could tell he was delighted, although perhaps not as delighted as he might have been. The war beckoned and he would be required to serve soon enough.

Emma dashed upstairs for her coat, hat and scarf. She was still pulling on her gloves as she headed out of the front door. She could see the top of a double-decker bus entering the street and she rushed to catch it. A brisk walk up Kingston Road and she was at Irene and George's in what felt like no time.

George ushered her inside and on upstairs to their bedroom. Irene was sitting up in bed. The midwife was still there and Emma exchanged a few hushed words. Irene looked as every woman did after giving birth, worn out and flushed. Emma's gaze drifted to the baby, all bundled up in a cot by her bedside.

'May I?'

She didn't wait for an answer. She reached in and lifted the little cloth parcel. Cradling the tiny new-born in her arms, Emma succumbed to a rush of feeling, her whole being consumed with an enveloping love. It was akin to a religious experience and so unexpected it took her breath away. Tears brimmed and her heart felt as if it would burst inside her.

'Little Margaret,' she whispered, placing her in Irene's outstretched arms. 'Well done.' She stroked her daughter's curly hair.

She sat for a while, asking about the birth and making small talk, until thoughts of her patient back at Cottenham House rushed in and she said she'd better get back and relieve Susan.

'I'll visit again tomorrow,' she said, hoping for more time off work. 'Is there anything you need?'

'I'm fine, Mum.'

'Just rest.'

When she arrived back at the house, Mr Holt informed her she'd been given the day off.

'That is unexpected,' Emma said, heading through to the kitchen, at a loss as to what to do with her free time.

'You've been holding off buying the new-born a present,' Mrs Stoker said. 'Why not catch the bus into Wimbledon and see what you can find?'

'That's a grand idea,' Emma said, wondering why she hadn't thought of it herself.

Something pink, perhaps, or yellow. A rattle? No, no, too young. Should I be practical? But Irene seemed to have everything she needed. Booties and mittens and bibs. She had all that. A teddy bear? What will Woolworths have?

She didn't wait long to find out. She was on the next bus into Wimbledon.

After a long time searching the shelves of Woolworths and finding nothing pleasing, she walked up the street and stopped outside the window of a toy shop, admiring the display. She entered and browsed and bought a small teddy bear with a pink ribbon tied around its neck. Thinking the gift too meagre, she also called in at Marks & Spencer and splashed out on a pink matinee jacket. Pink! A granddaughter! Her heart filled with joy.

Back out in the street, she saw her bus leave the bus stop. She had another fifteen minutes before the next one was due. She whiled away the time gazing in the windows of the shops nearby. One was filled with trinkets and curios and collectibles.

In one spot, between the displays of wares on metal stands, she was able to see into the shop itself, at the counter and the cash register.

A couple entered the shop and Emma watched as they made their way into its depths and disappeared. She looked up the street and checked the time. Others gathered at the bus stop. Confident she could not possibly miss the next bus, she returned her gaze to the shop window. The couple, who were partially visible to her, their upper bodies and heads obscured by a large embossed metal plate, approached the counter. As they neared, they came more fully into view. The woman pulled off her glove. Emma noticed the wedding ring on her finger. She felt for her own. Only then, as the woman, petite and fair-haired and in her mid-thirties or thereabouts, leaned forward and bowed her head a little, did Emma see the face of the man by her side, the man whose arm was linked with hers, a balding man with round spectacles and a perky, jowly face. It was Ernest.

She turned away and stood by the bus stop, hoping they would stay inside the shop a while longer. They didn't. In her side vision, she saw the shop door open. She faced the road, her mind in turmoil, her back stiffening. In her coat and hat and scarf she looked like any other middle-aged woman. He wouldn't recognise her.

She waited, giving them plenty of time to head off before she risked another glance back at the shop. She saw him strolling up the road with his pretty young wife on his arm as her bus approached. When it came to a halt, she pushed to the front of the queue amidst a few gasps of disapproval and stepped onto the platform and headed down the aisle of the lower deck. All the roadside seats were taken. She was forced to sit on the pavement side, forced across to the window by the passenger behind her.

The bus conductor pulled on the cord. The two quick dings of the bell rang loudly in Emma's head. It wasn't long before the bus passed Ernest. She couldn't bring herself to look at him. Ernest, not in Australia, not dead, but very much alive in Wimbledon. Remarried, no less. Illegally. And to a woman half his age.

She was more mortified than hurt. She, a widow no more. And not even a divorcee, as abhorrent as that would have been, but burdened with an unconscionable truth.

She wanted to erase ever having seen him. She wondered if he lived nearby or was just passing through. As the bus rumbled along towards Cottenham House there was only one thing Emma was certain of. No one must ever hear of this, not even, no, especially not her daughters.

The End

EPILOGUE

Emma's *Tapestry* is an imaginative re-telling of a period in my maternal great-grandparents' lives.

All my life, I have known I had a missing relative. That my great-grandfather Ernest disappeared out of my grandmother's life one day and no one knew what had happened to him. All we knew, or thought we knew, was that he had been a merchant with an interest in textiles, and he had travelled to Australia one day and never returned. One day in 2018, I was in my living room with my mother, who was visiting. I was living in a former textile worker's house at the time. She was seated below my great-grandmother Emma's tapestry, which she had had framed and given to me a few years before, and we were talking about migration. I looked up at the tapestry and said to my mother, 'Wouldn't it be funny if Ernest had migrated here and lived in this very house?' That remark precipitated a search for the truth about what happened to my great-grandfather.

We discovered that Ernest Taylor married Lucia Lackmann in 1922 in a registry office in Stratford, Westham, London, where my mother, in complete ignorance of this fact, married my father decades later. After his marriage, Ernest maintained a bigamous lifestyle for about six years before making his choice. In 1928, the year Ernest abandoned my great-grandmother and their two daughters, Ernest and Lucia departed for Australia. The family myth was that Ernest never returned.

Unbeknownst to Emma and the girls, Ernest was living right under their noses. In the late 1920s, the couple resided in a semi-detached house in a leafy street in St Margaret's, Twickenham. Before they left and when they returned from Australia, Ernest's commute took him through the suburb where Emma and the girls were living.

In the 1930s, Ernest became a podiatrist. I surmise the Great Depression may have precipitated the change of career. By 1939, Ernest and Lucia were living in a modest flat in Stockwell, near Brixton, a flat I used to walk past often one year in the 1980s, on my way to the Tube station. The Taylors moved again and in the 1950s, before his death in 1955, Ernest and Lucia resided in a detached house in Surbiton, only a few miles from where my great-grandmother, my grandmother and my mother and aunt all lived.

Lucia and Ernest did not have children. Lucia passed away in 1956.

After Adela Schuster passed away in 1940, Emma continued her work as a private nurse until she retired. Sometime in the 1950s she rented a flat above a butcher's shop in Carshalton, Surrey, from which she would commute by bus to the Wimbledon Spiritualist church. She also grew her own vegetables in a nearby allotment, and my mother remembers her as very kind and gentle, and frugal. I visited the flat as a child and have a vivid memory of climbing the metal steps behind the shops and fearing I would fall through between the treads.

My Aunt Gladys married Tom who is mentioned in this story, and they had one daughter Frances, who went on to marry and have a son. They all settled in Surrey.

Irene separated from her first husband George in 1946 when my mother was six. Irene then took on jobs as a house-keeper in Scotland before returning to London and becoming a bus conductor. She planned to migrate to Australia in the 1950s but her second husband failed the medical as he'd had tuberculosis. They eventually migrated to Australia in 1969 with their young son Steven.

By then, my family – my parents, my sister Michele and I – had already migrated to Adelaide. We arrived in Australia in 1968, leaving behind my mother's sister Sandra and her then young family. I never saw my great-grandmother again. She passed away on the twenty-night of January 1973, just ten days after my eleventh and her eighty-eighth birthday.

My grandmother Irene never got over the loss of her father. When she was in her seventies, she told me how her family went from riches to rags the day he disappeared. And her quest to find her father never left her. Wherever she went, she would visit cemeteries, scanning the headstones. She never knew that from the time he abandoned his family to the day he died, he was, for the most part, living in the next London suburb.

The silk tapestry Emma made and referred to in this book was destroyed by Irene after her attempt to have it framed proved disastrous. Emma's wool tapestry of the country cottage hangs in my writing room in a smart gold frame.

Dear reader,

We hope you enjoyed reading *Emma's Tapestry*. Please take a moment to leave a review, even if it's a short one. Your opinion is important to us.

Discover more books Isobel Blackthorn at
https://www.nextchapter.pub/authors/isobel-blackthorn

Want to know when one of our books is free or discounted?
Join the newsletter at http://eepurl.com/bqqB3H

Best regards,
Isobel Blackthorn and the Next Chapter Team

ABOUT THE AUTHOR

Isobel Blackthorn was born in Farnborough, Kent, England, and has spent much of her life in Australia. Isobel holds a PhD in Social Ecology from the University of Western Sydney for her ground-breaking study of the texts of theosophist Alice A. Bailey. She is the author of *The Unlikely Occultist: A biographical novel of Alice A. Bailey* and numerous fictional works including the popular Canary Islands Mysteries series. A prolific and award-winning novelist, she is currently working on a trilogy of esoteric thrillers.

ALSO BY ISOBEL BLACKTHORN

Novels set in the Canary Islands

The Drago Tree

A Matter of Latitude

Clarissa's Warning

A Prison in the Sun

Villa Winter

Dark Fiction

The Cabin Sessions

The Legacy of Old Gran Parks

Twerk

Other Fiction

Nine Months of Summer

A Perfect Square: An esoteric mystery

Esoteric Works

The Unlikely Occultist: A biographical novel of Alice A. Bailey

Alice A. Bailey: Life & Legacy

Other Works

All Because of You: Fifteen tales of sacrifice and hope

Voltaire's Garden: A memoir of Cobargo

Printed in Great Britain
by Amazon